Joe

Vampire

MJ Gardner

ꟼLP Palely Loitering Press

MJ Gardner
    Joe Vampire

ISBN: 978-1775048107

Palely Loitering Press
http://www.mjgardner.com/PalelyLoiteringPress/

He was not the man of my dreams because I had never dreamed up a tall, lanky, redheaded recovering addict with minor psychic powers. He was better than a dream because he was real.

- Evelyn's Journal

Intro

Hi, my name is Joe. Come on in. Yeah, this is my room, that little corner of MJ's head that I inhabit.

MJ? Oh, she thinks she made me up, like I'm not real. I don't know, maybe she did. Or maybe I'm real, and I made her up.

Anyway, pull up a chair. Yeah, I'll turn the music down. I got some stories to tell you like you wouldn't believe. Stuff about me and Evelyn. Yeah, some of it's kind of personal, but—hey!—maybe you need to know this stuff. Maybe someday you'll be in a relationship with a vampire too. Who knows?

Haven't read *Evelyn's Journal* yet? I highly recommend it. Just don't let Evelyn catch you.

TABLE OF CONTENTS

Acknowledgements

Thanks to my beta readers Chesley Giertz, Jason Justian, Brandy Kenny, Bryan Hamburg, and Carol Gardner for their insights, advice, trying to tape tin foil over a window, and above all, catching my typos and grammos.

And a big thank you to my partner, Karen, for her patience, support, and enthusiasm.

Evelyn

Sleeping Beauty

"You know," said Joe, "I really hate waking up alone." All six feet and two inches of him was sprawled across the bed, more on than under the tangled covers.

"You could get a puppy," suggested Evelyn gamely. Evelyn was on her stomach, huddled under the covers to soak up the warmth left in the bed. Her small breasts, plumped against the mattress, stirred desires in Joe that had only just been quenched.

Joe snorted. "Canine affection wasn't really what I had in mind."

Evelyn shook her curls. "You can't sleep with me."

"Why not?"

Her brown eyes held his green ones steadily. "I sleep in a trunk. There's no room. And you'd suffocate."

"A trunk?"

"Coffins are hard to come by, you know. It keeps out the light, and it looks innocuous."

"But you could sleep in a bed, right?"

"The light would get me."

Joe Vampire

Joe got up and looked at the problem. Two large windows on either side of the bed, plus lots more in the sitting room. He closed the door to the sitting room to see what kind of gap there was under it.

"What if we covered the windows with aluminum foil?"

"There's no point." Evelyn rolled over and sat up cross-legged in the middle of the mattress. "I'm dead from dusk till dawn."

"Dead? Like... stone cold?"

Evelyn shrugged. "I don't dream. I don't wake up. It's like no time passes at all. I pop—" she snapped her fingers to illustrate the immediateness of popping to another location "—I blink, and it's night again."

"But it could work...?"

Evelyn cocked her head to one side. "Why?"

"Don't you think it's romantic? I mean, sleeping together, you know, rather than *sleeping together*. Like a couple."

Evelyn's brown ringlets bounced as she shook her head. "We *are* a couple. But if you really want to, I'll give it a try."

Joe pulled on a pair of boxers and jogged downstairs to locate aluminum foil. Along the way, he wondered why he bothered with the boxers. It was only the two of them, the property was large and surrounded by trees, and there was no one around for miles.

By the time he came back after searching for, and finally finding, a roll of silver duct tape in the back of the pantry, Evelyn had straightened the bed. The covers were tucked with neat folds at the corners, the sheet was turned down so there was a perfect 4-inch band of white at the top of the designer coverlet, and the pillows were fluffed up and arranged. It looked like a bed in a hotel. Joe hoped she didn't expect to wake in a perfectly made bed like that.

He liked to sleep in an unanchored tangle of blankets, and sheets and pillow cases were a bit of a novelty to him.

"Here," he handed Evelyn aluminum foil and tape. "You do that one, I'll do this one."

"Just to be on the safe side we should do the doors too."

Joe popped the curtain rod off its brackets and began taping aluminum foil to the top of the window frame. He tried to hang the foil in strips, like a curtain, but the stuff was flimsy and awkward and the strips wouldn't hang straight and align with each other. Instead, he ended up covering the glass in ungainly rectangles sealed with lots of tape. Evelyn laid hers on the floor and taped it all together into a big shiny sheet.

When it was done the room was brilliant with reflected light. They sealed the doors with strips of duct tape.

Evelyn shut off the lights. The difference in the darkness outside inside was too subtle for Joe's eyes to make out, but Evelyn could see it, and added tape over any gap she found.

"You'll be up before sunset. You'll have to stay in here," she warned him.

"No sweat. I'll take a shower, watch some TV, catch up on Elementary Physics. Don't worry, I understand what sunlight can do to you. I won't leave you alone."

"Well... alright...."

"It's too late to back out now." Totally not true, he knew.

She slipped under the covers and laid down on her back. Joe climbed in beside her.

"What time is it?" she asked, not moving.

"Seven fifteen."

"The sun rises at seven seventeen." Her gaze was fixed on the ceiling.

Evelyn's rigid pose didn't invite cuddling. Joe stroked her cheek, hoping for some kind of affectionate response.

Evelyn's eyes flickered closed.

Well, thought Joe, I'm pretty sleepy myself. He closed his eyes. Not sleepy. He put his forearms under the pillow. Not comfortable. He turned his head to the right. No. He rolled onto his right side.

With a sigh, Joe rolled over to look at the clock. Seven nineteen, said the glowing red digits. When he closed his eyes he could see them floating, distorting. Joe turned restlessly on his side facing Evelyn. He half-opened one eye.

Evelyn was still laying on her back, her face perfectly composed. He could hear imaginary old women admiring her corpse: *She looks so peaceful—just like she's asleep.* Except that she wasn't breathing. No soft, comforting sounds came from her; her chest didn't rise and fall rhythmically. Her eyes didn't roll or flicker under her eyelids.

Joe opened both eyes. "Evelyn?" he whispered. "Evelyn?" And then out loud, "Evelyn?" Her naked shoulder was smooth and cool under his fingertips.

Was she really dead?

Joe pulled the neat covers askew kneeling beside her. He turned Evelyn's head gently from side to side. There was no resistance. He put his arms around her, under her back and shoulders, and lifted. She was completely limp. Her head lolled back, her arms hung loosely, like Juliet dead in Romeo's arms.

Joe bent his head over the graceful curve of her neck and pressed his lips to her cool skin. He kissed the hollow at the base of her throat. But there was no sigh and no smile as he laid her back down on the mattress.

I could do anything, he thought, *and she wouldn't even know.* But Evelyn's body, lovely as it was, wasn't much of a temptation with her not in it. What would be the point of parting her thighs, of loving her with his tongue, if she didn't moan and writhe?

He arranged her arms and her hair. Her bloodless lips were parted slightly, and he could not get her jaw to stay closed. Joe was suddenly sorry he had asked her to do this. Her vulnerability was disturbing. Even though he was not going to hurt her, and he was here to protect her, the possibility was still there. It would be so easy....

Just like Simms, said the Devil in his head.

The idea of someone dragging Evelyn out into the sunlight and her going up in blinding white flames like Simms made his throat clench. Was that love? Was that what love did, made you afraid to lose the other person?

Stop it. Nothing bad is going to happen. You wanted to sleep with her, so sleep.

Joe laid himself down at Evelyn's side, his head cradled in the hollow between shoulder and breast. He pulled her right arm around him and anchored it with her heavy hand on his rib cage. Her left arm wouldn't stay pulled across her body.

You're deluding yourself.

He wanted them to have that affectionate ease with each other that cats have when they sleep piled on top of one another. Joe had always slept alone—his parent's bed was not a place to creep to when frightened. He spent a lot of nights under the bed too. The darkness was his refuge.

Joe laced his fingers with hers and they rested together on her stomach. That worked. If he closed his eyes and listened, could he hear her heartbeat?

That's your own pulse in your ear.

Joe shifted and Evelyn's right hand slid off his side to fall heavily on the mattress. He disentangled his fingers from her left hand and pulled her arm back around him. As he reached to take her left hand again, the right one slid across his back.

5

You're deluding yourself.
Shut up!

Joe kept at it until he had Evelyn's limbs arranged the way he wanted.

"I love you," he murmured, careful not to disturb the arrangement. It was a nice little tableau: young lovers asleep together. He just had to stay perfectly still.

Joe fell asleep with tears sliding out of his eyes that he didn't really understand.

Trust Fund

Evelyn folded her arms across her chest. "I'm not doing it. It's silly."

"But Ev—"

"No."

"My therapist says—"

A tiny, fleeting frown creased her brow. "Joe, I don't want to be involved. If you think this therapy is helping you, great, but I'm not interested." She lifted her novel and went back to reading.

Joe crouched down so that he was peering at her over the top of the book and stayed that way until he had eye contact again. The frown was gone: she was softening.

"Please, Ev? Baby?"

Evelyn rolled her eyes.

"It's simple. Just an exercise to establish trust between us. You know I have trust issues. Come on, Ev, help me out. It's my homework."

She sighed. "You fall backward, and I'm supposed to catch you?"

"Yeah."

"And how does this prove anything?"

"It gives me the experience of trusting someone and having that trust validated."

"It sounds like a test to me."

"It's not a test. It's totally not. You'll catch me and I will be able to trust you more. That's all."

Evelyn gave him a long, inscrutable look, but then she placed a tasseled bookmark into her book and laid it aside on the couch.

"All right! You don't have to, like, take my full weight or anything. I know I'm a foot taller than you. I'll just lean back and you can stop me from toppling over." Joe turned his back to her, and shook out the tension in his shoulders. "Ready?"

"Ready." He resisted the urge to turn and check. The idea was that he had to trust.

He was halfway to the carpet when he realized she was not going to catch him. He tucked his head to avoid hitting it and landed with a thump absorbed mostly by his shoulders.

"You didn't catch me," he said from the floor.

Evelyn knelt down by his head and leaned over so that her face was upside down above his.

"This is not how this is supposed to—."

She put a finger to his lips to shush him. "What if I caught you, but then I sank my teeth into your neck while you were vulnerable and off balance?"

"You just hunted last night, I know you're not hungry."

"See," she sat back, "you don't trust me. You've been keeping track and you waited until you knew I wouldn't be hungry." She raised her voice to quell his protests: "And I think that's a good thing."

A good thing?

Joe sat up to give himself time to think of a response.

"It's not that I don't trust you, I just know better than to tease you."

"Because...?"

"Because... because it's not nice to tease a vampire."

"Because I might bite," she supplied. "Did you tell that to your therapist?"

"No, if I told him that I'd end up in the psych ward at County."

"It's not that I don't love you, Joey." She got up with a feline grace that Joe always marveled at. "You can trust me, as much as I can trust myself. But I don't know where the limits are. I haven't lived with someone and tried to not bite them before. I think maybe it's a good idea that you hang on to some of your trust issues."

"But I want to trust you. How can I love you and not completely trust you?"

Evelyn gave him a sad look. "I don't know."

#

The next day Joe was munching cold pizza at the kitchen counter and looking out the window over the sink at the lawn. His left shoulder blade was still sore from meeting the floor so suddenly. He was a little miffed at Evelyn for not catching him; he was a little miffed at his therapist for setting him up for failure, although, Dr. Jones could not have predicted that. Mostly he was mad at himself for being gullible and wrong. He had believed this activity could make him trust Evelyn the way he wanted to.

The thing was, he did trust her. He trusted her more than he had ever trusted anyone else, as long as he could remember, but something niggled at him, like a sand in his shoe.

Well, no duh, he told himself, *she's a freaking vampire.* But that wasn't it, and he wasn't sure what "it" was.

Joe reached absently into the box on the counter for another piece of pizza and found that it was empty. He brushed cornmeal and crumbs from his hands. Maybe the issue wasn't him and Evelyn at all. He felt adrift. For the first time in his life, there were no pressures on him. No school demanding his time and attention, no mother making rules, no father to avoid, no dealers to seek out and pay. He had no goals.

Time moved so much more slowly when he was clean and he had about five hours of daylight to kill before Evelyn woke.

I'll mow, he thought, looking at the overgrown lawn. Joe had discovered that the idea of an untamed meadow was much nicer than the reality. All that grass looked lush, but last year's tough, dry stalks hiding under the green were scratchy and sharp and could puncture a flip flop. The grass hid thistles and nettles and holes in the ground. And bugs! Joe was essentially an urban child: he had no use for the wildlife thriving in Evelyn's lawn. He laced up his high tops before heading out to the gardener's shed.

Once, the shed had been a nice dark green, but now it was flaking paint, especially the side that had been facing the cottage when it burned. Evelyn's grandfather— her other grandfather, the old groundskeeper—had probably been the one who painted it. Would he roll over in his grave if he saw how his garden shed looked now? Or the lawn? And what if he knew his son's bastard daughter was the lady of the manor? Joe chuckled at the irony.

Joe flicked a loose chip of paint and it spun to the ground. *Another project,* he thought and tried to muster up some enthusiasm for it, like the guys in ads for lawn mowers and power tools. He wanted to be a man, right? That was what men did.

There was a padlock on the big sliding door. Joe took out his laminated library card and popped the lock on the side door.

Sunlight slanted in through the dirt-hazed windows to reveal an enormous number of dead flies.

"Jesus!" breathed Joe. His feet stirred the air and sent their little dry fly corpses skittering across the floor. Those that didn't move crunched underfoot like cereal.

To the right was a workbench, and on a pegboard above it hung tools, orderly and dusty. Small square windows flanked the board. Their sills were heaped with insect carcasses that glittered metallic blue and green in the sun.

In front of the bench was a tarp-covered riding lawnmower. This was what he needed, but he'd never get it out without opening the sliding door. Maybe there were keys around here somewhere. At worst he could resort to a hacksaw, he supposed.

Beyond the lawnmower, the walls were lined with rakes and hoes and other gardening implements that Joe wasn't sure he knew how to use. Dusty sacks of fertilizer and weed killer sat in the corner, leaning against firewood that was stacked waist-high along the end wall of the shed. The piled wood was mostly covered with a blue tarp.

There seemed to be a lot of dead flies piled like a snow drift up against the firewood. Amongst their black bodies, something smooth and ivory caught Joe's eye. He fanned away the flies to get a closer look.

It was a bone. That was weird. Other than flies the place was neat and tidy. He couldn't imagine the gardener who kept this equipment so orderly would toss a chicken bone from his lunch on the floor and leave it.

Joe lifted the edge of the tarp. At first he thought he was seeing some old doll's hair, and then a Halloween skull, but the grey skin stretched over the skull was more realistic than any dollar store decoration he'd ever seen, and when he had lifted the tarp enough to see a strand of pearls and the neck of a stained sweater he realized it wasn't a prop at all.

It was a...

Body.
There was a....
Body.

....

Fuck.

Joe let the tarp fall. He vomited onto the dead flies. Then he ran outside and vomited into the uncut grass. He slammed the door so it locked again so that the thing could not get out.

It's dead, it can't get out.

Joe wiped his mouth with the back of his hand and spat to get the taste of regurgitated pizza out of his mouth. *Did I really see...?* When he blinked the image was clearly projected on the insides of his eyelids. But still.

Are you sure?

Joe grasped the doorknob, but it was locked. He could slip it again, but he really didn't want to.

What if you drag Evelyn out here tonight all scared like a kid and it's just Halloween decorations?

Joe let go of the knob. "No," he muttered out loud, "I saw what I saw." He'd had a good enough look at it. Her? He did not need to double check.

It was going to be a long wait for sundown. He needed something to calm himself down. Just a little. Nothing strong, no need to get stoned, just....

The medicine cabinet in the bathroom he shared with Evelyn contained only a razor, blades, ibuprofen, bandages, and athlete's foot cream. All his. He checked the medicine cabinets in each of the other rooms on the second floor. His fingers shook on the knobs and each time he looked at himself in a dusty mirror he was a little bit afraid he would see a face behind him, belonging to the ghost of the corpse in the shed.

All the medicine cabinets were empty, except for one small spider that he didn't disturb.

You don't want to do this, warned his conscience. *Stop looking.*

The third-floor servants' bathrooms were empty. Joe started going through the kitchen cupboards. Some cook or housemaid might have tucked away a little Valium or bennies or something.

Just a little something to take the edge off.

In the pantry, he ran his hands over the faces of cans and bottles gathering dust on the open shelves. At the back was a cupboard and inside it—

Sherry. Grand Marnier. Rum.

Joe took a step back. He'd watch a movie. He'd watch a couple movies to kill time until sundown.

He was not going to drink.

#

As color drained out of the sky Joe reluctantly shut off the TV and went up to their bedroom. Even though he was waiting for her he jumped when Evelyn appeared suddenly in the room.

"Joe?" Evelyn looked at him with her head cocked to one side.

He swallowed dry. No point beating around the bush. "I found a body." His voice sounded a lot younger than he felt.

Evelyn didn't move, not a muscle of her face betrayed surprise, horror, concern, disbelief, or any of the things you might expect a person to show when you tell them there's an unburied corpse on their property. She blinked once at him and simply asked, "Where?"

"In the shed."

"The gardener's shed?"

He nodded. It was the only shed on the property, as far as he knew. He hoped there weren't any others, hidden away in the trees, neglected and full of corpses.

"Show me."

That was the last thing Joe wanted to do, especially in the dark, but it wasn't right to ask her to go out there herself.

"I was going to cut the grass, and I went out to the shed, and it was locked, and...." The whole story tumbled out as he led the way. Evelyn kept up with his long-legged stride. Her feet didn't even rustle in the grass and she didn't say a word.

Joe didn't think to ask her for the keys and just forced the lock with his library card again.

"It's over on the wood pile," he said, stepping back. His stomach clenched and unclenched. Now that all the words of his story were gone all that was left in him was a pathetic and inappropriate giggle, like the bile you get when your stomach has emptied its contents. He swallowed it down.

Evelyn flicked on the lights and picked her way daintily through the flies. The tarp rustled when she raised it. She did not scream or gasp or anything. She seemed to stare at the body for a long time. When she stooped to retrieve the fingers Joe turned away. The memory of that little white relic he had mistaken for a chicken bone flitted through his stomach. It was going to be a long time before he ate chicken wings again.

"I suppose we'd better bury her," said Evelyn, stepping out of the shed.

Joe couldn't believe her coolness. "Her? How do you know it's a her?" he squeaked just as the image of those pearls appeared on his mental memory screen. "How...? Shit, Evelyn, how did it—she—end up here? Who is she?"

"Clara," breathed Evelyn solemnly.

"Clara," Joe repeated. He knew the name, or thought he did.

"The night we met. She drank your blood."

"Right...." In the back seat of Evelyn's car. He had been pretty out of it at the time. "But how...? Or who?"

"Simms," Evelyn all but whispered.

A shiver went down Joe's spine like a trickle of ice water. Just the mention of his name made Joe want to check over his shoulder. Even dead Simms was still finding ways to frighten and harass them. Joe tried to quell the fear that the memory of Simms stirred in his gut by remembering him going up in white-hot flames.

Evelyn laid a trembling hand on Joe's chest. She was shaking. Joe folded her in his arms and held her tight. He would never have known she was upset from her voice or her face.

"We should bury her," she murmured against his chest.

"Yeah...." That meant going back in there.

"We can't leave her there."

... Simms going up in white-hot flames. There had been nothing left of Simms to bury.

"What if... what if we just bring her out here? Sunlight will take care of the body. I think. I mean, if you don't think it's, like, disrespectful?"

Evelyn looked up at him and nodded. "Let's do that."

"But how do we get her out here?"

"There's a wheelbarrow." Evelyn pulled away from him. "You'll have to come in here and help me, I can't— ew, what's that?"

"Sorry, I ralphed earlier."

Evelyn scraped her shoe in a cleaner patch of grass. "I can't lift her myself."

Inside the shed, Joe trundled the wheelbarrow through drifting dead flies to the wood pile. He couldn't look at it.

This isn't happening, he told himself. *This isn't happening, this isn't happening, this—*

"I need you to lift that end," said Evelyn.

—isn't happening, this—

This was the chant that got him through scary situations in the past, like when his parents fought and things crashed and broke. Or when a gang shot at a car he was in. Or when he'd hidden under the bed and listened to the girl whose pussy he'd just been eating fuck her dealer boyfriend.

"Joe?"

Just do it. Joe took a deep breath and squared his shoulders. *Get it over with.*

Evelyn took hold of the tarp in two places by the feet and Joe did the same at the head. The tarp was under as well as over the body.

—not happening, this isn't happening, this is—

Things slid and scraped and crackled. The body was heavy, almost too heavy for both of them.

—isn't happening, this isn't hap—

Then something clunked to the floor near Joe's feet and rolled. Joe caught sight of brassy hair and an empty eye socket and dropped the tarp. He managed to run out of the shed before being sick in the grass again.

Pussy. That was his father's voice.

Fuck you, you'd run screaming too, he shot back.

Joe bent over, hands on his knees, trying to catch his breath and not throw up again.

"She's all in the wheelbarrow," announced Evelyn close behind him. Joe spun around. She held her hands out, fingers splayed, like Lady Macbeth dismayed by the spectral blood on them.

"That was...?"

"Yes, it was."

"Oh my God..." He swallowed to keep from dry heaving.

"She's all in the wheelbarrow," Evelyn repeated, "but I need you to move it. I can't. It's too heavy."

Joe straightened himself up, and took a deep breath. *Be a man. For Evelyn's sake.* For Clara, whom he didn't really know. Clara had been a victim of Simms, which made them allies, of a sort. She deserved his help, such as it was.

Think about something else.

Something else....

Like fucking what?

Joe stepped into the shed and turned his head very slowly so that the wheelbarrow came into view bit by bit. He planned to bolt at the first sight of any part of the corpse but Evelyn had arranged the tarp from the lawn tractor over the wheelbarrow so that there was nothing to see.

Joe lifted the handles and the contents shifted.

Nothing but a load of clay pots.

The barrow rolled smoothly across the concrete and bumped out the door. It was harder to move through the tall grass, and Joe rolled it onto the cracked concrete of the driveway that had once run to the gardener's cottage.

Tomorrow he would have to come back out and make sure everything burned up. Tomorrow. In the daylight.

Joe and Evelyn spent the rest of the night cuddling together on the couch while TV washed over them.

"He cut off her head," murmured Evelyn at one point in the evening. "That is how he killed her."

Joe snuggled Evelyn close, even though what he wanted, with the image of Clara's head rolling across the dead-fly-strewn concrete, was to get a glass of water to wash the taste of bile from his mouth, and a side of pills to wash the images from his mind.

At daybreak, Joe dragged himself out to the shed. His most valuable survival tools had been running away and hiding and he fought the urge to do one or both of those now.

It won't be so bad in the daylight.

The wheelbarrow, with its gruesome load, was sitting in the shade of the shed. *A load of clay pots.* Joe grabbed the handles and trundled it onto the sunlit.

Combustible clay pots. Smoke began to drift out from under the tarp.

"Rest in peace," he muttered.

The tarp blackened in the pattern of the bones underneath. Skull, ribs, something that was either a humerus or a fibula. He watched it smolder for a while, but it wasn't catching fire.

Joe inched forward cautiously, just close enough to get hold of the edge of the tarp with two fingers and flip it back. Dried skin sizzled like a handful of sparklers and then burst into white hot flames, sparking and spitting like a firecracker. Joe backed away from the heat. In no time at all the tarp was gone and the whole wheelbarrow was alight like it held a fallen star. Joe watched until there was nothing but twisted, glowing metal and ashes.

When Joe turned to go back to the house the familiar scene suddenly looked alien to him. Suspect. How many other secrets were buried—or not—on this property? Were there other corpses waiting to be found, with or without sheds?

Joe had buried some secrets here himself.

Only he hadn't.

In the bottom drawer of his desk, Joe kept what he considered his private possessions. Porn magazines, family photos he didn't want to look at and couldn't throw away, unnecessary condoms, a rusty switchblade, and Evelyn's satchel of journals, exhumed from its grave and wrapped in several plastic bags.

After they had defeated Simms and Joe had moved in with Evelyn, she had asked him to bury her school satchel. It contained the journals she had been keeping since she was small. That life was over and she wanted to start fresh, she had said.

Joe had duly buried them for her. And when he dug them up he reasoned that he wasn't committing any breach of faith until he read the journals. As long as they were shrouded in plastic in his bottom drawer they were just as safe as in the ground. Joe always had the option of destroying them.

You can't. She trusted you.

But she said you shouldn't trust her.

You should have thrown them into the wheelbarrow.

If this isn't the time, when is? whispered the little devil sitting on his left shoulder. *She won't even know.*

There was no angel on his right.

"Oh, hell," muttered Joe.

The books had been buried for three days before Joe dug them up again. Even now, a year and a half later, the satchel and its contents smelled earthy. The notebooks were sorted in date order; each one started in September. He opened the pastel blue cover of the first one. Ruled pages on the right were filled with fat penciled printing and unlined pages on the left were illustrated in crayon.

I wasn't even born when she started writing this, he thought, looking at the big round numbers of the date.

Last chance to back out, said his conscience.

Joe turned on his desk lamp and began to read.

#

For the next few days, Joe watched a string of mindless TV shows and went to bed early. Partly he hoped to drive the images of flies and finger bones and the sound of Clara's skull dropping on to the concrete floor from his head, and partly he wanted to drive out the plaintive words of the lonely little girl that he heard printed in pencil and then written in pen.

I want to go back to the nursery.

Maybe this holiday I can go home.

I wish I had Melanie's parents. I wish I had anyone's parents.

Why doesn't anyone love me?

It broke his heart. It made him angry. He thought his own past had toughened him against the sorrows of other people, especially rich little girls, but this cut his soul like a switchblade.

The worst part was that he couldn't tell her how he felt because he was supposed to have buried the journals.

Oh, the tangled webs we weave, smirked his conscience.

About midnight on the third night Evelyn came and sat in the wing chair kitty-corner from him. She aimed the remote at the TV like a futuristic weapon and killed it.

"Baby?"

"This is what I was talking about the other night." Her voice was grave and she was not meeting his eye.

"What other night? What—?"

"About trust. You don't trust me. And I suppose you shouldn't. I have done some things...."

Joe frowned. He knew a lot about her past now, but she wasn't talking about all of that. She didn't know he knew. So what was she talking about?

"I had my lawyer draw this up." She handed him an envelope.

Inside was a check book and a bank card and several stapled legal-sized pages. Joe looked at the lawyer's logo embossed at the top of the pages and began to be afraid. Lawyers, like the police, never boded any good.

"These are papers for a trust fund." She sat with her knees primly together.

"A... a what?"

"It will pay you enough to live on and go to college for four years. I can't touch the money; the lawyers are administering it."

"Oka-ay." Joe blinked at the papers in his hand.

"This way you don't have to worry."

"About what?" asked Joe, baffled.

"About any of those things you read."

Joe blinked, then his eyes widened.

Lie! Lie! urged the devil.

"Read where? What are you talking about?"

Evelyn's head came up slowly, then her big brown eyes, and she just stared at him. He couldn't lie. He shouldn't lie. Lying was just instinct.

Tell the truth, whispered his conscience, or maybe there was an angel on his right shoulder. *If you love her, tell her the truth.*

It's not in your makeup, to be honest.

Joe swallowed hard. "I read your journals."

Evelyn sat mute and unblinking.

Joe slouched down into the chair. What was he going to do now?

"I can't change what I did," said Evelyn, "or the danger I put you in. I'm not sure I'd take it back if I could anyway. But, this is.... This way you're free."

Joe froze.

Freedom's just another word for nothing left to lose.

"Are you cutting me loose?" Joe's voice cracked in the middle of the sentence.

"No." Evelyn was quiet for a minute selecting her words. "I'm making it so you can leave if you want to. I just want... do you want to leave? After the other night, I was afraid...."

"No, no, I don't want to leave you," protested Joe.

Evelyn looked down at her hands loosely clasped in her lap. "I want to protect you."

"Me? From what?"

"You could have an ordinary life, Joe. You could be safe from vampires. Safe from people like Simms. Safe from me."

Joe leaned forward and took her hands in his. "I read them. I read what you did. I'm still here. I'm not afraid."

It wasn't a lie.

"Why did you read them?"

Joe let go of her hands and sat back. He opened his mouth and shut it again. *Oh fuck.* He ran his hands through his hair.

"I just—I wanted to know.... How did you know, anyway?"

"I smelled something earthy. I followed my nose."

"Oh."

"When did you dig them up?"

"Uh...."

What was he going to do now? He couldn't lie about it; he couldn't even think up a good lie.

And then it struck him. He had read it and it had not hit him at the time.

"Simms did this."

Evelyn didn't say anything and didn't move.

"So he'd have something on you. Ev, that is not why I read them. That is so not why. I wanted to know what happened with Simms and Clara and all of it. I wanted to know where the bodies were buried, like Simms said. It has nothing to do with not trusting you. Baby, I trust you."

And he knew it was the truth. He trusted her.

"You shouldn't."

"Stop saying that. You aren't a monster. You aren't," he insisted when she turned her face away. "Being a vampire doesn't mean being like *him*. You put yourself in danger for Clara. You threw yourself at that maniac to protect me."

Her eyes finally rose to look at him. "I tried to help Clara by picking up a stoned teenager from a park and tricking him into my car where she dined on him till he passed out. And then I brought him back here, where Simms might have finished him off. Or I might have. You know this. You read it."

"You called me a puppy."

She answered with a little smile. "You were too sweet to finish off. You told me you liked black girls."

"Uh.... yeah...." Joe felt himself blush. He looked at the papers in his hand again. "Evelyn, baby, I don't need this."

"Yes, you do. You and I both need this."

"Why?"

"So that we both know that you are here voluntarily, Joey. Ever since I've known you you've been in captivity: your parents, the courts, the foster home. Lack of money is keeping you from the education you want. Money frees you. I want you to be free. I don't want you to stay because you're financially dependent. I don't want you to ever feel one-tenth of the helplessness Clara felt."

Joe looked at the papers in his hand.

"Even though I could leave?"

"Yes."

"Even though I read your journals?"

"Especially because you read them."

Joe's vision began to blur and he blinked at the tears. Evelyn slid into the space between him and the arm of the couch.

"Nobody has ever...." All his life, when anyone had given him anything, there had been strings, expectations, conditions, take-backs, but mostly just empty promises. And now, with his future handed to him, Joe felt horrible.

"I don't deserve this."

"It's not about deserving. It's a gift."

"I'm sorry," he whispered. "I'm sorry I dug up your journals. I shouldn't have."

"Hush."

Joe bent and pressed his head into her shoulder so she couldn't see his face.

It wasn't Evelyn who wasn't trustworthy after all.

COLLEGE LIFE

Faking It

When Joe got back from the campus tour, his dorm room was open a crack. Someone, who ought to be his new roommate, was standing at the foot of the other bed, his back to the door. Close-cropped black hair with a side part razored into it, dark brown neck, blue button-down Oxford shirt and beige Dockers. Joe pushed the door open and the guy wheeled around.

"Hey, you must be Joe Carter," Joe said, pointing to the name on the paper taped to the door.

"Yeah, hi." Carter stuck out his hand. "And you're, um...?" The button-down shirt was indeed buttoned down.

Joe shook the proffered hand. "Joe Cheney. Oh, sorry about that," Joe grabbed yesterday's clothes off what was now Carter's bed and tossed them on his own. "I'll try to keep my mess on my own side. So, where you from?"

"Newark." Carter just stared at his bed. He had a hand on each of his bags, an overstuffed backpack and a ratty oversized gym bag filled to bursting.

"So, um, your folks left, then?" They were all over campus: fathers in navy blazers and grey slacks, and mothers in flowered and shoulder-padded Laura Ashley dresses, delivering their precious offspring for higher education.

"Naw, I came on my own."

"Really?

Awkward silence reigned. Carter stared at his bags. Joe stared at them too for a minute, but they were not that interesting.

"Did you just get here?" asked Joe.

"Yeah. Went to the registrar," Carter gestured to a thick packet of papers on the bed between his bags, "and then I came up here to find my room."

Joe nodded. Silence again.

"I was going to head over to the bookstore and get my textbooks. I just did a campus tour, so I think I know where everything is. You want to come? Or you want to unpack first? I can wait."

"Uh.... Yeah, I guess. May as well have everything at once to put away."

"There's a books and materials list in that stuff from the registrar. You aren't one of those neatniks, are you? A place for everything and everything in its place?"

"Um, yeah." Carter finally moved. He rifled through the carbonless pastel pages from the registrar until he found his book list.

"Do you make your bed every morning?" Joe dumped the contents of his back pack onto his bed. Underwear, CDs, a pair of runners, and a paperback joined the mess of clothes, headphones, deodorant, a damp towel, and sunglasses.

"Yes. I do."

"Man, my girlfriend does that. Tucks in the corners and everything so tight you could bounce a quarter off of it, just like in the military. It's like trying to sleep in an

26

envelope. I have to tear it all out before I get into bed."
Joe swung the empty pack over one shoulder. "Well,
maybe we can pick up a roll of masking tape at the
bookstore," said Joe.

"Why?"

"So we can divide the room into your neat and tidy
side and my mess."

Joe grinned at him but Carter didn't smile back.
Waves of anxiety poured off of him. Joe could cut him
some slack. He had been on campus for two days, and
when he first arrived he had felt like he was in an alien
universe. Everyone looked rich to him. It was the way
they dressed, the way they carried themselves. A sense of
entitlement and a lack of caution. They weren't dressed in
ragged jeans, faded AC/DC jerseys and canvas runners
with holes. Carter certainly looked the part, with his
suburban, preppy clothes and clean-shaven face. Joe had
been out shopping a few times, intending to reinvent
himself as Mr. College Student, but each time he returned
home with clothing more suited to an Abercrombie &
Fitch model.

He was afraid that someone was going to call him
out, like Donald Sutherland at the end of *Invasion of the
Body Snatchers*, at least until he had met with his
academic advisor. She had looked at him over her half-
moon reading glasses and said, "You don't feel like you
belong."

"Uh...."

"I'll let you in on a secret." She took off her glasses
to emphasize the importance of this secret. "Nobody does
when they first get here. And here's another secret: fake it
till you make it."

"Fake it....?"

"Pretend you belong. Pretend you are Joe Student.
It will come. In a few weeks, you will know the campus

like the back of your hand and you will have made new
friends and settled in. It will feel like home."

Joe suspected that she gave the same speech to all
the freshmen, but he did as she said. As soon as he relaxed
and started looking around, he realized that she was right.
He didn't just look, he listened in on their thoughts when
he could catch them, like snatches of song on the breeze.
His psychic eavesdropping told him all about their
anxieties and excitement, their lusts and confusion. He
saw himself through their eyes, and some were
contemptuous of his unkempt appearance, but because of
it, no one took him for a freshman. Freshmen were
conspicuous in their neatly pressed new clothes and their
stiff postures. Like Carter.

As they walked across campus Joe pointed out the
various buildings, to which Carter said, "uh huh," like he
was trying to cram for an exam he was afraid of failing.

The bookstore was built into the side of a hill.
Grass grew on its roof and a sign proclaimed it an eco-
building. Despite the glass and steel doors, it felt a little
like entering a cave.

Joe was glad he had Carter with him, even though
Carter was so uptight. Being in the company of buttoned-
down Carter helped him feel more legitimate, and Joe
needed that more than ever in the bookstore. Faking it was
all well and good if you had an idea what to fake.

As a kid, Joe had gotten his school supplies
through a process of scrounging, borrowing, and
liberating goods from the lost and found. Sometimes he
liberated things from stores. The school insisted that he
have such and such so he told himself he had no other
options. He'd been caught stealing pens once when he was
eleven and gotten a lecture from the store manager, a
scolding from his mother, and nothing but a guffaw from
his father. At fourteen he'd been banned from the local

28

Whirlmart for six months and warned if he was caught again they would call the police.

The key word in that phrase for Joe was "caught." He had managed not to get caught again. Ironically, when he entered the college bookstore with a fully loaded bank card, an official printout of the text books and lab equipment he needed, and a list of school supplies in Evelyn's beautiful handwriting, he felt more nervous than he ever had shoplifting. Joe imagined campus police stopping him, kicking him out or arresting him. Or something.

You don't belong here.

Joe followed signs and picked up text books. He could not believe the prices. He was tempted to put them back and go see if he could get them at the library. But everyone else around him had arms loaded with shiny hardcovers.

Amidst the psychic noise being kicked out by dozens of students humming with excitement and uncertainty, Joe suddenly caught a warm blast of attraction, followed immediately by a voice piping, "Hey Ginger. You can put those up on the checkout if they're getting too heavy." It came from a girl with hair as red as his and a spattering of freckles across her cute little turned-up nose. Her bookstore employee name tag said, Anne.

"Uh, yeah, thanks." Joe smiled. Her blue eyes twinkled. He caught a quick image of himself from her mind, in his tight black jeans and thought, *damn, I look good.*

Joe left his tower of textbooks at Anne's register and went back for supplies. A cute girl smiling at him was an even better boost to his self-confidence than dragging Carter along. It was certainly more fun.

Evelyn had written him a very specific list after he had said, "Oh, I don't need anything."

One package black ballpoint pens. Joe looked at the clear plastic pens lined up in their cellophane wrapper. They were so new and shiny. No one else had put teeth marks on the caps yet.

Two coil-bound notebooks. Five one-inch binders. Evelyn had a system, she said, for taking notes in one book and then putting the pages into binders by subject. Less to carry and still organized. Joe doubted he was going to use the binders, but he dutifully picked out five different colors.

One scientific calculator. Now he felt like a pro.

Two red ballpoint pens. Really? The voice of Evelyn-who-lived-inside-his-head answered firmly: *Really.*

One package mechanical pencils.

One combo pen and pencil eraser. Did she expect him to edit his notes and make corrections? Joe just crossed things out and kept writing. He was not being marked on penmanship.

Ponytail holders. Okay, now she was just having fun with him. His hair was not that long.

Backpack.

He already had a backpack, but the ones covering the rear wall of the store had the university crest on them. Here were cheaper one-color bags with the crest printed in white, nicer bags made of a heavier nylon with the crest in full color, and then there were the retro leather and canvas bags with the crest embroidered on.

I want that.

You can afford it, answered the Devil or Evelyn, he wasn't sure which. He picked out a bag with brown leather trim and an embroidered crest.

"Let's see, Ginger," said Anne as she rang his purchases up. "You're a chem major." She didn't ask him for ID to verify that the bank card was his.

"Yeah. I like your hair."

30

Anne laughed, like little bells tinkling, thought Joe. He caught a vision from her, of him and her at a house party, in a dark hall, and him leaning down to kiss her.

"Are you a student?"

"Sophomore. I'm sure I'll see you around." She looked up at him coyly through her lashes. "I work weekends here."

Joe grinned. "I'm in Taft Hall. 5C. Come on around and visit."

She just laughed again, but the bells were broken. "I'm at Kappa Chi. And sophomores don't date freshmen."

"Well, what about next year? Do juniors date sophomores?"

She gave a little shrug. She had stopped making eye contact.

"Well, if we're going to date next year, we ought to get to know each other now."

Anne shot him a look and he got the feeling that she wanted him to pursue her, but Carter joined him at the register. Joe could almost taste the anxiety coming off of him.

"You okay?"

"I can't believe how much these books are."

"I know!" Joe packed his into his new backpack as Anne rang up Carter's purchases. "What are you studying?" asked Joe, looking at the stack of books equal to his own.

"Chemical engineering."

Joe gave Carter his old, empty backpack to load his books in. Once they were outside Carter looked back at the bookstore doors and said, "You're a real mover. The term hasn't even started and you're already hitting on coeds."

"Coeds?"

"Isn't that what they call girls here?"

"I just call them girls."

"Didn't you say you have a girlfriend?"

Joe thought he liked Carter better when he was not talking. "I'm just flirting, you know, I don't mean anything by it. You have to keep in practice. Anyway, there's enough to go around. I won't steal 'em all," teased Joe.

Carter snorted. "I wasn't worried about that. You know, she's in a sorority, she isn't going to be seen with a guy who isn't pledging a frat."

"Yeah?"

Carter shrugged. "That's my understanding of what 'I'm at Kappa Chi' means."

Joe smiled to himself. If only he could tell Carter that what he picked up from the girl. Maybe she wouldn't be seen out on campus with a non-frat freshman, but he could still get her into bed. If he wanted to.

"Let's drop these off and get some dinner," suggested Joe.

"Dinner. Yeah."

They walked along in silence for a while and then Carter blurted out, "I came here on the bus."

Joe stopped and they looked at each other. "Okay," he said. The lowering sun cast the grass and the pale brick buildings golden.

Carter made a face, looked around, and then started walking again. Despite the background buzz of student psychic noise, Joe caught a distinct set of words from Carter: ... *white boy never been on a Greyhound in his....*

"From Newark. That's a long ride."

"Yeah."

"So your folks didn't bring you."

"No."

"Mine neither."

There was silence for a few minutes, but when they got to the dorm door Carter asked, "How come?"

Joe stopped with one foot on the first stair and turned for appropriate dramatic effect. "My folks are dead." Then he turned and continued up, and Carter followed after a pause.

"I'm sorry, man. I didn't know. I mean...."

Joe waved the apology away. It wasn't really a lie: they were dead to him. And it would curtail any questions about his family that Carter might want to ask.

Carter dropped his books on his bed with a groan when they got to their dorm room.

"Want to go out?" Joe grabbed his car keys off his desk. "There's a place off campus called Lenny's. They've got video games and—"

"Um no, well, no, I, uh, I'd rather go to the cafeteria. You know, get the lay of the land."

Joe sensed a lie in that, and he caught a vision from Carter of coins. Change. Maybe that was all he had on him.

"Yeah, sure, we can do that."

"You can go without me."

"Naw, that's okay, another time."

"Gentlemen!" A round, blond guy with a clipboard stepped into their room. "You must be.... Joe Cheney?" he read off the clipboard and pointed at Carter with his pen.

"He's Cheney. I'm Carter."

"Carter. Cheney. Check. I'm Ethan." He extended a hand to each of them. "I'm your don."

"Great!" said Joe. "What's a don?"

"It's like a housemother," answered Carter.

"No," said Ethan crisply, pointing his pen at Carter. "I will not bake you cookies, I will not pick up your dirty socks, I am not your mother. I am your don. You can come to me with any problems you are having with your laundry, your roommate or the food in the caf, although there isn't much I can do about the food. You can come to me with academic problems or alcohol or drug problems, or if you feel suicidal—or homicidal, I guess—and I will refer you to the proper agency and see that you get help."

"So, you're kind of like a... housemother" said Joe.

Ethan gave a dramatic sigh. "No," he repeated. "I will not bake you cookies, I will not pick up your dirty socks, I am not your mother. I will, however, tell you that that kind of mess is not allowed in here, Joe."

"No, no," said Carter. "I'm Joe. He's Joseph."

"I am not Joseph. I was here first, so I get to be Joe. You can be Joseph."

"Mm-mm." Carter shook his head.

"Joey?"

"No way."

Ethan looked from one to the other. "You can be Cheney and you can be Carter. Do you guys have any questions? Do you know where the caf is? You know all this stuff, Cheney, right? You've been here a few days already."

Joe nodded.

"Well, then, gentlemen." Ethan snapped his heels and gave them a salute and held it until they followed suit.

#

In the cafeteria, Joe loaded up his tray with two burgers, a plate of fries with gravy, and a tall glass parfait dish full of blue Jell-O cubes in whipped cream. His favorite part about meals in the campus cafeteria was slurping down Jell-O.

"You know, you don't look like a chem major," said Carter after they had been eating in silence for a while.

"No?"

"When I first saw you, I thought drama. Or art. Something like that."

Joe looked at his round, mirrored sunglasses sitting on the table beside his tray. They had cost over a hundred dollars.

"You know," he said, in the same tone of confession that Carter had used earlier, "I didn't come here on the bus."

"Mm."

"I drove myself here. But I was not always the suave playboy you see in front of you now. I grew up poor."

Carter gave a little snort of disbelief. "How poor?"

"Poor enough that I think this is good." He held up his hamburger. "And this," he pointed at the Jell-O, "this is a luxury."

Carter chuckled. "I'm not keen on Jell-O. Once a week, on grocery day, my Mama would allow me one treat. I always chose chocolate milk."

Joe nodded. Finally, he had Carter talking to him like a real human being.

"I spent most of my childhood eating cold cereal straight out of the box."

"There have been times when I've gone to bed with nothing but a slice of bread and margarine in my stomach."

Joe gave Carter a level look. "I've gone to bed hungry."

Carter sat back. "You aren't making this up, are you?"

Joe shook his head and sucked a Jell-O cube off his spoon.

"So what happened? You don't look like you're poor anymore."

"Someone died and left me money." *In a roundabout way.* "I got enough to get me through college, and then I have to make good on my own. Honestly? I can't believe I am here."

Carter nodded slowly. "You and me both. It's kinda scary. What if I can't make it? What if I flunk out? What if I am not cut out for this?"

Scary? thought Joe. *No vampires, no drug dealers, no psychopaths like Simms.*

This is a piece of cake.

So what have you been worried about?

Joe settled back in his seat. "Fake it till you make it, man."

Auld Lang Syne

Joe sat on a bench with Evelyn's many shopping bags gathered around him. Evelyn's closets were full to bursting, but she could always find something she wanted to buy. For that matter, so could he. It was August, Joe's junior year had not started yet, and already the mall was full of sweaters, mittens and scarves, and Halloween costumes.

Waves of psychic noise rose and fell around him, depending on how many teenagers were nearby. They broadcasted louder than anyone else. After living in the quiet of Evelyn's remote house he really noticed it here at the mall and on campus.

A little boy went by, hanging on to the side of a stroller. His little jeans were turned up at the bottoms and red lights blinked on his runners like the landing lights on a plane. The baby sleeping in the stroller was no more than pursed lips in an old woman's face afloat in a sea of pink and white ruffles.

It wasn't until the stroller stopped and turned that Joe looked up at the mother. She was bulging out of her faded leggings. The sleeves of her oversized T-shirt half-hid a tattoo on one arm. When he got up to her kohl-rimmed eyes, Joe realized that he knew her.

"Hey, Joey Cheney, is that you?"

The last time he'd seen Therese she'd been living with a dealer named Ricardo. They had a one-room apartment in a house not far from his. Joe had crashed there for nearly a month one summer.

"Therese?"

"Hey, I haven't seen you round the hood in, like, forever."

"Yeah, well, you know." Joe broke eye contact and thought: *Go away.*

Therese laughed. "You're as bad as ever."

Joe shook his head. "I don't do that anymore."

"You don't party no more?" she asked in astonishment.

The little boy just stared at him with the same big brown eyes as his mother, minus the makeup. He'd just been a baby when Joe hung out with Therese and Ricardo, and he'd spent most of his time with his grandmother. Ricardo used to sneeringly refer to him as Therese's "nigger baby." If she objected, Ricardo just said he was comparing her sweet little boy to the licorice candy.

"Man, we're getting old. Giving up partying, getting married, getting jobs." She thrust her hand under his nose to show him a wedding band sunk into one fleshy finger. "Me and Rick, we got married before my little Suzie-Q was born."

"Congratulations," said Joe, but he was thinking, *oh my God, Ricardo has procreated.*

"Rick—well, Ricardo—only he don't like to be called that no more, ain't in that line of work no more neither. We got a townhouse up on the north side and he's working at Valley Plastics."

"That's good." Joe nodded.

"So what you doing?"

"Going to school."

"Ain't you had enough of that?"

Joe chuckled. "I'm studying chemistry."

"You was always good at chemistry," she said coyly.

Okay, now she was flirting with him, on the heels of telling him that she was married to a guy who would kick his ass some days just for existing. Not that Joe had anything against extracurricular activities, but not with Therese. He was happy to forget whatever chemistry had gone on between him and Therese and Ricardo. In fact, there were things he couldn't remember, and he had decided some time ago that was for the best.

"You working?" asked Joe, cutting his eyes and pretending he had not heard the subtext.

"Me? No way. That's part of the deal: I stay home and take care of my babies. Darnel is living with us now instead of his Grandma."

Darnel just looked at the floor and said nothing. Joe wondered if the drugs Therese had done while pregnant with him had left him brain damaged.

"You got any babies, Joey?"

"Me? No, no way."

"At least none you know about," she teased.

And there was Evelyn, checking out. He so did not want these two to meet.

Aren't we the snob?

Old life, new life, no overlap. It was the only way to steer clear of temptation, although right now Joe's discomfort was not in any way related to a desire to slip back into that life, and he knew it.

Joe stood up. "Well, it was nice seeing you."

"Whoa, Joey, you have grown!"

"Yeah," he agreed. When he'd last seen her he'd been tall for his age at five-foot eight. Now he was six-two. Joe gathered the bags by their handles and hoped Therese was going to take the hint and depart before Evelyn finished checking out.

But no. By the time he had snagged all the handles, there was Evelyn, with yet another shopping bag.

"You must be Joey's girlfriend," Therese bubbled like ginger ale as Evelyn joined them. "I was afraid he was shopping at Victoria's Secret for himself." She laughed at her own joke.

"Pleased to meet you," said Evelyn with a practiced smile.

Therese looked at Evelyn's extended hand for a minute, as if she didn't know what to do with it, then responded with a giggle.

"Well, Joey, I'll see you round." Therese turned the stroller and Darnel nearly tripped over his light-up shoes trying to keep up. "I'll tell Rick I saw you," she called back over her shoulder.

Evelyn watched Therese walk away and didn't say anything.

"Can we go home now? I don't want to run into her again."

"Sure," agreed Evelyn easily.

#

It was late Saturday afternoon when the phone rang. The phone ringing during the day was something of an oddity in Evelyn's house. Joe grabbed the extension in the kitchen.

"Hello?"

"Joey? Hey, this is Rick Gutierrez, how are ya?"

"Uh, Ricardo?" Joe would never have realized from the energetic voice that this was the same guy he'd known three years ago.

"Well, I'd rather be called Rick," the caller replied solemnly. "I left behind my old life and my old name, praise the Lord!"

Joe pulled the receiver away from his face and looked at it for signs that it was connected to an alternate universe. This could not be the Ricardo he had known on the other end, the Ricardo who had told Therese to get her ass out on the sidewalk and earn him some cash.

"Uh, how'd you get my number?"

"Well, Terry called your folks and your Mom gave her a number for... Martin Selesnik? And he gave me this number."

40

"Oh." It was a good thing the mob wasn't after him if he was that easy to track down.

"Terry tells me you've gone straight. She said you're in school."

"Yeah, I'm going to college."

"Good, good!" Ricardo sounded genuinely enthusiastic and Joe felt the warmth of approval.

"We'd love to see you."

The feeling of warmth didn't extend that far. "You would?" was all Joe could think to respond with.

"We thought maybe you and the little missus would like to come over for a barbecue on Saturday," Ricardo charged on cheerfully.

"Little—?" Joe could just imagine Evelyn's response to being called *the little missus*. "Uh huh. Well, I don't know Ricardo—Rick. I'll have to talk to Evelyn and get back to you."

"Joey, you're not letting your little lady boss you around are you? You are the man of the household. What you say goes."

"Uh huh. Well, see Evelyn's pretty busy during the day...."

Ricardo tsk-tsked. "You ought to be supporting her, Joey, so she could stay home and tend to the house and the kiddies as God intended."

As God intended...?

"Like I said, I'll have to get back to you. Give me your number."

Joe wrote down the number on the notepad Evelyn kept by the phone and said goodbye. Why had he written it down? Why on earth would he want to visit Therese and Ricardo, even if they had gone straight? He considered his own recent transformation, from poverty-stricken druggie with no future to college student, pretty remarkable, but this went way beyond that. Ricardo a God-fearing family man was on par with a talking dog.

Joe tore the page off the notepad and crumpled it.

#

Ricardo hoovered up a line of coke with a fat McDonald's shake straw. One line was left on the mirror half of Therese's broken compact. The other half sat off to the side, its tin pan caked with peachy face powder. Both were on a coffee table that was even stickier and grimier than the rest of Ricardo's tiny apartment.

"You want it, Joey?"

Joe wanted it, but he knew better than to reach for it.

"You want it, Joey? You want it, you gotta be my li'l bitch."

Therese was giggling, stoned, in the background somewhere. On and on and on.

Joe got on his hands and knees, but instead of the compact mirror and coke, Ricardo placed a fast food shake in front of him. He was going to get sodomized for runny ice cream. He didn't dare get up or object, and he had an uncomfortable erection.

"Mr. Cheney, why are you on the floor?"

It was his high school chemistry teacher, Mr. Balfour, an older man with half-moon reading glasses and no sense of humor. Only now he was standing at the head of the lecture hall where Joe took organic chemistry with three hundred other freshmen, and Joe was on his hands and knees half way up the sloped aisle.

Naked.

Joe woke with a sheen of cold sweat on his forehead. He glanced over at his roommate, Joe Carter, but Carter snored on. He'd once slept through a fire alarm, so that was no surprise.

The clock said it was six a.m. Not dawn yet, Evelyn would still be up. He tugged on sweat pants from the tangle of clothes at the foot of the bed and went down to the common room to call her.

"Hello," said her smooth, if slightly puzzled voice.

"Hey, baby." He closed his eyes and pictured her on the other end of the line. He tried to put himself in the room with her so that he would not be in that lecture hall anymore.

"What are you doing up?"

"I just wanted to say good morning to you." He didn't want to tell her he'd had a nightmare and needed comforting because he really didn't want to tell her what the nightmare had been about.

Evelyn chuckled. "I miss you too, Joey," she purred. "But I have to go."

"We'll get a phone installed in the trunk."

"I'll see you Friday night."

Well, Joe was awake now. Evelyn's warm caramel voice hadn't quite driven visions of Ricardo from his mind and he didn't want to go back to sleep.

I am over this. This is the past.

Are you?

Joe went back to his room and dressed, grabbed *Of Mice and Men*, and headed to the cafeteria with it under his arm. Catching up on his reading, and the prospect of an upcoming quiz, should be enough to drive away any phantoms of the past.

#

That evening when Evelyn called her voice was unusually cool.

"Someone called for you," she said.

"Who?" *Therese,* he thought, but he didn't want to give the thought voice.

"Someone named Rick something or other. He wanted your phone number. Said he was an old friend. I didn't give it to him. I didn't like the sound of him."

"Did he leave a message?"

"Just for you to call him. He left a number." There was a pause. "He kept calling me *little lady*."

Joe chuckled. He didn't think Evelyn would appreciate what an improvement that was on the things Ricardo had called Therese back in the day.

"Do you want the number?"

"Um, no. You remember Therese that we met in the mall? That's her old man."

"Her father?"

"Her husband, although he's almost old enough to be her father."

The next night when Evelyn called she ended the conversation with, "Oh, that guy called again."

"Again? Did he say what he wanted?"

"No, but he called me *honey*."

"Do you still have his number? I'll call him back so he stops calling you."

"I would appreciate that."

"Sure thing, honey," he teased. "Can't let the little lady get flustered."

"Careful, or you may not get to see my *little lady* this weekend."

Joe laughed. He was about to come back with something about Evelyn's *little lady*, but then he caught sight of Carter, sitting at his desk with his back to him and just said, "That would be a tragedy."

Joe wrote the number on the back of a notebook, and after he hung up he sat looking at it.

You told her you would call.

What was the harm in a phone call? Ricardo couldn't do anything to him over the phone.

If you're really over this then it's no big deal.

44

Joe dialed. He imagined the phone ringing in Ricardo's old apartment. It was red, with the buttons arranged in a circle, like a rotary dial phone, and the receiver had a piece broken out of it from a time when Ricardo had hurled it across the room. He didn't like bad news.

"Hello!"

The voice was loud and the greeting was so aggressive Joe hesitated a beat before saying, "Hi Rick. It's Joe."

"Hey, Joey!" Ricardo's—Rick's—voice was unnaturally happy. "How are you?"

"Fine."

"You never called me back about the barbeque."

"Oh, you know, midterms. It totally slipped my mind. I still haven't talked to Evelyn."

"Really? I've talked to her, but, you know, not to make any plans or anything. For that, I got to talk to you. So, how about this Saturday?"

"Uh, like I said, I have to talk to Evelyn...."

"Joey, are you a man or not?"

At one time Joe had wanted to please Ricardo, to be seen as adult and cool and all those things in Ricardo's eyes. He had not realized back then that Ricardo knew his approval was a leash around Joe's neck that he could tug on any time with a sneer or a few well-chosen words. And here was Ricardo, supposedly reformed, still trying to jerk that leash.

"Look, Ricardo..."

"Rick! Rick! Call me Rick. You gotta get that situation in hand, boy. It sounds like you're letting your little lady lead you around by the nose. Well, you know, maybe it's not your nose...." Ricardo sniggered.

"It's not like that."

"Well, then, we'll see you both on Saturday. About five o'clock?"

Go. Face it head on. That's what they teach you in therapy.

And then he will stop pestering you.

Joe closed his eyes. "Yeah, five, sure." It wouldn't be dark yet, but Evelyn wouldn't want to go anyway.

"You got a pen? I'll give you our address."

What the hell. He was man enough to go and visit Ricardo and Therese. Ricardo held no power over him anymore. Ricardo was an upstanding family man now, so there would be no drugs.

It would be fine.

#

On Saturday Joe dragged his heels and left the house after 5. It took him a while to find the address—a tall narrow townhouse in the middle of a block of identical townhouses, in a subdivision that was a maze of twisted streets with cutesy names. The building was cement block. Windows on the second floor peeked out from black shingles of the Mansard roof like someone peering through overgrown bangs.

Therese answered the door with the baby on her hip. "We was about to give up on you." She picked up a pacifier from the floor and wiped it on her jeans before stuffing it back into the baby's mouth.

Joe was relieved to see that this place contained nothing he remembered from the old apartment. He didn't recognize any of the furniture, what he could see of it under a litter of toys, clothes, baby bottles and dishes. From the front door, Joe could see straight out the back to where Ricardo was stationed in front of his grill.

"C'mon out back. Ricardo's so happy you decided to come."

The "back" consisted of a ten by twelve patio wedged between wooden privacy fences. Beyond the ten feet, it opened onto a common yard that was leveled more by kid's feet than anyone's mower. A rusty hibachi was smoking on the patio and a card table and lawn chairs spilled onto the grass.

Darnel sat at the table in a high chair, eating chips and a hotdog without enthusiasm. He was the quietest little boy Joe had ever seen.

"Joey!" Ricardo greeted him with an arm-pumping hand shake. "Terry was right, you're just about a giant," he said with a big gap-toothed smile.

Ricardo Gutierrez, the son of Cuban refugees, had to be nearly thirty-five years old, by Joe's reckoning. He'd had long hair and a straggly goatee when Joe knew him and wore the same sweatshirt for days on end. Now his hair was short and slicked back, revealing a hairline receding like the tide retreating from a beach. He wore khakis and a clean polo shirt in a pattern that would have made Escher go cross-eyed. The eyes Joe remembered as sleepy were wide open, and the sneering mouth was grinning.

Far from being afraid of Ricardo, Joe thought, *Do I even know this guy?*

"Hey, man, how are you?"

"Just fine. Get Joey something to drink, honey," he ordered Therese, who had just seated herself in a lawn chair. "We've got caffeine-free cola and orange soda."

"Uh...."

"No beer here!" Ricardo scraped at the grill and flipped the burgers he had just flipped thirty seconds ago.

"That's okay, I don't drink. Coke is fine."

"It's not Coke," Therese warned him, handing him a can of generic cola from an ice-filled cooler he could have reached himself.

"A cup?" Ricardo reminded her sharply.

Oh, yeah, I do know this guy. That was the old Ricardo, peeking through the genial façade.

47

"That's okay, I can drink it from the can." said Joe.

"Suit yourself. So, Jo-ey! What have you been up to?"

"Where's your girlfriend?" asked Therese.

"Oh, she's tied up at the office, she'll come a bit later." Joe had given Evelyn a non-invitation, the sort that went, *You won't want to come. I probably won't stay long.*

"You know, we don't feed people who can't show up for dinner on time." Ricardo chuckled, but Joe sensed that he was completely sincere about enforcing that rule. Ricardo had always enforced his rules, even if he made them up on the fly.

"I don't think that will be a problem."

"She doesn't want you to pick her up?"

"Uh, no, she has her own car. Two, in fact."

"You should see what Joey's driving, Rick," sang Therese.

"New car?"

"Beemer," answered Joe. He wanted to be able to brag about it, but it didn't seem sporting, and besides, it wasn't really his.

"No!" Ricardo dropped his spatula and trotted out through the house to take a look. Joe watched him go.

"Hey, Joey," whispered Therese, eyeing her husband through the screen, "you wouldn't have a joint on you, would you? For an old friend?"

"No." Joe shook his head without looking at her.

"Shit."

"Mama, I'm done," piped Darnel. "See? I ate everything."

"What a good boy," she said without even looking at him.

"Can I go play?" he asked.

"No, Darnel, you know Daddy wants you here 'cause we have company."

Darnel gave a sigh.

Ricardo came back and laid a hand on Joe's arm and looked into his eyes with a gaze that was too sincere. "I do hope, Joey, that that car is not the product of any illegal or sinful occupation."

Joe shook his head. "The Lord has been good to me," he managed with a more or less straight face. On the edge of his vision, he saw Therese turn her lips inward to keep from laughing.

"Wonderful! Have a seat, Joey. Hamburger or hot dog?"

"Burger'd be fine."

"May I be excused?" asked Darnel.

"No, you stay at the table until dinner's finished," answered Ricardo without even looking at the boy.

"But I'm done."

"Darnel!" snapped Ricardo.

Darnel's eyes went big and round and he was silent. Joe's stomach twisted.

"He's done eating, let him get down," argued Therese with some irritation.

"He has to learn to be polite," answered Ricardo testily. "And discipline is my department."

Therese sighed. "How about some more chips, baby?" She plucked the bag from the middle of the table. She'd put the little girl down in a stroller and she was now fast asleep.

"No, thank you," Darnel answered sadly.

"Don't make him stay on my account," said Joe.

"The boy has to learn," responded Ricardo. Joe remembered—nauseously—hearing those same words from his own father. The only lesson he'd learned was to stay out of reach.

Therese served up the plates that Ricardo filled, although he could have reached the table from where he stood. There was very little conversation during dinner. No matter what he said about teaching the boy, Ricardo's own table manners had not improved. Darnel put his head down on the tray of his high chair and was soon asleep.

"I'm going to put Darnel to bed," said Therese. Ricardo gave her a sharp look and she rolled her eyes. "Can I put Darnel to bed?" she asked.

Ricardo looked over at the boy and nodded.

"C'mon, dumpling," she said, hefting Darnel into her arms. He put his arms around her neck without opening his eyes.

"Turn on the light, huh?"

An orange bulb snapped on over the door as Therese passed through.

"So, I bet you're wondering what caused such a change in me Joey." Ricardo settled back in his lawn chair. "I'll tell you. I used to be the scum of the earth. I was mean, I was depraved," he counted his faults off on his fingers, "I was slovenly, I was disrespectful. I hated the world and the world hated me. And worst of all, I dragged others down with me. Kids like you." He poked an index finger at Joe's chest.

This is what I want to know, said the Devil on Joe's shoulder, and Joe agreed.

"It happened in prison. Sometimes you have to get to rock bottom before you'll let the Lord pick you up again. We had a ministry come in: Brothers Arm in Arm. I just went to get points, you know, to help with my parole hearing. But Jesus had other plans for me, praise His name. For the first time in my life—" he knocked on his skull "— something got through. And I began to see that I had been doing it all wrong. I hadn't been taking responsibility for my life and the things I'd done, and I had to start facing up to them like a man. I needed to get on the straight and narrow path or I would surely die."

Joe slapped at a mosquito. This was similar to the things he had learned in therapy. Similar, but not the same.

"So-o... what did you do?" asked Joe.

The day had been hot, but darkness was bringing a chill with it. Therese had left a blanket draped over the end of the stroller and Joe reached over and pulled it up to the baby's chin.

"First, I gave up drugs. Cold turkey. Then when I got out I proposed to Terry." He shook his head with the exaggerated sorrow of a TV preacher. "I fornicated with that girl. I ruined her. It was my responsibility to make an honest woman of her."

You fornicated with me too, thought Joe.

"And of course we took in little Darnel. It's only right that he be with his Mama, in a good Christian house."

Joe heard a gentle knock and the murmur of voices at the front door.

"I don't approve of the commingling of the races," said Ricardo in a low, very serious voice. "But what's done is done."

As coolly as he could, Joe said, "I hope you didn't bring me over to propose to me too."

Ricardo leaned forward, elbows on his knees. "What we did, Joey, it hangs heavy on my heart. I've prayed about this. I've prayed to the Lord for guidance, and he has delivered. He put you in Therese's path at the mall."

"Um, yeah...."

"Look who's here!" announced Therese

The screen door opened and there was Evelyn, commingled races and all.

Oh my God no.

"Let me just move this high chair and get you a seat," sang Therese. Joe watched Ricardo's eyes widen.

"I'm Evelyn. Pleased to meet you."

Ricardo just grunted in response.

"You want a drink?" asked Therese. She seemed far too happy with the situation. This wasn't an answer to Ricardo's prayer; this was Therese setting them up for drama. Nothing had changed there either.

"No, thank you, I'm fine," said Evelyn, smoothing her skirt down as she sat.

The baby began to kick at her blanket and fuss. All at once she spit out her pacifier and wailed.

"Whassa matta," cooed Therese in a voice reserved for the parents of infants. "Does my little dumplin' need—ew, I guess you do need a diaper change."

"Why don't you go along," said Ricardo with a grin that revealed the gap where one of his front teeth was missing. "I know how you girls love to fuss over a baby."

"Babies don't take to me," answered Evelyn. She crossed her legs and sat upright in the lawn chair as regally as if it was a throne.

"Well, you wouldn't be interested in the guy talk going on out here."

"I'm sure it will just go over my pretty little head, but I've been cooped up all day and I really need a breath of fresh air."

"I, um, didn't think you'd be able to make it," said Joe.

Evelyn smiled at him sweetly. "I wouldn't want to miss out on meeting your old friends."

Would it have been better if he had told her that "old friends" wasn't really the right term? He hadn't wanted her to know what had gone on because that would have meant talking about it, and it was embarrassing enough just to have to see Ricardo and Therese as they were now.

"So how do you know Joe?" asked Evelyn.

"We used to do drugs together," said Ricardo boldly, "back before I found the Lord, and Joey, well, what did turn you around, Joey?"

"A brush with death, and a stay at County General."

"ODed?"

"Very nearly. My father beating the shit out of me didn't help."

"Being a parent is hard work," sighed Ricardo.

A piece of the plastic arm on his lawn chair snapped off under the pressure of Joe's fingers.

Time to leave.

"Evelyn, pass me a soda, there," ordered Ricardo, gesturing at the cooler beside her.

Evelyn opened it a little. "Empty," she said. Joe could see the shiny primary colors of cans inside it, but from his angle, Ricardo couldn't.

"Ter-ry!" called Ricardo.

"I'm giving the baby a bath," she replied from an upstairs window.

Ricardo grumbled and got up from his lawn chair. While he was inside Joe leaned toward Evelyn and whispered, "Why did you come? Let's go."

"Only orange soda left," complained Ricardo as he pushed through the screen door.

"So, Ricardo, it's been great—"

Ricardo cut him off. "Has anyone talked to you about accepting Jesus Christ as your savior?"

"Yeah," answered Joe, "but, uh, I'm not really religious."

"You know, neither was I. I hadn't been in a church since I was baptized."

"We should really be going."

Joe stood up and Evelyn did not follow suit. *Don't embarrass me in front of this jerk,* thought Joe.

"Before you go, let me pray with you. I've done you a lot of wrong, Joey, and I need to make it up for it. You need a mentor. Let me pray with you that Jesus will come into your heart and the scales will fall from your eyes and you will see the error of your ways."

"Uh, no, I'm good." Joe turned to Evelyn. "You ready?"

Evelyn took her time standing. She brushed off her backside and fussed with her jacket.

"Joey, at least let me give you some literature. I've got a Bible for you. I've been reading the Bible, and I believe that's where the truth is to be found. Have you read the Bible, Joe?"

"I think we already have one. Isn't there one in the library, Ev?"

"I'm sure there is," she answered.

Ricardo looked from Joe to Evelyn and back. "You two... live together? But I don't see no wedding ring. You know, fornication is a sin," intoned Ricardo very seriously.

"I bet you've done lots of sinning in your time," said Evelyn in a low, silky voice.

Joe started. Business Evelyn turned off and Seductive Evelyn turned on. Seductive Vampire Evelyn.

Ricardo was momentarily flustered. He sucked air in through the gap in his front teeth. Joe got a quick flash amidst the psychic white noise always present in his head of what Ricardo would like to be doing to Evelyn, and it wasn't saving her soul.

The headlights from a car parking behind the townhouses flooded the little patio and reflected brightly in Evelyn's widened irises. Even Joe could see the glow from beside her.

"I bet you still remember how," she continued. Her fangs were down. He could hear it in her voice.

"Get thee behind me, Satan!"

The headlights went out, leaving Joe temporarily night-blind. He touched Evelyn's elbow. "We should go."

Therese was bustling in the kitchen, talking nonsense to her baby.

Thankfully Evelyn acquiesced and let herself into the townhouse through the screen door. Joe was right on her heels.

"Are you guys going already? Oh, I didn't even get a chance to visit."

"Another time," lied Joe. "It's okay, we can let ourselves out."

But Therese thumped down the front walk after them. Evelyn got into the driver's seat and started the car.

"Nice car, Jo-ey!" commented Therese.

"Thanks. It's Evelyn's."

"Well, but, you drove it here. Where's her car?"

"Uh... Ev took the bus," he lied.

Evelyn revved the engine but Therese didn't want to let him go.

"I was going to say you could do better, hey? But she's got money."

"Gobs and gobs," said Joe wearily. He looked back at the house to see that Ricardo was watching them anxiously from the door.

"You know I'd like to see more of you, Joey," said Therese quietly, gazing up at him with big soulful eyes. Joe didn't find Therese particularly attractive, but she did have big, soft brown eyes.

"You're married now, Therese," he reminded her, barely moving his lips.

Therese slid her eyes back toward the house. "We used to have fun, Joey. Rick ain't no fun no more." She leaned in and whispered, "He'll only do it missionary and most of the time he can't get it up like that."

Joe shook his hair back, trying to dislodge the words from his ears. "I'll see you around, Therese."

"What'd she want?" asked Evelyn as they drove away.

"To relive the good old days," he answered.

"Were they good old days?" asked Evelyn.

"No. How did you get here? Where's the Jag?"

"I just popped into this car. I got the house on the first try. Thank you for parking right out front. So, do you want to tell me about the good old days?"

"Not really."

"Confession is good for the soul."

Joe sighed. "I used to hang with them, mostly one summer when I was fourteen, the year before I met you. They were into a variety of drugs and kinky sex. Ricardo was a small time dealer and worked real jobs off and on. Therese was his girl—you know, servant and whore mostly--like she is now. He used us...."

"Used you?"

Joe ran a hand through his hair. He didn't want to have this conversation.

"Used you how?"

"Um...."

"He had sex with you?" Evelyn's eyes flicked between him and the road.

"Um... yeah...."

"Sex or rape?" asked Evelyn in a quietly serious voice.

"It was... I never, like, said no."

"Really?"

"Well, no, I mean, I didn't always want to, but.... Look, Ev, I did a lot of things to feed my habit. Things I don't want to think too hard about, and talk about even less."

Evelyn was silent while she digested this news.

"That's all behind me now," he sighed. "And I want it to stay there. I don't want to think about it. I thought that if I faced him, well, he'd be less scary."

"Him? Scary?"

Joe chuckled. "I used to think he was. Now I wonder why."

"They're such a lovely couple," said Evelyn with saccharine sweetness. "We should have them over for dinner."

"Ohmygodno!"

"We could roast that baby up and serve it with mashed potatoes and little baby carrots," she continued in her cheery voice.

Joe laughed.

It was over. The past was the past. He had been in Ricardo's presence and not been intimidated or tempted to fall back into old habits. He was fine.

Everything was fine.

#

Thursday Joe and Carter moved into their dorm room ahead of classes starting on Monday. They had talked about getting an apartment, but being on campus was just so convenient, especially for Carter, who didn't have a car. On Friday night when Joe was just drifting off to sleep the phone on his desk rang.

"It's not for me," mumbled Carter from his bed.

Joe frowned sleepily. He had just talked to Evelyn before he got into bed.

"Hello?"

"Joseph, we need to have a talk." It was Ricardo. Ricardo sounding like a stern father figure. "A serious talk. Your soul is in danger."

Joe rolled his eyes. "Ricardo, I need to get some sleep or my grades will be in danger."

"I wasn't sure that I saw what I saw the other night. So I did some investigating."

Joe had been about to hang up, but that caught his attention. "What kind of investigating?"

"Are you aware that your girlfriend has been involved in two murders?"

"Yeah, I am. Her grandparents were killed. I don't think Evelyn was *involved* in the investigation. She hadn't had any contact with them for years." None of that was a lie.

"Is that so? And there was a guy who disappeared while delivering pizzas. Your house was the next stop on his run. He never made it that far."

Joe remembered that entry from Evelyn's journal: Simms' method of ordering in.

Joe's stillness alerted Carter, and Joe heard the question form in Carter's mind, *what's happened?*

"When his body was found, he had been bled to death."

"What's your point, Ricardo?"

"I think you've got yourself mixed up with some bad business, Joey. Satanic rites. I think you are involved with a succubus. I've been reading—."

You were bad business, thought Joe, but he didn't say it out loud with Carter there. "I can run my own life, man."

"Jesus should run your life."

"I gotta go," he said, and hung up.

"Who was that?" asked Carter.

"Don't ask. If he calls again, I'm out, man."

"Now, how can I lie for you to this guy if I don't know who he is?" asked Carter.

Joe didn't answer.

"You in trouble?"

"No," Joe sighed. "Just somebody I used to know who wants to save my soul."

"Save your—?" Carter fell back in bed laughing. "*Your* soul Cheney? Ha! Good luck to him."

#

Two weeks later on a Saturday night, Joe sat in the library at Evelyn's house reading a hard-bound copy of *Of Mice and Men*. He had left his copy at school. The room was dusty and deathly quiet, so when the phone rang he jumped. He hadn't even known that there was an extension in this room.

Before he could say hello a hysterical female voice panted, "Joey?"

"Therese? What's—"

"He's on his way over!"

"Who?"

She moaned. "Rick has this idea in his head that your girlfriend's some kind of demon or something. He's on his way over, Joey! He made a big cross out of slats from our fence. Oh, God, don't tell him I called you. I didn't know what to do...."

"Call the police, Therese." Joe hung up the phone. A cross? What the fuck did he think that would do? And then he wondered, *Could a cross hurt Evelyn?*

"Evelyn!" he called, but his sentence was punctuated by pounding on the front door.

The drive from Ricardo and Therese's subdivision, out of the city to Evelyn's place, would have taken at least half an hour. Therese had certainly taken her time in warning him.

"What is that?" Evelyn asked as she materialized in the front hall.

"Ricardo," Joe sighed. "Therese just called, he—"

There was a thud, like someone ramming the door with a shoulder. Evelyn frowned in annoyance, popped across the marble-floored foyer, and opened the door.

Ricardo did not fall in, like a slapstick comedian. His eyes widened and he thrust a home-made cross at Evelyn.

"Get thee behind me, Satan!"

59

Evelyn turned casually to Joe. "What were you saying?" she asked.

Joe tried to match her coolness, "That, um, that...." but he couldn't help focusing on the railroad spike in Ricardo's other hand. It was brown with age and rust, except where the point had been ground sharp and shiny.

Ricardo took a step forward, cross in front of him. "You've been sleeping with the Devil!" hollered Ricardo. "Repent, Joseph Cheney!"

Evelyn planted her feet and crossed her arms. Without raising her voice she said, "That's right. I am the Devil, and I am going to suck your soul out if you don't get out of my house."

Joe joined Evelyn and clutched her elbow. "Get us out of here," he muttered. They could call the police from elsewhere, who could deal with the nutcase.

Evelyn didn't take her eyes off of Ricardo. "I'm not leaving. This is *my* house and he is trespassing."

"In the name of the Father and the Son and the Holy Ghost!"

Evelyn pushed the cross aside with an irritated huff and Joe rushed Ricardo, hitting him sideways with his shoulder. He grabbed the wrist of the hand that held the spike.

"Drop it!"

"No! Joey, your immortal soul is in danger!"

Joe wished Evelyn would come to his aid. He couldn't see what she was doing behind him, but it didn't seem to be anything to stop Ricardo from wrestling with him and whacking him with his stupid fence-slat cross.

"Joey, you'll thank me for this. You are in thrall to a demon! A succubus!"

Joe twisted Ricardo's hand back, but he couldn't get him to let go of the spike. They fell to the floor, locked together like they were spooning.

"Repent!" shouted Ricardo. "You're going to be damned to Hell! It's a sin!"

Joe didn't waste his breath in argument. He just had to pry that damn thing out of Ricardo's fingers.

And suddenly Ricardo went slack. He didn't drop the spike, but Joe was able to pull it out of his grasp. He rolled away from Ricardo, who was staring up at Evelyn.

Who was holding a gun.

She held it in two hands as if she knew how to shoot.

"Get up," she told him. Her voice was still calm.

Ricardo clambered gracelessly to his feet. His lower lip quivered and shone with a slick of saliva.

"I told you to leave, but no. Joey, tie him up."

"With, um, with what?"

"There's duct tape in the pantry. Come on. Into the kitchen. If I accidentally pull the trigger, I don't want the mess in my front hall."

"I—I—" gibbered Ricardo.

Joe reached out and grabbed a handful of the back of Ricardo's shirt and guided him toward the kitchen. He was bigger than Ricardo now. Taller. Able to manhandle the man who had handled him as a boy.

Evelyn trailed them with the gun and Joe hoped that she had it pointing at the ground. Just in case.

In the kitchen, Joe shoved Ricardo towards the banquette. "Sit."

Joe grabbed the duct tape out of the pantry as quickly as he could. He didn't want to let Ricardo out of his sight. He didn't trust him, gun or no.

When he came back Evelyn still had the gun trained on him and Ricardo was sweating and fidgeting in his seat. A confusing medley of images and feelings came off of him—sex, violence, shame, righteousness, fear—ever-changing, like the shapes in a kaleidoscope as you turn the lens.

"Joey! You don't really need to do that, Joey!"

The ripping sound the tape made was jarring.

"Shut up. Give me your wrists."

Ricardo held out his arms, but as Joe started to wrap tape around them Ricardo leaned in conspiratorially. "I just have your welfare at heart, Joey. I came to save you. You're not safe here, Joey. Your soul is going to burn in Hell if you go on this way."

"My name is Joe. You don't get to call me Joey."

"Joe. Yeah, that's good. That's good. A fresh start deserves a changed name. Joe, look at me, I'm a changed man. I want to do good. And that's why I'm here. For you, Joe. Cause I'm worried about you. I wasn't going to do no one no harm."

"Give me your feet."

Ricardo obliged. "You need me, Joe. You do. You don't know it yet, but you do. You don't have a father. I mean, I know you do, but you don't, you know? You need someone to show you how to be a man. Someone to make sure you stay on the straight and narrow. Someone who understands what you been through, eh, Joey?"

"Joe. And if you don't shut up, your mouth is going to be next."

"Well, now, what should we do with him?" mused Evelyn once Ricardo was bound. She put the gun on the counter.

"The police are on their way. Therese called them. She called to warn me and I told her—"

The phone rang. They all looked at it.

Evelyn stepped over and picked up the kitchen extension, and in her smooth alto, as if there was nothing out of the ordinary going on, said, "Hello? .... Why, yes, he is here, but he can't come to the phone right now. He's tied up."

Ricardo snorted.

"It's not a fucking joke!" Joe hadn't meant to yell but it burst out of him.

Evelyn raised an eyebrow at him. "Oh, yes," she said into the receiver. "Really?" She covered the mouthpiece with her hand and said to Ricardo, "Your loving wife wants to know if we could accidentally shoot you."

"Terry!" bellowed Ricardo. "You bitch!"

Joe grabbed the receiver from Evelyn's hand.

"...would look like an accident." Therese was saying. "He was breaking in, after all, I mean, it's self-defence, isn't it?"

"I'm going to hang up now," growled Joe, "and call the police." He slammed the phone home so hard it bounced out of the cradle and clacked against the tile floor where it dangled, buzzing.

Ricardo was on his feet, teetering. "You see what's happened, Joey? She's infected Therese! That's not Therese talking—it's the Devil!"

"Sit," ordered Evelyn. She had the gun again. Ricardo swallowed and did as he was told.

The buzzing of the dial tone was like bees nesting in his brain. Joe grabbed the receiver from the floor and tried to hang it up, but the phone was uncooperative and he was clumsy with anger. It took three tries and once he got it he wanted to hit the stupid thing, but that would knock it off again, so he thumped his fist against the wall beside it. The receiver jumped a little but didn't fall.

But it wasn't the phone he was angry at. Or Evelyn. Or even Therese. Joe turned towards Ricardo.

"What a model citizen you are. Husband! Father! See how much your wife loves you!"

"That miserable whore! She's sold her soul to the Devil."

"Whore? You made her a whore, Ricardo. You pimped her. You beat her when she didn't bring home enough money! You fucking raped her and humiliated her and... fuck!"

"I admit I was a sinner—"

Violence and more violence. Abuse was probably how Ricardo ended up this way in the first place. Nothing Joe said had changed the jumble of thoughts and emotions coming out of Ricardo's mind. He was stuck. He was always going to be exactly like this.

"How are you not still in prison? You are the lowest fuck on the face of the planet! You don't deserve a wife. You don't deserve to be a father. You don't deserve to have a home. You're no better to those kids than you were to me. You were an adult. You took advantage of me, and Therese, and a bunch of others like us. You used us. Not just to get money and drugs. That I could understand." Joe gave a humorless laugh, and then cut it off before it turned into a sob.

"I—" began Ricardo.

"Shut up," ordered Evelyn.

"You used us to make you feel like a big man. You got all these kids looking up to you, wanting your approval and your respect, willing to do anything for you, and you haven't changed at all. All you've done is find an excuse to hide behind. You've changed the tune, but you still expect us to dance. You got Therese on a chain, and now you want me on one too."

"Here," said Evelyn. She was holding out a big butcher's knife, handle towards him. Joe recognized it: her lucky knife. The one she had armed herself with against Simms.

The one she had used to kill her grandparents.

"No! Joey no! I'm changed. I am, I really am. Just let me go, Joey. Just let me walk out of here and I won't bother you no more. You don't want the cops involved."

Joe turned away from both of them and leaned on the kitchen island. The wood under his hands felt solid and stable. He wanted to dig his fingers into it, to keep himself from flying into a rage or sinking into tears.

"I understand you're hurt, Joey. I know I've done some awful things. And you're mad at me, and I get that. But really, Joey, you got to listen to me. You got to—"

There was a sharp crack and Joe turned around to see that Evelyn had backhanded Ricardo across the face.

"Stop talking," she ordered. "No one cares what you have to say."

Ricardo craned his head around her to appeal to Joe. "Joey? Joe? Let me go, huh?"

Joe took two long strides to the table, tore off another piece of tape and clapped it firmly over Ricardo's mouth. Now all he had to deal with were Ricardo's wide and pleading eyes.

"Ah," sighed Evelyn. "That's better."

Joe leaned against the kitchen island and contemplated Ricardo. The past was the past, but....

"I don't think she called the police. They would be here by now," said Evelyn. "So what are we going to do with him?"

"You're the one who said tie him up!" Joe shouted in exasperation. He took a breath. Yelling at Evelyn was not going to help. "I don't know. If we let him go he'll just go home and beat on Therese."

"Mm!" objected Ricardo. "Mm mm!" Sweaty locks of hair flew as he vigorously shook his head.

Evelyn pointed the knife at him like a teacher with a pointer. "Quiet."

"You have a gun," Joe reminded her.

"Yes, but that's not loaded."

Ricardo snorted like a bull about to charge.

"Besides, I prefer this." Evelyn turned the blade. "See how the edge gleams," she said to Ricardo. "That's sharp."

Ricardo's wide eyes turned from Evelyn to Joe. Joe knew him well enough to know what he was thinking. *She's psycho, man!* Maybe he was hearing Ricardo's actual thoughts; he wasn't sure.

Fear. Ricardo responded to fear. If not the fear of God, then the fear of the Devil. Or his representative.

"Ev, baby, would you do something for me?"

Evelyn lowered the knife to her side and sidled up to Joe, looking up at him with her big brown eyes and a lovely smile.

"Anything you want. Does it involve using my knife?"

"No."

"Is there any blood involved at all?"

"Oh, you can have a drink, if you like. Drink away! But what I wanted to ask you, was, will you take him home?"

Evelyn cocked her head to one side, questioning.

"Have a nice long drink and then pop him home. To his own back yard."

Joe bent, hands on his knees, so that he was on eye level with Ricardo. "Here's the thing: you were half right. Evelyn is not a succubus or a demon. She's a vampire. And I would willingly let her drink my blood, but she doesn't like to do that. It kinda hurts. But yours, hey, she won't have any qualms about that. So you are about to make a blood donation."

Ricardo was making increasingly louder and more panicked noises behind the duct tape and Evelyn thrust the knife towards his face, stopped with it inches from his nose, and he subsided into a wheezing whimper.

"Evelyn is going to take you home. And you are going to be a model husband and father from now on. If you touch a hair on Therese's head, we're going to come after you. If you say one nasty word or raise your hand to

Darnel or that little girl, we will know about it. Do you understand?"

Ricardo looked at Evelyn for permission to answer, and she withdrew the knife. He nodded vigorously.

"One more thing," said Evelyn. "I am going to pull off this tape and you are going to say one thing to Joe, and one thing only. You are going to say, 'I'm sorry.' Understood?"

Ricardo nodded.

The tape came away with some of Ricardo's stubble and a lot of his spittle. "I'm," he gasped and sniffled, "I'm sorry. I—"

Evelyn slapped the tape back on. She grabbed Ricardo by the front of his shirt and hauled him to his feet. Then she held the knife blade just under his chin as she sauntered around to stand behind him.

Ricardo was not much taller than Evelyn. That suddenly surprised Joe. In his mind, Ricardo was always bigger than him, larger than life, and he was really just a runt.

Evelyn's free arm, the one not holding the knife, went under Ricardo's chin to tip his head to one side for a bite.

Joe didn't stay to watch. He walked back to the front hall.

The hall had always been his favorite part of the house. It was the most impressive, with its marble floor and the intricately carved round table in the center. The table could easily seat eight for dinner, but the hall dwarfed it, and made it seem like an occasional table, the kind you might put in the corner of a living room to hold a plant.

It was all a question of scale.

As a kid, Ricardo had seemed so impressive, and so cool to Joe. He had his own apartment. He let the kids who crashed there do whatever they wanted, just like they were adults. Now, Joe saw that Ricardo was just a whiny little pedophile who needed to prop up his ego by destroying other people.

Shouting at him had changed nothing about Ricardo, but it had changed something in Joe. He felt hollow. Cleansed. A little shaky too, but altogether better.

The past really was the past.

Blood Money

F at ducks splashed in the stream that ran behind Joe's dorm. It was just the end of March, but they hadn't flown south for the winter. Living here, with students feeding them popcorn and cafeteria leftovers, was too easy. Watching them was currently more interesting to Joe than reading about Cubism for his elective course in art history. He might look like an arts major, but Joe was a chemist at heart.

All at once the ducks started quacking like lunatics, and flapped and waddled their way across the lawn; someone on the ground floor was feeding them.

Joe sighed. It was Saturday afternoon. He'd finished his lab work. He'd eaten brunch in the caf. He'd done his laundry. He was bored stiff and the stash of pot he had hidden, stuck to the bottom of a drawer, was calling to him.

Can't get through one weekend without her? taunted his conscience.

Evelyn had said, "If you'd just let me pop you back and forth you wouldn't have to drive home and back every weekend." This was an argument they had had several times through his freshman year and now into his sophomore junior year. Joe didn't want her popping into his dorm. Someone would see. Besides, it wasn't like he needed to come home every weekend. Sometimes he just wanted a little space. And he had decided that this weekend was one of those times.

So here he was, bored and lonely. The dorm room seemed tiny, compared to Evelyn's mansion. It was pretty small, so small that everyone tacked posters to the ceilings because there wasn't enough wall space. Joe had a movie poster of Francis Ford Coppola's *Dracula* that he had talked the ticket-taker at the Student Union theater into giving him, and Carter had the periodic tables. Joe actually liked the colored squares of the periodic tables better than *Dracula*—he often recited them to himself instead of counting sheep—but he would never have admitted that to Carter.

"Hey, Joey." Carter came in and bounced a backpack full of library books onto his bed.

"That's not my name," sang Joe. They were still having this contest in their junior year, even though it no longer mattered because everyone called them by their last names.

"Aw, come on. That's what your girlfriend calls you."

Joe gave him his best Clint Eastwood look and said, "You aren't my girlfriend."

"Damn straight!" Carter's voice jumped an octave.

"Besides, I know what your mama calls you," teased Joe.

"What?"

"Sweet potato!"

"You been eavesdropping?" demanded Carter with mock indignity. "Cause what's said between a man and his mama, that's sacred, man. That's like confession in the Catholic Church."

"You ready for dinner?" Joe slipped into his goose-down ski jacket.

"Ready? I'm never ready for that slop. You know," Carter sighed as he locked the door behind them, "my mom can *cook*."

"Yeah, yeah." Joe had heard all about Carter's mother's cooking; he had even eaten some of it in the form of leftovers that Carter brought back to school after holidays at home.

"You never talk about your family," observed Carter, practically shouting over the clang and echo of the iron stairs and the open cement stairwell. "Only Evelyn."

"Don't have a family," said Joe.

They'd reached the bottom and Carter pushed the door open with his forearm. "What happened to them?"

"Nothing."

"Come on man. We've been roommates for two years now and you have never told me anything."

"Nothing to tell."

"How can there be nothing to tell? Did somebody just drop you off as a baby at an orphanage? Did the stork leave you under a cabbage leaf?"

Joe gave a long sigh through his nose. "I would have been better off as an orphan. That's about all I want to say." Joe turned and strode away so Carter had to jog to keep up.

They came around the corner of the dorm and into the brunt of the wind. It was probably forty degrees out but the wind cut like January. Joe turned his back to it and snapped up his jacket.

There wasn't any lineup in the cafeteria; even students that hadn't gone home had gone out. Joe loaded up his tray quickly with sloppy joes, fries that had gone pasty and soft under the pink glow of the heat lamps, and took two of the ever-present rainbow assortment of Jell-O cubes in sundae dishes. Carter picked over the steam-heated bins, making faces the whole time.

"This's good," said Joe around a mouthful of sloppy joe when Carter joined him with his tray.

"For a skinny white boy, you can really pack away the food. Evelyn cook for you?" asked Carter.

Joe laughed, nearly spilling a mouthful of food. "No, man, Evelyn doesn't cook."

"You look that fine, you don't need to cook."

Joe looked up in surprise, and Carter suddenly found his mashed potatoes very interesting.

Joe laughed. "I know she's gorgeous, that's not news to me. I can't figure out what she sees in me, but I'm not going to question that too deeply."

"Sorry, man. I didn't mean nothing by it, but, uh, can I say something about her?"

Joe cocked his head to one side. "What?"

"No, no, never mind, forget I said anything."

"What? Go ahead, tell me."

Carter poked around in his fruit cocktail, picking out the grapes and exiling them from the bowl. "I don't have anything to say."

"Come on," urged Joe. "What? You aren't going to tell me I ought to be dating white girls, are you?"

Carter snorted. "No! Okay, well, I don't know but... there's something just as little....odd about her. She's just—" Carter stared across the empty cafeteria. "It's like she's too still sometimes. Like she's watching you, or me, or someone else, and she's so still. She just, like, fades into the background like there's no one there, like a cat stalking a bird and just waiting for the bird to get close enough to pounce."

"Hmm." Joe absorbed the comment and mulled it over. He'd grown used to Evelyn's stillness. Was she forgetting to blink and to breathe because she didn't need to? He hadn't noticed, but he made a mental note to pay more attention.

"You don't see it?"

Joe shrugged and slurped Jell-O off his spoon.

"How long you been going out with her?" asked Carter.

"Three and a half years."

"So you're, like, high school sweethearts?"

Joe chuckled at the notion. "Evelyn's a few years older than me."

"Yeah? She's going to be wanting to get married soon."

Joe didn't answer. What Evelyn wanted was not a white dress and 300 guests.

Carter laughed. "You scared?"

"Sometimes," Joe blurted before he could stop himself.

"You must love each other," said Carter, "to go out that long. I mean, it ain't as if you're both ugly and can't find nobody else. In fact, you seem to *find* girls all the time."

Joe shrugged that off and changed the subject. "There's a movie on at the Student Union. *Attack of the Killer Tomatoes*! You want to go?"

Carter shook his head. "No, man, I just spent all my money on lab supplies."

"It's only a buck. I'll treat," offered Joe. When Carter didn't answer he pulled a dollar in change from his pocket and wiggled it enticingly in front of his roommate.

Carter looked at the quarters shining between Joe's fingertips. "I am not one of the ducks."

"Well, then, I won't throw popcorn at you. Come on, live a little."

"Alright," he conceded. "If you're going to make me. I'll pay you back later."

"Whatever," shrugged Joe.

#

"Damn, it's cold," complained Carter as they came out of the Student Union. He stuffed his hands into his jeans' pockets.

"Attack of the Killer Tomatoes!" sang Joe at the top of his voice. "Attack of the Killer Tomatoes!"

"Cheney, knock it off. Man! You tone deaf or what?"

"Let's hear you sing," challenged Joe.

"I'll pass on that."

They'd reached the dorm. The fat ducks were snoozing in a group on the edge of the brook.

"Man, there's ice on the stream and it's practically Easter," observed Carter while Joe fiddled with the key. The doors were locked in the evenings, and their key didn't work unless you put it in and then backed it out an eighth of an inch.

"They don't start serving better food in the caf, I might just try my hand at French cuisine," said Carter. "What do you think about roast duck for Easter dinner?

Joe opened the door and sprinted up the staircase. "Last one's a dirty rotten egg!" he called back over his shoulder.

"Hey, no fair, man," Carter's voice echoed behind him.

Carter passed him on the third-floor landing, sailed through the hall door just ahead of Joe, and ran full tilt down the hall to slide up to their door like a baseball player stealing home. Joe came up behind him, panting and shaking his head. He had longer legs; he ought to be able to run faster than Carter.

"What's that smell?" asked Carter as Joe unlocked the door to their room. "Oh, that must be Joe Cheney, he smells like a dirty, rotten egg," he chuckled.

The room was in darkness and just as Joe's finger touched the light switch he saw a black silhouette move against the blue darkness of the window. The next instant he'd flicked the light on and there was Evelyn, shading her eyes from the brightness.

Carter, beside him, jumped a little.

"Evelyn!"

"How did you get in here?" asked Carter.

"I gave her a key," lied Joe.

"It wasn't locked," said Evelyn at the same time. Then she smiled softly at Joe. "I missed you."

Carter tossed his coat on his bed. "Well, hey, I'm going to go watch Letterman."

Joe shut the door after him. "You popped in here?" he asked.

Evelyn shrugged. "I wanted to come. You keep telling me I ought to be more impulsive."

"Don't you think Carter's going to wonder how you got in?"

"Oh, please," she said, rolling her eyes. "It can't be that hard. Maybe you left the door unlocked."

"Well, next time try using the door. And dress for the weather. You know, if we'd found you waiting in the hall...."

"I *did* miss you," she said archly, folding her arms across her chest.

Joe kissed her until her arms unfolded.

"It's been a bad week..." she sighed.

Joe sat on his bed and pulled her onto his lap. Her cold fingertips combing through his hair made him shiver pleasantly.

"Tell me about it," he invited, wrapping his arms around her to warm her up. She was cold and pale. He offered her his upturned forearm.

"No, baby. I'll hunt later. I just want to be with you now." Her fingers stroked up the back of his neck, making him shiver some more.

#

Carter opened the door and slipped in quietly so he wouldn't wake Joe. He felt around in the dark for the gooseneck lamp that grew out of the headboard of his bed like some weird flower and turned it against the wall so all it made was a dull orange glow.

A slight rustling caught his ear and he looked over to see two cat's eyes glowing at him in the dark. It was Evelyn, in Joe's bed beside him, her naked shoulders and head visible above the blankets.

"Sorry, I didn't mean to wake you," whispered Carter when he had regained his voice. He'd never seen a person's eyes reflect the light like that.

"I wasn't asleep," she said.

So now what? There was the grotty couch in the TV room. He could sleep there, he supposed. He grabbed his towel and shaving kit and was about to reach for his pillow when Evelyn started to get up.

She moved with the silent grace of a cat. The blanket slipped off her naked body and she stood between the beds, facing him.

"You don't have to leave," she said in her lovely alto voice.

Carter's mouth dropped open. Yeah, she spooked him sometimes, but there was no denying that she was hot, in her short skirts, and especially now, in nothing.

"He sleeps like a log." She stepped up onto Carter's bed and walked across the foam mattress without sinking in at all, like Christ walking on water. Carter could only stare.

Her hands rested lightly on his shoulders. "Uh...." said Carter. Her breasts were right at the level of his mouth.

"Don't you want me, Carter?" she asked, her hands sliding up his neck, up over his short carpet of hair. Her fingers were cold and made his skin tingle. "You do know how, right?"

She leaned forward and Carter looked up at her face. Just a kiss, that was all. He really wanted to know what those lips felt like. Just one kiss, and then he'd say—

That was when he saw her teeth.

Evelyn grasped his shoulders with surprising strength and bit his neck. It hurt. Carter flailed his arms, but he didn't dare touch her. She was Cheney's girlfriend, for chrissake, and there was Cheney not six feet away.

"Stop!" he hissed. "Let go of me!"

She pulled him off balance and toppled him onto the bed and knocked the wind out of him. Her mouth never lost its grip on his neck. The cat had pounced and Carter was the prey.

What in hell was she doing? What kind of kink was this? She seemed to be latched onto his neck like a leech. God, if that was what she called a hickey, he wasn't going to let her mouth near any parts he prized.

Carter tried to pull away but Evelyn had him pinned with her weight. He didn't know if it would be better if Cheney woke up and saw this or not. He would intervene—wouldn't he?—but which one of them would he be mad at? Maybe he should just lay still. If he didn't respond she was bound to stop. He was not going to touch her.

The initial stabbing pain he had felt in his neck had dulled to discomfort. Was she... swallowing? Carter's eyes fell on the *Dracula* poster and a rush of panic filled his belly. He tried to push Evelyn off of him, but the strength seemed to have gone out of him. His body was relaxed when he was sure it shouldn't be feeling that way.

And then he just felt fuzzy.

And then he blacked out.

#

Joe woke to daylight filtering through the heavy drapes and Carter's curved, sleeping back. He'd slept the whole night? Shit. He hated waking up to find that it was day and Evelyn was gone.

The clock said 12:31. Joe hopped out of bed and pulled on sweatpants. If they didn't hurry they weren't going to make lunch in the caf, but he wanted to run down the hall and take a quick shower first.

"Hey, sweet pota... to...." The words died in his throat.

Carter was asleep in the fetal position, like usual, but he was fully dressed and uncovered. His skin was ashen and his breathing was rapid and shallow.

"Carter?" Joe poked him in the leg. "Hey, man."

Carter smacked his lips a few times, mumbled, and rolled onto his back. And Joe saw the blood staining the pillow and smeared on the side of Carter's neck. No holes. No, of course not, Evelyn would have healed those.

"Sonofabitch!" Joe muttered fiercely. Had she really been hungry enough to vamp his best friend? He had offered his own blood. It looked like she had taken a lot, too. Joe leaned in for a closer look. Carter wasn't comatose or something, was he?

Carter snorted and his eyes popped open. "What you—" His voice came out as a rasp. "What you doing?" he whispered.

"It's okay. It's okay, you're going to be fine."

"What the Hell—?" Carter started to sit up and fell back on the bed.

Joe stared hard at him for a minute. "It's just a hangover, man. You were really wasted last night." He turned away so Carter wouldn't see just how embarrassed he was to lie to his best friend.

"I need some water." Carter started to struggle out of bed.

"I'll get it," offered Joe.

"I'll get it myself, man."

Joe pulled on a sweatshirt, sat on his bed and waited for his roomie to come back from the bathroom.

Carter was going to see the blood. He'd fill his cup at the sink, look up at himself in the mirror and....

The door burst open and Carter slammed it behind himself. "What the hell is goin' on?" he demanded.

"You came home bombed. You must have cut yourself somehow—"

"Don't shit me!" Carter's legs were shaking.

"Let me get you some water."

In the bathroom, Joe filled Carter's forgotten plastic cup and looked at himself in the mirror.

What are you going to say?

Tell him a lie?

What lie?

Carter had an uncanny knack for spotting lies.

Tell him the truth?

He won't believe that either.

And what was the truth anyway? Evelyn had bitten Carter and drank deeply. Joe wanted to believe that there was a good explanation for it, but he couldn't think of one.

Carter was back on the bed, his hand over his eyes, and Joe hoped he had fallen back to sleep, but he hadn't.

"Evelyn. What the hell is she?"

Joe gave him the water and watched while Carter drank. That was the most important thing, to rehydrate.

"I'll go get you—"

"Answer my question," insisted Carter.

"You won't believe me."

"You going to tell me she's a vampire?" demanded Carter. "This is bullshit, man! She ain't no vampire, just some twisted, superfreak—"

"Yeah, and what about those teeth?"

Carter stopped short and blinked.

"You'll be fine. Rest, drink lots, eat. I know." Joe advised.

"Your girlfriend bit me on the neck and drank my blood!" Carter's voice jumped up an octave.

"What'd you do to her?" asked Joe.

"Nothing, man! I came in here, into our room, *my* room, and she was in bed with you there, so I decided to grab my stuff and sleep on the couch, and then she came at me." Carter turned his eyes away from Joe's.

Joe looked down at his feet. He had never really thought that Carter had done anything to provoke Evelyn.

Give him the truth. He deserves it.

"She was hungry," said Joe lamely.

"Weren't you enough for her?!"

Joe really wished Evelyn was here to defend herself. She deserved to get this chewing out, not him.

"She doesn't understand that we're friends. She just sees other people as... dinner... sometimes." *The longer one is a member of* that club, *the less regard one seems to have for non-members.* "Look, I promise you it won't happen again."

"No wonder you don't want to marry her! No wonder you're afraid of her," said Carter. He laid down on his side. "I'm asking for another roommate."

Joe heard, *Water, I need more water*, clearly in his head.

"I'll get you some water." Joe was glad to escape.

It was noon. Joe had hours before he could confront Evelyn, and then it would be by phone.

He went down to the first floor and bought Carter a Gatorade out of the vending machine. When he came back to the room, his roommate was asleep.

#

Carter dreamed that he got up for a drink. He shambled sleepily down the hall to the washroom. The sound of the water filling his plastic cup made him even thirstier. He raised it to his mouth and tipped it back...

... and there was nothing. Only air.

80

Carter woke with a sticky mouth and sat up. The last thing Joe had said was that he was going to get water. Carter turned toward his desk to look for it and found Evelyn sitting there.

"Ahh!" He grabbed his pillow to shield himself with but Evelyn sat, perfectly still, and didn't even blink. "What are you doing here?"

"I came to apologize."

"Where's Cheney?" he demanded.

"He went to get you some dinner. He said you slept through it."

Yes, it was dark outside. What time had it been when he woke up earlier? He looked back at Evelyn. She wasn't making a move, just sitting there like a china doll.

She was a vampire.

"You're not breathing, are you?"

Just as he said it her chest did swell with a breath. "Only to talk," she said. Then she bowed her head and began playing with the hem of her dress. "I'm sorry that I bit you."

"Uh-huh." She didn't sound sorry. She sounded like she was here because Joe was making her do it. Carter spied a bright blue Gatorade on the desk near Evelyn's elbow but was afraid to reach for it.

"Don't be mad at Joe," she said. "He had nothing to do with it."

"No? He invited a vampire into our room."

"Well he doesn't understand everything about being a vampire, and I didn't understand that you were friends. And I didn't mean to drink so deeply. But," she smiled at him coyly, "you were so compliant."

"I didn't want Cheney to see you naked, doing... what you were doing."

"Joe knows how I hunt."

Carter's mouth was dry enough he decided to risk Evelyn getting a little closer. "Can you hand me that bottle?"

Evelyn handed it to him.

"You won't bite me again?"

She raised one eyebrow. "Not unless you want me to."

Carter gave a nervous laugh. "You drink Cheney's blood?"

"I have. I don't do it on a regular basis."

"Why not?" asked Carter. The Gatorade tasted of chemicals and corn syrup and it was the best thing he had ever drunk. It soaked into him like he was a dry sponge.

"Blood and relationships don't mix."

Joe came in, filling the room with the deceptively good smell of fast food.

"Feeling better?" asked Joe.

Carter just glared at him.

Joe handed Carter the grease-splotched paper bag and another Gatorade, this one ruby red. "That'll help rehydrate you," he explained. "And there's a chocolate bar in there too."

"Mmf," mumbled Carter around a mouthful of burger that was mostly bun, lettuce, and dressing.

"So, is everything okay?" Joe asked cautiously once he had settled himself at his own desk.

Carter looked from Evelyn to Joe. "Not exactly."

"Then maybe I should go," said Evelyn perfunctorily.

"No," protested Joe. "I mean, let's talk, okay?" He turned to Carter. "Evelyn's never told anyone before. I mean, besides me."

"Really? I can't imagine why not."

"Tell her what's really bothering you," urged Joe. "What you told me before."

Carter looked up at Evelyn, who was still standing. "Joe," he growled, but then he decided that he did want to say his piece. "You took my blood! Like—if you don't understand how invasive that is I don't think I can explain it. At least the Red Cross gives you juice and a cookie."

Evelyn gestured at the fast food rapidly disappearing from the torn open bag.

"They don't just attack people in their bedrooms and stick a needle into them! You have to volunteer. I did not volunteer."

"I'd better go," said Evelyn.

"Evelyn," pleaded Joe, "come on, sit down and talk."

"Joey, stop being a therapist," she snapped at him, then turned on Carter. The way her eyes flashed at him made him wish he had something more substantial than a half-eaten burger and a bottle of blue freshie in his hand.

"I drank your blood because I was hungry. Yes, I know how invasive it is. How do you think I got this way? I didn't know you were friends. I didn't... I won't do it again."

Joe had his forehead resting on his hand, his fingers pushing his hair up in tufts.

Carter stared at her. "How can you be...? I don't believe in vampires."

Evelyn said nothing, just stared at him. She didn't blink, she didn't breathe; she was dead. It made shivers run down Carter's spine. She had *touched* him with dead hands.

"See, that's what I mean," said Carter to Joe, who looked up at Evelyn.

Joe looked at her. "You're not breathing," he said. "You're not blinking. You're giving yourself away."

Evelyn turned to Carter and gave a slow, deliberate blink, and then suddenly vanished.

"Shit!" Blue Gatorade splashed over his legs and his sheets.

"Yeah," said Joe, running his hands distractedly through his hair. "She does that."

#

Joe unsnapped his jacket as he walked. There was an unseasonably warm spring wind blowing—it was going to rain for sure. He almost didn't mind that his evening class had been canceled and he'd made the trek across campus for nothing.

Joe's long legs easily took the iron stairs two at a time. An evening off. He'd been wanting that for a while, but now he wasn't sure what to do with the time. It seemed a shame to waste it studying.

He grasped the doorknob to his dorm room and hit his shoulder against the door when it wouldn't open. It was locked. The light was on and Carter had been there fifteen minutes ago when he'd left.

"Carter?" He knocked, but there was no answer, so he took out his key.

"Don't come in!" called his roommate as Joe opened the door.

He expected to see Carter naked with a girl. It would be a first, but it was damn well time. But Carter was fully dressed and the flash of a small, shiny blade in Carter's right hand drew Joe's eyes to blood on his left wrist.

"Carter!" he squeaked, "What the hell are you doing?" He made a grab for the knife and Carter blocked him by turning his back toward him.

"Hey, man. Hey! You're going to make me spill it. Close the damn door."

Blood dripped in a steady rhythm into a glass measuring cup.

Joe backed up until his hand contacted the door and he closed it without taking his eyes off the dripping blood. "Have you lost your fucking mind?" he asked.

"Oh, please. You're the one with a vampire for a girlfriend."

Joe blinked. "Is that who this is for?"

Drip drip drip....

"Yeah," answered Carter crossly. "Aren't you supposed to be in class?"

"Canceled." Joe eased out of his jacket and sat down in his chair, still watching the measuring cup. "That's an awfully generous gift."

Drip drip drip....

"Gift?" snorted Carter. "Ain't no gift."

"How much is she paying you?"

"I get 20 bucks an ounce."

"Are you sure it's worth it?"

"You think I ought to ask for more?"

"That's not what I mean," said Joe.

Carter's eyes narrowed. "I've been poor all my life. So, yeah, if this is what I have to do, it's worth it. I told my mom I got a part-time job on campus, so she could quit her second job. If I had more blood I'd sell it. I'd sell your blood, Cheney."

Drip drip drip....

Carter set down the penknife and started massaging his inner forearm downwards, pushing blood out. He was a picture of clinical indifference. The level in the cup crept up and up

"I take it this isn't the first time you've done this."

"Every Wednesday, while you're in class." The blood flow slowed down and Carter deepened the cut with the knife.

Joe winced. "How can you do that?"

"It took a little practice."

"I prefer to give blood the old fashioned way," said Joe.

"I don't want to know about it." Carter pressed a tissue over his wrist and raised it above shoulder level to stop the bleeding. "Look, Evelyn's going to be here in a few minutes. You want her to see you?"

"Me?" laughed Joe. "I got nothing to hide."

"Me neither," responded Carter defensively.

"Then why did you keep this a secret?"

"I didn't think you'd be real comfortable with it. I mean, it ain't like sex, but maybe you like being the only one she drinks from."

"Evelyn rarely drinks from me."

"And maybe I didn't want you to know how desperate I am," Carter continued. "I don't know what kind of scholarship you got, but all mine covers is dorm fees and tuition. I got to scrape up money for books and phone and laundry. I can't even afford a goddamn movie at the Student Union. I am not one of the ducks. Ain't nobody giving me a handout, so I gotta fend for myself."

"Are you saying I am a duck?"

"I'm not talking about you at all, Cheney. But, if the feathers fit...."

Joe snorted. "You think it's embarrassing to be poor? You think it's embarrassing to take charity?"

Carter glared at him.

"I grew up with nothing, too," Joe reminded him "I'm here because Evelyn is paying my way, and Evelyn's money scares me more than your desperation."

"Really? I didn't know it was the money that scared you, Joey." Evelyn was standing inside the closed door.

"One-twenty," said Carter. Evelyn handed over a Gatorade and a chocolate bar and counted out six twenty-dollar bills from her purse.

"That's not too much?" she asked Carter, nodding at the cup.

"Naw, I didn't even get dizzy this time." Carter stuffed the money in his pocket.

Evelyn moistened a tissue with her spit and handed it to Carter, who wiped it over the cut. Like magic, it was erased.

"I'm out of here." Carter grabbed a hanger from the closet along with his jacket. "Here," he hooked it on the outside doorknob. "Take this down when it's safe to come back," he told Joe pointedly, and closed the door.

"You mind if I drink this while it's warm?" asked Evelyn, seating herself on Carter's desk with her feet on his chair. She took a paper-wrapped straw out of her purse.

Joe shrugged. "I'd have thought you preferred Waterford Crystal to —" he checked the side of the measuring cup, "— Pyrex."

"I would, but none of my crystal is marked in ounces." Her eyes dilated as she sipped Carter's blood through the straw.

Joe tipped back in his chair and rested his feet on his bed. "Tasty?" He glared at her from under his shaggy hair.

"You want a sip?" Her voice was husky in a way that Joe found undeniably sexy.

"I don't have twenty bucks," Joe snapped back. This was no time for fooling around.

Evelyn took a drink and licked her lips. "I knew it would bother you," she said around her fangs. "But I don't understand *why* it bothers you."

"Why? Gee, you don't think this is a little bit exploitive?"

"He proposed the arrangement," she said, tipping the cup and herding together the last droplets with her straw.

"He did?"

"He said, 'I've got blood; you've got money. We could do business.'" She slurped up the remaining blood in an unladylike fashion. "It's the perfect arrangement. We both get what we need."

"You attacked him and drank his blood."

"I paid him for that."

"You *paid* him for that? That makes it okay? It's not right," said Joe, shaking his head. "It's exploitation. It's like poor people in India selling their organs."

"It's like buying groceries," she objected. Her eyes strayed hopefully back to the empty measuring cup. "Does the farmer say he's being exploited? The grocer? No. You think this is worse than assaulting people and stealing it? Because that's what I do, you know."

Joe stared back into her unblinking eyes. No, on an objective scale, taking blood by force was worse than buying it. A lot worse. But Carter was his friend and the other men she bit were faceless strangers.

"Drink my blood."

"We've been through this, Joey."

"Drink my blood," insisted Joe again.

Evelyn's nostrils flared. "Don't tempt me, I'm still hungry."

He lifted the hair off his neck. "Instead of Carter."

"He'd just be angry with you," she said, getting up from the desk. "It's easy money, and you'd be taking that away from him." She stopped suddenly. "If I wasn't wealthy, would you mind then? If I had a job and I paid $20 an ounce for blood, would you think it was exploitation then?"

Evelyn with a job—well that was a laugh. But a vampire who wasn't wealthy...?

"I don't know. Maybe it wouldn't be as bad."

"Well, then, if you take the groceries analogy—"

He cut her off, "You been reading Socrates again?"

Evelyn gave a small smile. "So you get my point?"

"Yeah. I guess. That doesn't mean I'm convinced and it doesn't mean that I like it."

She came over to him and stroked his hair. "It's a good arrangement for both of us. It's cut my need to hunt in half. If I could find—"

Joe offered her his wrist.

"No."

He stood up and came close to her with his head tilted to one side to provide easy access to his neck.

"I got Carter into this. Assuage my guilt."

But Evelyn just took his face between her hands and kissed him.

Joe Vampire

Graveyard Shift

Joe followed Evelyn up the steps of the funeral home, feeling uncomfortable in his new suit. It had taken both of them to tie his tie.

Yesterday Evelyn had called him at school to tell him that Celia, her half-sister's mother, had died.

"What do I do?" she asked. "I've never known anyone who died."

Joe had to explain about visitation, and funeral homes, and funerals.

"Did Asha tell you what the arrangements are?"

"Arrangements," Evelyn repeated with distaste, like she was trying a new food she didn't care for. "I haven't talked to her yet. Some aunt called and left a message during the day. Poor Asha! I just want to pop right to her apartment now, but—."

"No, no, no! This is not a time when you want to freak her out." Joe dug around in the pile of books and papers on his desk until he found his exam schedule. He'd have to beg for an extension on his geriatrics medications final. "Listen, you call Asha and get the details on the arrangements. I'll head home and we can go together."

"You'll come with me?"

"Of course!"

Evelyn had called Asha but got her Auntie Louisa instead, who had all the details, so now, here they were. He had to bring back an *In Memoriam* card or something from the funeral service to prove to his geriatrics prof he had really been at a funeral. He was a junior now. All the "chaff" as his academic advisor called them, had been "winnowed" out of the program and it was time to "buckle down" and take things seriously. She was a font of clichéd advice.

"Tulliver?" said Evelyn to the man who stood by the door like a maître-d. Her normally smooth voice was just a touch higher.

"Tulliver?" he repeated. "Do you mean Johnson? Ms. Johnson is in the Rose Room." He pointed out the door.

In the Rose Room, everything was muted—the lighting, the colors, the noise. Everything but the sound of a little girl crying. Less than a dozen people stood in little clutches and spoke in hushed tones. From what Joe could pick up it was not about the dearly-departed. The crying was louder in here, but Joe couldn't see any children.

Just inside the door, an elderly man reached out for Evelyn's hand. "So glad you could come," he all but whispered. His eyes flickered up Joe's tie to his face and he blinked, but shook his hand and repeated the same thing.

"Is Asha here?" asked Evelyn in a subdued alto.

"Pardon?" said the man, leaning in and cupping his ear.

"Asha Tulliver," Evelyn repeated a little louder.

"I'm sorry, I can't quite hear...."

Joe pulled her away. "There," he whispered, aiming Evelyn towards the end of the room.

Asha was sitting on a loveseat just to the right of the coffin. Her broad face was totally blank and Joe recognized the work of tranquilizers in her dilated pupils. No one was with her.

"Asha?" said Evelyn quietly as they approached.

Asha raised her red-rimmed eyes slowly to her half-sister's face. "Evelyn," she said in wonder, and then her blank composure crumbled into tears.

Evelyn stiffened.

"Maybe you could take her to the john," suggested Joe in a whisper in her ear.

Evelyn crouched in front of Asha. "Why don't we go freshen up, hmm?" she asked as if she was talking to a child. Asha nodded.

"Thanks for coming," said the old man at the door as they walked past him.

"There's a room..." said Asha, pointing down the hall. The child's crying followed them.

At the end of the hall, a little brass plaque denoted the Grief Room. It was dimly lit, had three couches facing each other, and a large stock of tissues. Evelyn sat down on one of the couches with Asha.

"I'm glad you came," said Asha miserably leaning into Evelyn's shoulder. Evelyn didn't seem quite sure what to do at first, and put her arm gingerly around her sister.

There was only him and Evelyn and Asha in here. It wasn't a child, Joe realized. The crying was coming from Asha; he was hearing her inside his head.

"It's going to be okay," soothed Evelyn.

"I'm all alone now. Don't got nobody...."

"Then who are all those people?" chided Evelyn gently.

"I don't know."

"Who's the old man shaking hands at the door?"

"My uncle, great-uncle...." Asha stared straight ahead unseeing.

"Come on now," said Joe, squatting down in front of her. "You've got the Tullivers, and Evelyn here, and me." *And whoever gave you the tranqs*, he thought. Somebody had overdone it.

"They want me to shake hands and talk with everybody that comes in," complained Asha. "I don't know these people."

"They must have known your mother," suggested Evelyn.

"I guess," Asha sighed.

Evelyn squeezed her tighter and rested her cheek on Asha's head. "It's going to be okay," she repeated.

"These people, they're here for you," said Joe.

"Ain't nothing they can do," murmured Asha, doe eyes staring off into space.

"You aren't alone," said Evelyn. "I'll take care of you."

Joe stood up. It was hopeless trying to talk to her while she was stoned. "Are you ready to go back?" he asked.

Asha just stared into the distance.

"Maybe you could find some coffee?" suggested Evelyn.

Joe shook his head. "Won't help. It just has to work out of her system." He found a washroom and came back with wet paper towels. Asha let Evelyn wipe her face and hands.

"That feels better," she said. "You going to come with me?"

"I'll stay with you all night," promised Evelyn.

The Rose Room had been deserted. Only the deaf uncle remained, and two elderly women sitting on a couch, clucking and murmuring to each other. As they walked into the room the elderly uncle shook Joe's hand again. "So glad you could come."

Asha glanced at the coffin. "I want to go home," she said.

"I don't think we can do that yet," said Joe.

"Of course we can," declared Evelyn.

One of the elderly women heaved herself up from the couch and came over. "Asha, honey, how you doing? Those pills I gave you helping you out?" she crooned, but she was looking at Evelyn and Joe with open curiosity.

"I guess," murmured Asha.

"Now, who are your friends?"

"This my half-sister Evelyn," said Asha, putting her arm around Evelyn's waist.

"How do you do," said Evelyn, and shook hands.

"And this Joe," added Asha.

"I'm Louisa Johnson, Celia's aunt," she said with a nod toward the coffin. Joe noticed for the first time that it was closed. "I'd be the one called. I thought I was Asha's only relative, other than her father," she said with a disdainful sniff. "We've been doing what we could to help out. Are you going to be staying?" she asked hopefully.

"Yeah?" asked Asha, "are you?"

"As long as you like," Evelyn smiled.

"Well," said Auntie Louisa, smiling. "That's good. It's good to have family around you."

"So glad you could come," they heard the uncle say again and looked over to see Justin Tulliver.

Louisa snorted and retreated to the couch and the company of the other woman.

"Daddy?" whimpered Asha in a little girl's voice. The crying in Joe's head was echoed by audible sobs.

"Oh, baby," he answered and enfolded her in his arms, where she broke down crying again. "It's going to be okay, sweetheart, everything's going to be okay. Somebody—" he looked around the nearly empty room, "— somebody takin' care of you?"

"Evelyn came."

Justin hadn't even noticed his other daughter. "Evelyn!" He blinked at her a few times. "How you all doing?"

"Joe, right? Nice to see you again." Justin gave him his salesman's smile and reached around Asha to shake hands.

"Excuse me, Mr. Tulliver," said a low-voiced funeral home employee who had glided up behind Justin. Justin managed to detach Asha and stepped away to speak to the man.

"Asha, they need to know some things for the funeral tomorrow," he said, coming back.

"Would you come with me?" Asha asked Evelyn, looking shyly at her.

"Sure."

"Well, you don't have to," protested Justin, following as they turned to go without him. "I've helped out with all the other arrangements, I can take care of this too."

"If Asha wants me to go with her, I'll go," responded Evelyn, smiling coldly.

"Well, Asha, who do you want?"

Asha stopped and pressed her hands to the side of her head like it was going to explode.

"We'll both go with you." Justin threw a warning look at Evelyn, who nodded in agreement.

Joe sat down on the loveseat Asha had occupied. He looked around. The coffin was closed. How had Evelyn said she'd died? A traffic accident of some sort. Must have been messy. He repressed a shudder.

The feeling of eyes on him made him turn to find Auntie Louisa alone and staring at him. He smiled.

"Are you Evelyn's fella?" she asked.

"Uh, yeah."

Louisa got up and shuffled over to sit with him.

"You know, I don't know how this is going to be paid for," she confided to him.

"Didn't she have insurance?"

"Insurance won't pay. Coroner ruled it suicide."

"Suicide?"

"Asha don't know and I trust you not to tell her," said Louisa, staring at him like she'd hex him if he breathed a word of it. "Celia had cancer. Didn't tell nobody, neither, but she knew and her doctor knew. The truck driver said she stepped out in front of him deliberately. The coroner ruled it suicide and the insurance won't pay."

"Was it?" asked Joe. "I mean, you knew her, would she have...?"

Louisa straightened up and took a noisy breath in through her nose. "She was independent. She didn't want to be a burden to nobody, least of all Asha. So I reckon maybe she did."

"How did you keep this from Asha?"

"Oh, that was easy," she said with a wave of one gloved hand. "She's just been, you know, cata- whatsis? She just lay on her bed and stared into space these last few days."

"Catatonic."

"That's it. Don't eat, don't do nothing, don't talk much. Grieving. I had to take her cigarettes away 'cause I was afraid she'd set the bed afire. Hell, Celia was her whole family, except her daddy, and he don't count. I answered the phone, I talked to the coroner, and the insurance and the doctor, so she don't know nothing about it. Justin, he knows, and he agreed to keep his mouth shut."

"She's going to find out sooner or later."

Louisa shook her head. "Not as long as the funeral's paid for. I understand Evelyn's got money."

Joe nodded. Yes, Evelyn would pay. He knew she would.

"Justin, he says he can't pay for it," continued Louisa. "He says he might be able to pay half, but don't tell his wife. He wants me to come up with the other half, but I don't have that kind of money."

"You really ought to talk to Evelyn," said Joe.

"You tell her to call me." She rummaged in her purse until she found an orange plastic pill bottle and handed it to Joe. The label was smudged and faded. "I was going to give these to her sister. You hang on to that and you can give Asha one or two if she needs them, only don't let her have the bottle because I'm afraid of what she might do."

Joe nodded and pocketed the pills.

More rummaging turned up a box of Chiclets. Auntie Louisa offered Joe one, then tore off the flap and wrote her number on it. "And don't dare say anything about this to that poor girl.

#

Joe lay staring at the ceiling, his feet up on the arm of the couch. No matter what he tried, there was no comfortable way to sleep on it. When you're over six feet tall, couches just won't do.

Asha shuffled into the doorway. She looked dumpy and old in her terry-cloth robe, bunny slippers, and sleep-matted hair.

"Hey, you awake?"

"Yeah. How'd you sleep?"

"Okay, I guess," she answered in her whispery soft voice. "Where's Evelyn? She up already?"

"Uh, she had a meeting with a banker or investment broker or something. She'll be back."

"Oh. You want some coffee? I'll put it on." She shuffled away before Joe could decline.

When Joe had first met Asha she had been fourteen and looked like a child next to her sophisticated older sister Evelyn. Even when Asha turned eighteen, the same physical age Evelyn had been when she died, Evelyn had more poise and maturity. But now, grief had aged her. Asha looked much older than her sister.

The bathroom was tucked under the eaves and Joe had to stoop the whole time he was in there.

"How you like your coffee?" The machine was burbling away on top of a filing cabinet turned kitchen counter.

"Uh, none for me, thanks."

"You don't drink coffee?"

"Naw, I'm afraid if I start I'll be having ten cups a day and getting the shakes without it." Joe seated himself at the little white table. It was under the eaves too, in front of a gable window that looked out over the street and the two-storey gingerbread houses that lined it.

"Evelyn said you... 'kicked the habit,'" Asha euphemized.

Joe nodded.

The coffee maker stopped and Asha loaded her cup with sugar and a teaspoon of powdered milk.

"'Cept for the occasional smoke. You know. But that's not addictive."

"Yeah," Asha said with a little sigh. She sat down and stirred her coffee until the little white granules disappeared. "I used to toke up once in a while when I was in school. But I'm a grown-up now."

"Not me," bragged Joe with a grin.

"My—" Asha choked back a sob and stared into her coffee. "My mom wanted me to go to college. Ain't no point. I'm not dumb, but I was never good at school."

Joe shrugged. "You got a good job, right?" Evelyn had told him that Asha worked for one of the big car companies, putting minivans together on the assembly line or something.

"Yeah. I work the graveyard shift. Pays better, but sometimes I don't see the sun all week. Anyway, they gave me a week off. HR guy said if I need more time to come in and talk to him and I could have it. But he said sometimes it's best to get back to work. Something to do, something else to think about. Nice enough guy, only he talked down to me. I don't know if it's 'cause I'm young, or I'm black, or I'm a woman. Or maybe all three."

Joe shrugged. "Doesn't matter what he thinks. You want me to cook some breakfast?"

Asha took a little slurp of her coffee, trying not to burn her lips. "I'm not hungry, but help yourself."

Joe's stomach was twisting inside him. Neither Evelyn nor Asha had thought of dinner last night, and he hadn't found an appropriate time to suggest it.

In the fridge were bacon and eggs, and there was pancake mix in the cupboard. After wrapping the cooked bacon in a paper towel, Joe fried pancakes in the grease left in the pan. It was a trick he'd learned from Carter.

"Maybe I will have some," said Asha. "It smells good. I didn't know you could cook."

"I can't," answered Joe. "This is it. And macaroni and cheese out of a box."

"I can't cook," she replied, eyes on her plate. She drowned her pancake in syrup and added a squirt to her coffee for good measure.

"When will Evelyn be back?" she asked as they ate.

"Uh, I'm not sure."

"Will she be back in time for the funeral?"

"Uh..." Joe knew she wouldn't be. The funeral was at four in the afternoon and the sun didn't set until six. Asha was staring at him. "I'm not sure."

Whassup with her? Joe heard in Asha's mental voice, but she didn't ask it out loud, so he didn't answer.

"Is somebody coming to take you?"

"I don't know."

"Well, I've got my car...."

Asha frowned. "You got the car, where's Evelyn?"

"We brought two cars. She knew she had to go back...." He hoped Asha never asked to see that second car.

Asha frowned at her plate and Joe could feel the unasked questions. Just as well, he thought, it would keep her mind off her mother.

"Anyway, I thought you might want to go with your father...."

"Naw, he'll have Joleen with him and the kids. I got my own car."

"Hey, I'm not going to let you drive yourself."

"I can drive," said Asha quietly.

"Come with me," coaxed Joe. "It's okay."

"I was hoping Evelyn would be back. I was going to ask her to do my hair," she said shyly, running a hand over her head.

Joe got a mental picture of Asha sitting at this table, her mother doing her hair. Asha at five with twisted pigtails; Asha at ten with cornrows; Asha at twelve with a pink foam roller in her bangs. Her mother doing her hair and morning sun gilding the table, coffee scenting the air.

The little-girl-lost sobbing was starting again, and Joe remembered being woken by it in the night.

"I'll do your hair," he said.

The crying stopped short. "You?"

"You think I don't know how? Evelyn wouldn't have a clue. Come on, she's whiter than I am."

Asha laughed a little and nodded. "But you know how I do my hair? You can do that?"

"Yeah, I've done it before. I did Evelyn's hair all up in cornrows one night, but she hated it." He smiled, remembering. Cornrows were decidedly not Evelyn.

"No, I can't see it," agreed Asha.

The crying started again, in Joe's head. Big tears streamed down Asha's face.

"Hey, it's going to be okay," said Joe, reaching across the table to take her hand. "You're going to get through this." It was nice to reach out for a hand and feel a warm one pulsing with life, he thought.

Asha snuffled and wiped at the tears on her cheeks with the sleeve of her bathrobe. She shook her head. "I don't feel... I don't feel like I'm going to get through it. How am I going to go to the funeral home? I can't stop crying, I see that coffin, and—"

"It's okay. You can cry. Come on, now, why don't you get a shower. That'll make you feel better. And I'll do your hair."

Asha chuckled through her tears. "Okay."

#

A chocolate skinned girl with a big, reddish afro closed in on Asha as soon as she and Joe came in the door of the Rose Room. She had a tall skinny boyfriend whose arm was draped over her shoulders like he was a permanent attachment. Joe was relieved to see that Asha's friends had turned up at the funeral. It was going to soften the blow of Evelyn not showing.

"Asha, honey, how you doing? Why didn't you call me, girl? You know I only found out this morning?"

"Call you?" said Asha faintly. "I thought... my auntie said she called everyone."

A girl with a big belly and her husband, whose suit must have been borrowed from someone larger, had joined them. The tall girl barrelled on while they hugged Asha and murmured their condolences.

"Well, she didn't call us, hon," said the girl, as if it had been a social slight. "Anyway, we're here to take care of you now. So, who made the arrangements? Your auntie?"

"My daddy," answered Asha. Her voice had gone even softer. She seemed to shrink and fade into herself.

"Yo' daddy!" squeaked the girl. "You been staying with him?"

"No."

"Who done your hair, girl?" she demanded.

Joe guessed she was trying to be helpful, but she came on more like a bully. He laid a hand on Asha's shoulder to remind her that she wasn't alone.

"Who's this?" demanded the girl.

"This is Joe," said Asha, brightening a little. "You remember, I told you about my sister Evelyn? Joe is her boyfriend."

"Where is she?" demanded the girl.

"Hi, I'm Al," said the expectant husband pushing in between the tall girl and Asha to shake hands with Joe. "This is my wife, Neda. We all went to high school together."

"I'm Yasmin," declared the girl, "and this is my boyfriend Dexter," she said, with a smile and a little hip swing.

"An' I'm Frog," croaked a voice to Joe's left. He turned to find a guy who was too pale, with sparse dishwater blonde hair on a large, lumpy head. Pale grey eyes blinked from behind thick glasses. The nickname suited him, thought Joe, and the guy blinked straight at him. Joe decided he'd better keep his thoughts quiet.

"How are you, Asha?" he rasped.

"Okay, I guess," she sighed. "Joe been looking after me."

"You could have called me," said Frog. "I'd have come right over, helped you out, done whatever."

Asha shook her head mutely, unwilling to meet Frog's earnest gaze. Yasmin was staring at them.

"Yeah, well," she said into the leaden silence that followed, "we're all here for you now, girl."

Asha straightened with a deep breath, as if being called "girl" reminded her that she was a full grown woman. "I'm okay."

"So where's this Evelyn?" Yasmin wanted to know.

Asha looked to Joe.

"I don't know." He glanced at the window. The shadows were long, but it wouldn't be dark for another hour yet. Evelyn was curled up in a locked trunk in the boarded-up closet of a locked room, dead to the world. "She ought to be here any minute," he lied.

"So where you going after the service," asked Yasmin.

"Going?" said Asha. "Well, home, I guess."

"Usually someone has an open house after. A wake, like," said Neda, absently rubbing her belly.

"My god, don't tell me this your first funeral!?"

Asha nodded.

No wonder she was so lost, thought Joe. "Didn't Justin say something about his house?"

Asha shrugged, focused on the floor. Joe hadn't even given her any tranquilizers, though the bottle was in his pocket.

Justin came out of the chapel with the funeral director. "Asha? Hi," he said, including the group of her friends in his smile. It was so broad and bright Joe was afraid he was going to pass out business cards. "We're about ready to start if you want to come in and take a seat. Your friends going to sit with you?"

"'Course we are," declared Yasmin for the whole group.

"Joe, we could use another pall bearer."

"Sure."

"And, uh, we need one more...."

"I'll do it," said Frog, and coughed.

"I'll do it, man," interjected Yasmin's boyfriend. "We're more evenly matched, anyway." He eyed Joe's height like it was a challenge.

"Yeah, Frog," agreed Yasmin, "you stay with Asha."

"I can—" he started to protest, and then gave up with a sigh. "Alright, yes. Come on." He took Asha gently by the arm. "You have to sit at the front. It's sort of like a wedding."

Joe went as far as the front of the church with the group, then seated himself on the left with Justin and Dexter. Two other men joined them, nodding, and lastly the old uncle who had been at the funeral home.

"He's not going to be a pall bearer, is he?" whispered Joe to Justin.

"I couldn't talk him out of it," Justin whispered back. "Don't worry, we'll put him in the middle."

The service was short. Joe had seen Celia several times, but her absence didn't really mean anything to him. It wasn't until he lifted the coffin, and felt the weight of the body within shift, that Joe felt it was real.

This will never happen to Evelyn. Except that it happened every day when the sun came up.

"Are we going to the cemetery?" asked Joe as they slid the casket into the back of a long grey hearse.

"No, Asha didn't want to." Justin stepped back as the funeral director swung the back doors of the hearse closed.

The final click of the doors seemed to cause something to break in Asha. With a wail she started to cry in earnest, not caring that she was with her friends, not caring that she was in a parking lot on a busy street. Frog caught her as she crumpled, and Joe and Justin both hurried over.

Neda and Yasmin were stroking her back and her hair, both talking at once. Frog croaked comforting things, and tears were streaming from under his fogged-up glasses.

"Uh...." Justin looked on helplessly. "We're going to have an open house at our place," he said to Joe.

"I think I ought to take her home and let her collect herself first," said Joe.

"Where's your car, Asha?" asked Frog. "Hey, come on, where's your car, we'll take you home."

Asha's sobs had subsided to hiccups and weeping, but in his head, Joe could hear her shrieking. It wasn't childish sobs anymore, it was a terrified wail mixed with claustrophobic images of coffins and graves. He stopped himself halfway to covering his ears and smoothed his hair back instead.

"I brought her," said Joe.

"Come on, now, girlfriend, you got to be strong," said Yasmin, but it came out as a whisper.

"Take me home," pleaded Asha, lifting her head from Frog's shoulder.

"We'll see you at the wake," Frog told the others, wiping his eyes. "Okay if I go with you?" he asked Asha and Joe.

Asha didn't answer, but Joe was glad for the help. He really wished Evelyn was here.

#

The shrieking in Joe's head became a mournful wail as they pulled out of the funeral home's lot, although on the outside Asha was calm and dry-eyed. She stared straight ahead. In the back seat, Frog was noisily blowing his nose. Joe offered him a package of tissues from his pocket.

"No thanks," he rasped. "I got my own."

Asha gave a little chuckle and the shrieking wound down to a sob.

"Frog's an environmentalist. He uses handkerchiefs so he don't fill up the trash dumps with tissues."

"You know how many I go through," he answered.

"Ask him how he wipe his bum." Tears spilled out of her eyes as she gave a half-sob, half-laugh.

"Oh, Asha!" whined Frog. "Don't."

Joe mentally rolled his eyes. No, this was not a discussion he wanted to get into with a complete stranger, but it was distracting Asha from her grief and that had to be good for her.

"Oka-ay, how do you—?"

"With toilet paper, like everybody else, thank you. Hundred percent recycled post-consumer content."

"But he used to do it like a baby."

"Not like a baby," answered Frog with exaggerated indignation. Joe got the feeling he was playing along to get Asha talking and to get her to think about something else. Frog must be a good friend. Joe just wished he wouldn't lean forward between the seats and breathe on him. His breath was sour. The windshield started to fog up and Joe had to turn the defroster on.

"Environmentally conscious parents use cloth diapers, and instead of commercial diaper wipes, they use washcloths and launder them with the diapers. So I figured, why not do the same thing? Get a couple dozen cheap washcloths...."

Asha chuckled to herself.

"So why'd you stop?" Joe forced himself to ask.

"Well, I'm allergic to detergent, and bleach. And borax."

"Frog is full of good ideas," teased Asha as they got out of the car.

"Okay, so that one backfired." He held Asha's door for her.

Joe clicked the car alarm on. Nearly dark now. Could he stall long enough for Evelyn to arrive?

"I'm going to go wash my face," Asha muttered as they entered the third-floor apartment. Her good humor was gone as soon as she looked around at her mother's furniture, her mother's photos on the wall, her mother's home.

Frog was gasping with the effort of climbing the steps. He rested with his hand on the door knob for a few minutes. "She was a good woman," he panted. "She was a good mom." He turned and blinked his magnified eyes at Joe. "So, what do you do?" he asked abruptly, and led the way into the living room.

"College," said Joe, perching himself on the broad arm of a worn velvet armchair. "I'm studying to be a pharmacist."

"Yeah?"

"Joe's the same age as us," said Asha from the doorway. Little beads of water sparkled in the hair around her forehead.

"You feel better now?" asked Frog. "Are you ready to go to your dad's?"

Asha sighed and sat down in a chair beside the door, although the couch next to Frog was conspicuously empty.

"I do not want to go," she said in a soft but resolute voice.

"Well... you kind of... have to," said Joe.

"Who'll be there?" she asked.

"Anyone who was at the funeral. Your friends'll be there."

Asha rubbed her forehead. "I don't think I can take Yasmin just now."

"She's just trying to help," offered Frog.

"I know. But I just want to tell her *to shut up* and maybe tonight I'll do it."

"So?" croaked Frog. "I tell her all the time, she doesn't listen." Joe was beginning to wonder if that was his normal voice.

Joe took the tranquilizers from his pocket and looked at the label. They would make the evening easier, but did she need it? This was why pharmacists just dispensed medicine, he thought. His definition of when you needed a drug to make you feel better was probably different than a doctor's. Well, maybe not Elvis's doctor.

"Your dad's going to be real upset if you don't go," said Frog, eyeing the pill bottle in Joe's hand.

"I know. And he's been doing so much for me. Only I wish everyone would leave me alone. Not you guys. Just... my auntie and my dad and all these people I don't know."

Joe held the bottle out to Asha. She looked at it and shook her head.

More for me, said one of the voices in Joe's head.
Stop that.

Joe tucked the pills back in his pocket.

"You don't have to stay long. I'll run interference for you with Yasmin and anyone else who gets in your face," said Frog. "Well," he announced when Asha didn't answer, "I'm going to use the... you know."

When he was gone Joe leaned confidentially forward. "What's wrong with him?" he asked.

"What ain't?" replied Asha. "Asthma, allergies. He passes out if it's too hot and he gets sick all the time. He don't have no sweat glands. He's real smart, though. Going to U of M, full scholarship."

Joe was suitably impressed.

Asha got up and looked out the window over Riverside Park.

"If I don't go, Daddy'll be mad. Joleen'll be mad for sure," she sighed.

"Just go for a little while. After tonight it'll all be over."

"Yeah, it will all be over," she said, resting her forehead against the glass.

Joe wished he hadn't phrased it that way. "Think of it like a new life. Not exactly what you wanted, but a beginning, not an end. A new adventure."

"By myself."

"No," protested Frog from the door. "Look, there's Yasmin and Neda and Al. And Joe's here, and your sister's coming. And me. And maybe your dad isn't the best father in the world, but he's trying."

"Yeah," she breathed, her breath fogging the glass. Asha turned to Joe suddenly. "You reckon Evelyn's okay?"

Joe was startled by the question. Of course, he knew she was okay, but he should fake some concern, shouldn't he? He glanced at his watch and involuntarily at the window. Dark, finally.

"Uh, maybe I ought to call."

"She's been gone all day for one meeting," commented Asha with a hint of resentment.

"Well, it was in Ohio."

He'd started dialing the phone when there was sharp rap at the door. Evelyn walked in without waiting for anyone to answer it.

"Here you are!" she said, like she had been looking for them. "I'm so sorry Asha. I couldn't get here any sooner."

"How come?" Asha demanded in a sullen voice. She'd come half way across the room before remembering she was upset.

"My car broke down on the interstate. It took forever to get a tow truck, and two rental agencies were out of cars. I ended up taking a cab here."

"You took a cab? All the way from Ohio?"

Evelyn shrugged. "I had to get here. And I knew Joe had his car. I'm so sorry, this is the earliest I could come." She pleaded with her eyes for Asha's forgiveness. Or belief.

"S'okay, you here now."

Frog cleared his throat and Joe saw that he was openly staring at Evelyn.

"This is Frog," said Joe. "He's a friend of Asha's."

"How d'you do," said Evelyn, offering him her hand.

"Pleasure," he rasped, his voice almost gone. "Asha's talked a lot about you."

"We was just on our way over to Daddy's," said Asha with a marked lack of enthusiasm. "I don't want to go but... I guess I better."

"Why? If you don't want to go, let's not go," said Evelyn.

"See?" laughed Asha. "This is why I need my sister here. She lets me do whatever I want."

"We have to go, baby," said Joe gently.

"I don't think I'm welcome there."

"It's an open house," rasped Frog, "Everyone's welcome."

"Justin and I don't really get along," said Evelyn.

"She called him out on his colorism the first time she came over," explained Asha. She stood up. The little girl was not crying anymore. "Okay, I guess I gotta go. And then I want to come back home and sleep."

#

The Tullivers' house was much as Joe remembered it from his first and only visit at that uncomfortable Thanksgiving five years ago: clean and neat and crowded and a bit showy. And surprisingly empty of people.

"You're here!" said Justin loudly as Joe, Evelyn, Asha, and Frog trooped in the front door. The drink in his hand winked gold light at them. It gave Joe a sick feeling in the pit of his stomach to see Justin drunk.

"Where is everyone?"

"Hardly anyone came. I guess Celia wasn't too popular."

"They came to her funeral," Asha ground out, staring at the floor, "they just don't want to come to your house."

"I'm sorry, baby girl." Justin's shoulders sagged. "I didn't mean anything by it. It's been a long day."

"Where's Amy?" asked Asha. "And Michael?" Amy and Michael were Asha and Evelyn's younger half siblings, Justin's kids with his wife Joleen. Joe had not seen them since his last, uncomfortable visit to this house either.

Justin waved vaguely, then seemed to realize his gestures were not accompanied by any words. "Amy went over to her friends. Figured you were a no-show. I'll bring her around tomorrow. She wants to see you."

"And Michael?" asked Evelyn.

Again the vague wave. "Somewhere. I never know where he is anymore."

Asha snorted like a bull. "Don't feel like you have to bring *him* around to see me."

"Aw, baby girl, don't be that way."

"Nobody came?" asked Frog.

"Your friends were here. That loud girl and that young couple. They just left, in fact. We all figured you weren't going to come."

"What about Auntie Louisa and Uncle Ben?" asked Asha.

Justin shook his head. "That woman hates me. Wouldn't step foot in my house for nothing. She blames me 'cause your mother wouldn't marry me."

"What?" asked Joleen, suddenly appearing from the kitchen with a box of plastic wrap in her hands.

"Louisa. Celia's aunt. Blames me cause we didn't stay married," he amended, looking into his drink rather than at his wife. "The others, I think they were all folks Celia used to work with, long time ago."

Joleen didn't look like she believed him. "I was just wrapping up the food, but if you'd like anything...."

"No, we going to go on home," said Asha, turning to the door.

"Let me put together something for you to take home." Joleen disappeared into the kitchen.

"Let's go," said Asha.

"But, um—" began Frog.

"Let's. Go."

"I'll phone you tomorrow," called Justin as they went down the walk.

"I won't be answering the phone," muttered Asha under her breath.

In the car everyone was quiet. Joe glanced in the rear-view mirror and saw Frog reach for Asha's hand. She tucked her hands into her sleeves and looked out the window.

"Well, back to the apartment?" asked Evelyn.

"Yeah, I guess," sighed Asha. "I don't want to kick nobody out, you know, but I really wouldn't mind some time to myself."

"Are you sure?" asked Evelyn, half turning to see her.

Asha nodded. "Been so many people around all weekend...."

Joe cruised onto the interstate. Except for Frog's occasional bouts with his handkerchief the trip was quiet. The crying in his head was gone too, Joe realized with some relief. Asha had turned a corner somewhere.

"Can we drop you somewhere, Frog?" asked Joe as they came into Ypsilanti.

"You can just let me off with Asha. I can walk from there, it's only a block."

"It's three," said Asha.

Joe Vampire

"Why don't we just drop you off," offered Joe. "You've already got a cold."

Frog's voice was muffled by a handkerchief. "It's just allergies."

"Turn down here," Asha told Joe, "it's the last house on this side."

"Thanks, Ash," said Frog with glum sarcasm.

"I don't need nothing," she told him as Joe pulled up to the curb.

"If you do, you call me. Seriously. Even if it's the middle of the night."

Asha didn't answer and Frog got out with a sigh.

"So, you really want us to go?" asked Evelyn as they pulled away from the curb.

"I know you just got here, but I need some time to myself," she answered shyly.

"No problem," Joe assured her. "We understand."

Inside the apartment, Joe gathered his stuff from the living room while Asha sat and smoked in the hall chair.

"I'm really sorry I missed the funeral," Evelyn told her. "You can call us if you need anything."

"I just... you know, I been feeling so low, but now I need to pull myself together. Don't worry, I won't need anything, and Frog, he come if I call."

"What...." Evelyn paused to phrase her question. "What exactly is your relationship with him?"

"Frog? We've known each other since kindergarten. Seems like we've always been friends, 'cause I don't remember a time when I didn't know him. And, well," her voice descended to mutters Joe could hardly hear from the next room, "a couple of weeks ago he told me he's in love with me."

"You don't feel the same," said Evelyn.

"No. I love him, but I'm not *in* love with him."

114

"He is kind of...." Joe could tell she was looking for an inoffensive synonym for 'repulsive.'

"No, that ain't it. It's like he's my brother or something. It just don't feel right."

"I'm ready," announced Joe.

"You're going to be all right?" Evelyn asked again.

"I'll be fine. Don't you start fussing too." She put out her cigarette and hugged them goodbye.

#

"You think we should have left her alone?" fretted Evelyn as they pulled away from Asha's apartment.

"You heard her," said Joe. "She's tired of people, she just wants to be alone." He stopped at a red light and started to wriggle out of his jacket. "You know, if I drive back to campus tonight, I can make my geriatrics final. If you don't mind, you know, popping home."

"I can do that. But...." She sighed. "I'm worried about Asha. She's taking this awfully hard."

"Some people love their parents."

"Would you grieve like that if...?"

Joe shrugged and stared ahead at the road. "I love my mom, even if she was crappy to me. I don't like her, or a lot of the things she did, but... she's my mom."

"You didn't want to live with her. You chose foster care."

"And I still think that was the right choice. You can love someone and know that they are bad for you. And it wasn't so much her as, you know, the environment."

"Readily available painkillers."

"Yeah."

"I don't get it," she said, shaking her head.

"I know."

Evelyn said quietly, "That's what I'll be like when I lose her. Or you."

Joe glanced at her. Was that fear he heard in her voice?

"Well, you know, she isn't going to live forever, and you are."

Evelyn was quiet.

"Baby?"

"Hm?"

"Asha isn't going to live forever."

"Maybe," she whispered.

COMMUNITY

The Vampire Council

On his drive home for Thanksgiving weekend, Joe thought about all the Thanksgivings he had managed to survive as a kid. They involved feuding relatives, drunken car rides, food poisoning, and 911 calls. This was his year of lasts: the last time he would eat a pre-Thanksgiving dinner in the caf, the last time he would drive home from college for the long weekend, and the last time he would have to endure Carter pining for Christmas holidays for a month beforehand. He was thankful that this weekend was just four days off, four long November nights with Evelyn. There would be no drunkenness, no turkey, no relatives, and no fights.

Evelyn greeted him at the door with kisses that were warm despite the coldness of her lips.

"You, um, you going out somewhere?" asked Joe.

Evelyn smoothed down her navy skirt. It was topped by a double-breasted matching jacket with gold buttons.

"I got a call from Otto last night."

Joe had never met Otto, and his brief impression of the man, or vampire, the few times he'd spoken to him on the phone, had been that Otto had a rake up his butt.

"I've been invited to a Council meeting."

"What council?"

"The Vampire Council of Ohio."

"The...?" Joe snickered. "The Vampire Council of..." he said in a Bela Lugosi voice, "Ohio!"

Evelyn folded her arms across her chest and gave him a mock stern look.

"So, what do they do?"

"Well, I asked Otto that, but I didn't get a clear answer. He said they do a lot of bickering, and they have a rule about no bloodshed."

"I suppose that's a good rule to have."

"And sometimes the *Mater Omnium Lamia* attends."

"The what?"

"It's Latin for 'Mother of All Vampires.' Didn't you take Latin in school?"

"Latin? Ha! No. I took a year of Spanish so I can say *no hablo ingles* with a convincing accent."

"The Mater is like the head vampire. Otto says that if they are inviting me to come, they will invite me to be part of the council."

"So, you get to be one of the cool kids."

"Something like that I guess."

"Can I come with you?"

"Are you serious? I'm not even sure I want to go."

"Aw, c'mon, Ev. The Vampire Council of Ohio! How can you miss that? Aren't you curious? I know I am."

"I don't know...."

She shook her head and turned away, but Joe ditched his backpack and laundry bag and danced back into her line of sight.

"If I am ever going to decide if I want to be a vampire, I need data. I need to know what I am getting into."

"Otto did say Richie would be there."

"Richie?" Joe knew the name from reading her journals, he was.... "The bloodling?"

Evelyn nodded. She was watching him. Joe remembered how she had written about their night together, about wanting to see him again. He just smiled at her.

"Now you have to take me."

"I suppose," she agreed.

"It'll be fun," Joe assured her, although he had no idea what it might be like at all.

#

Joe had imagined the Vampire Council would meet someplace elegant and exclusive—some rich vampire's mansion, the ballroom of a once-elegant but now boarded-up hotel, or maybe a castle high in the mountains. Only Ohio didn't have castles. Or mountains. But no, it was the back room of a rundown bar called *The Lazy Susan*. Evelyn parked the Jag a block away, around the corner, and set the alarm.

"If there's any trouble...."

"Yeah, yeah, I know, grab you and we pop. A room full of vampires, what kind of trouble could there be?"

Evelyn still didn't move to get out of the car.

"They have a rule about no bloodshed," Joe reminded her.

"It worries me that they *need* a rule about bloodshed."

Joe opened his door. "We're here now," he said before she could change her mind, grab his arm and pop him back home.

The unusually warm November night smelled like worms. *The* Lazy Susan sat between a boarded up storefront church and an empty lot. Neon beer signs reflected on the shiny wet street and dingy lace café curtains obscured the lower two-thirds of the windows.

The minute Joe walked in the door he was bombarded by psychic noise. People were laughing, crying, singing, shouting, and talking. But it wasn't the people actually in the bar. The weeknight crowd was sparse. There was a table of older women dressed to the nines, smoking cigars and drinking serious, non-girlie drinks from tumblers. One drunk snored by the window, his hand wrapped around a bottle, and a couple of men at the bar were arguing in mutters. Or maybe they were agreeing with each other. There was no way so much noise was coming from the few people in the bar.

"Why Miss Evelyn!"

From a stage made of plywood and pallets, a man perched on a stool was grinning broadly at Evelyn. His teeth were very white in his dark face, and he had a head of shiny black curls, like Lionel Ritchie in the '80s. There were dull spots on the saxophone in his hands where the finish had worn off. This was not Otto.

"Richie!" Evelyn crossed the room and the sax player took her hand and kissed it.

"You are a vision of loveliness, as always."

"You never called me."

Joe barely noticed Evelyn was flirting: he was too distracted by the psychic crowd.

"Another night with you would have taken decades off my life, and I did not feel that I could afford that."

"Well, you've missed your chance now. This is my boyfriend, Joe Cheney. Joe, this is Richie."

120

"It's a pleasure to make your acquaintance." Richie shook his hand.

Evelyn was watching his face for his reaction, so Joe tried to be as bland as possible. "Yeah, same here."

Joe recognized Richie from Evelyn's journal and the old fashioned way he addressed her as *Miss Evelyn*. Richie, the bloodling who had lived two hundred years. If he was telling the truth.

Evelyn leaned close to Richie, and Joe caught a vivid flash of memory from him. It was Evelyn's naked breast and the feel of her nipple in his mouth, only not his mouth. Richie's. Joe looked around the bar to hide his flush.

"Are you here for the meeting?" asked Evelyn *sotto voce*.

"I'm not a member of *that club*, Miss Evelyn. Mayhap I never will be. Not a day I look forward to. So, they want you to join?"

"I guess."

"And..." Richie's eyes moved to Joe, "you brought them a snack!"

"Hey, I'm not a snack," protested Joe.

"Miss Evelyn, Miss Evelyn." Richie shook his head. "He'd best stay out here. Unless," he looked at Joe, "you *want* to be a snack?"

"Uh, no."

"They aren't big on asking first."

"He's my guest," said Evelyn.

Richie shook his head. "No guests. Otto didn't tell you that? Well, let me tell you: breathers who go in don't always come out. Not vertical, anyway."

Evelyn gave him a worried look and Joe rolled his eyes.

"Maybe you'd better go home."

"I can wait here." Joe looked at Richie. "I'll be okay out here, right?"

Joe Vampire

Richie shrugged. "Yeah, sure. According to the rules members of *that club* are supposed to come and go through the back door and not come out here."

"Oh! Otto told me that and I forgot," exclaimed Evelyn.

"And deprive me of seeing your lovely self? You can use the front door, Miss Evelyn. Consider yourself my guest. But now you best go on in. Down the hall there. Otto gets touchy if anyone is late."

Evelyn squeezed Joe's hand and gave him a worried smile.

"I'll be fine," he assured her. He didn't want Evelyn to have to run him home like an overtired toddler up past his bedtime.

"Leroy," Richie called to the bartender, "set the gentleman up. Order whatever you like, on the house."

Leroy the bartender looked like he ought to be laying in a casket, not upright behind a bar. He was bald and liver-spotted on both his hands and his head. His dress shirt and dinner jacket hung on him like his shoulders were a wire coat hanger.

"What can I get you?" asked Leroy in a papery voice.

"Just a Coke," answered Joe. Richie played some jazz riffs on his sax. Leroy placed Joe's glass on a cocktail napkin and Joe took it to a table near the stage and sat with his back against the wall.

Joe tried to focus his psychic ears and sort out all the images and sounds and sensations, but there were too many. If he closed his eyes, he could almost feel the crowd.

There was a sudden hush in the noise and Joe opened his eyes to see a biker, all leather and denim, heavy boots, American flag bandana tied around his head, a ZZ Top beard, and dark sunglasses, striding along the bar toward the rear hall. Joe knew he was another member of *that club*. It wasn't just the sunglasses after dark–he could somehow feel it. The biker slowed down as he passed the bar and Leroy backed into the tiny space between the counter behind him and the ice machine. Joe saw the sneer lift the end of the biker's mustache but he didn't turn his head or break stride. The bar seemed to be holding its breath. The whole place let out a sigh when he disappeared down the hall.

"Play Misty for me," called one of the women, when the biker was gone.

On the makeshift stage, Richie launched into a slow, sweet rendition of the song. Joe could hear Ella Fitzgerald singing along, just as if her ghost was there on stage. Richie played with his eyes closed. He moved on to *Dream a Little Dream*, and a few other tunes Joe didn't recognize. Joe had never listened to jazz before, and now he wondered why not. When Richie finished his set he went to the table of ladies and flirted and made them laugh and blush.

"You all enjoy your book club night," he told them as he walked toward Joe's table. Leroy brought him a whiskey and replaced Joe's empty glass with another Coke.

"You're really good," Joe told him. "You should be playing someplace better than this."

Richie gave him a level look. "I own this place."

"Oh..."

"There was a day, it was a better place. It was a speakeasy back in the '20s. I'm waiting for real estate prices to rebound."

Joe thought that was unlikely.

"So, you are Miss Evelyn's boyfriend."

Joe nodded.

"Are you out of your mind?" asked Richie.

"Excuse me?"

"She's in a dangerous business."

Joe snorted. They'd taken on Simms and won, but Richie didn't know anything about that. "I know what I'm getting into."

"Do you, now? No offense, but Evelyn is a babe in the woods, and we're talking really dark and dangerous woods. And you, well, you are what we call a snack."

"Who's 'we'? I thought you weren't part of *that club*."

Richie gave him a grudging half-smile. "I am part of that world, whether I like it or not. Look, the longer one is a member of *that club*, the less regard one seems to have for non-members. Even for younger members. In fact, I would hazard to say that the best way to continue to be a member of *that club* is to have a certain amount of disregard for human life. It's too much of a moral dilemma otherwise."

The women were standing up, getting ready to leave. "You all have a pleasant good night," Richie called out to them. "And tell your husbands I said what lucky men they are." The women giggled on their way out the door.

Only the drunk was left, still in the same position on his table, and old Leroy behind the bar, who was reading the newspaper.

"So, you're a bloodling."

"I am a bloodling. Someday something will happen to me, a jealous husband probably, and then I will be a member of *that club*. Look, this is not—"

The biker came striding out from the back hallway. He looked around, saw Joe and grinned. "Ah, Joe, there you are. Come on, I got something to show you."

He had radiated menace when he came in, but now Joe felt absurdly happy to see him, like they were old friends. He stood up.

"Got something to show you, outside. C'mon, you'll like this."

Out of the corner of his eye, Joe caught Richie reaching for him. He turned to see that Richie had his mouth open, but nothing was coming out.

"Richie? Are you okay?"

Richie's mouth moved, but still, nothing came out. He frowned and touched his throat.

The biker gave a laugh full of bonhomie. "Never mind him, he'll be fine. Come on."

Joe wanted to go, but Richie did seem to be in distress. "Richie?"

Richie looked up and locked eyes with Joe. *Do not go with him*, Joe heard in his head very clearly.

That happy, trusting feeling in Joe's chest evaporated.

"C'mon, Joe," urged the biker, all good ol' boy friendly. Joe felt his friendliness, like a soft and cozy blanket, trying to envelop him. He kept his eyes on Richie.

"Something's wrong with Richie. I'm going to stay here and make sure he's okay," said Joe, pushing the table away from the wall so he could get it between him and the biker. Where was Evelyn when he needed to be popped home?

Richie coughed and croaked, "What you think you up to, Claude?"

Claude grinned and showed his fangs. "Just helping myself to a little snack, seeing as our newest member was so kind as to bring one along."

It was gone. No more warm and friendly sensations were flowing over Joe.

"I am not a snack!" declared Joe. He had been hoping it would come out in an intimidating roar, but instead his voice cracked.

And then Evelyn popped into being just in front of the bar, blinked out again, and was suddenly between Joe and Claude.

Claude took a step back and began to swear.

"What is going on?" demanded Otto as he burst into the room. Joe knew him by his voice and German accent. Other faces appeared in the doorway. Other vampires. They didn't venture into the room, just watched from the doorway.

"Did you see that?" asked Claude. "Did you see that? She can transport."

"*Ja*? So?"

"Well, who else do you know that can do that?"

There was silence for a minute.

"Only the Mater," hissed Claude. "What are you playing at? What is the Mater playing at?"

"What were you about to do with Joe?" asked Evelyn, her voice quiet and icy.

"Immaterial!" declared Claude, waving his hands in the air.

"This is why we have a rule about not bringing pets to the meetings," said Otto.

"Richie is here," Evelyn pointed out. Joe was happy to hear a touch of exasperation in her voice. He wanted to declare that he was not a pet or a snack, but he was afraid his voice would crack again.

"I am not a pet!" growled Richie, his voice still gravelly. He got to his feet. "Look, this is my bar, and I let you all use it, against my better judgment, but if there is going to be bloodshed—again—I might just decide—"

From the corner near the window, the drunk raised his head. "Are there goddamned vampires in here again?" His voice was as deep as Barry White's.

Claude turned and gave him a Hollywood-style fanged snarl. The drunk's eyes widened and he scurried out the door with his bottle.

"That was my only customer," complained Richie.

Joe squeezed Evelyn's hand, but she didn't take the hint and pop them to the car, or home.

"Claude, were you going to break the rule about bloodshed in the bar?" asked Otto in a patronizingly patient voice.

"Why, no." Claude grinned. "I wasn't going to do anything *in* the bar. I mean, that is the extent of the boundary of this rule, right?"

"He tried to get Joe to go outside," explained Richie.

"I was just going to have a drink, like I said. Just having a little fun at the newbie's expense. Call it an initiation. But then your pet interfered—"

"I am not a pet!" spat Richie.

"—and then she suddenly, and I mean suddenly, like—" Claude snapped his fingers, "—she appeared. She can transport."

"What is the big deal about transporting?" asked Joe.

"What is the big deal, Claude?" asked Otto. "Different bloodlines, different powers....?"

"No," Claude shook his head. "Only one bloodline ever had that power, and it's extinct, except for the Mater and—" Claude stopped and crossed himself.

"The Inquisitor," supplied Otto.

"Who is the Inquisitor?" asked Joe.

Claude pointed an accusing finger at Evelyn. "She's his bloodline!"

"Don't be ridiculous," said Otto. "She told us who her maker is. A piano teacher at private school hardly sounds like the Inquisitor.

"Who is the Inquisitor?" repeated Joe, more loudly.

In his head, he heard Richie say, *Hush, son. Snacks don't talk.*

"A piano teacher?" sputtered Claude. "I am supposed to believe that she got that ability from a piano teacher? She's a spy!"

"Do you want to fight about it?" challenged Evelyn.

Joe squeezed her hand, trying to convey *no, no, no!*

Claude chuckled. The reptilian malevolence that he had been radiating before was back. "Brown Sugar, I could rip your lungs out, but the rules of this meeting house do not allow me to touch a hair on your pretty little head. Here. Now. Ha!" Claude turned away, threw aside an innocent chair that was in his path, and stomped out of the bar.

Otto shook his head. "Move to adjourn?"

Someone from the peanut gallery made the motion, at least three others seconded it, and they all disappeared down the back hall as Otto declared, "Meeting adjourned."

Joe watched them go. He remembered the drunk scurrying out. *Goddamned vampires.* He had been an idiot not to be afraid of them. And, of course, the ones in the bar now were a lot less frightening than Claude, who might be waiting for them outside. Or had Evelyn's transport power scared him off?

"Are you okay?" murmured Evelyn.

"Yeah, I guess. That was really weird."

"Claude is old," said Richie, "He's powerful."

"Not someone a fledgling should challenge, Miss Evelyn," advised Otto.

Otto came towards Joe with his hand extended. Joe had imagined him as a jackbooted Nazi, slim and precise in his movements, but Otto was soft and pale and blond— rather dumpy looking, really.

"I am Otto. We have spoken on the telephone."

They had to reach around Evelyn to shake. She wasn't moving out of reach of Joe.

"*Ja*, so, that's a typical meeting of the Vampire Council. I am sorry I did not tell you not to bring anyone. It did not occur to me that you would."

"I won't do it again," said Evelyn.

Richie clapped a hand on Joe's shoulder. "Come back and see us sometime. In the daylight. You and I should have a chat. Unless, you know, you already changed your mind."

"Uh, thanks," muttered Joe. He turned and took Evelyn's hand in both of his. "Could you pop us to the car?"

Evelyn gave a brittle laugh, and they were standing in the front hall before she finished saying, "I'm popping us home."

#

For the next week, Joe made sure he was safely in his dorm before nightfall. He hoped he was safe there. The thought of Claude lurking in every shadow and around every corner clung to him like a dark and chilly fog. On Wednesday he had no afternoon classes, so he drove over to the Lazy Susan. There was a yellowed cardboard "Closed" sign hanging on the door, but he knocked and Richie let him in.

"So, still ain't got no sense?"

"Did you invite me over here to lecture me?" asked Joe.

"Maybe. Some. Have a seat. What can I get you to drink?"

"Just a Coke."

"Just a Coke. The teetotaler's drink. Ha! You know they used to make this from coca leaves, the same plant you get cocaine from?"

Joe nodded. "I'm majoring in chemistry."

"It hasn't been the same since they switched to caffeine."

"So, you're a bloodling."

"Mm-hmm. I drank from the fountain of youth and here I am 200 years later, still young and sexy." He grinned.

"You're not selling me on the *run away* bit right now.

"Mm." Richie's face turned thoughtful. "You know it comes with a price. There is a cost to everything. Nobody is ever really immortal. You need to know that. Not me. Not vampires. I've seen vampires killed. I've seen bloodlings, who thought they were immortal, die. You know, most vampires don't last long, not without help. Miss Evelyn is something of an anomaly."

"She's very determined."

"Anyway, that's not what I invited you here about, though you can ask me about it if you like."

"What did you invite me here for?"

"You ever see the movie *The Shining*?"

"Yeah. For about a week after I freaked out every time I saw the Lawrence twins." Joe smiled at the memory of his horror of his two little first-grade classmates. "I was six."

"You were watching horror movies like *The Shining* when you were six?"

"I wasn't adequately supervised at home."

"You remember what 'shining' is? The other night, I told you not to go with Claude. Only, I didn't say it out loud. And you heard me, didn't you?"

"Um, yeah. Loud and clear."

Richie leaned forward, arms resting on the bar. "You hear other people too, or just me?"

"I hear a lot of things. For instance, I hear voices in here, and there's no one here but you and me. It's not so bad now. Not like the other night."

Richie nodded slowly. "It gets louder after dark. Round about 3 a.m. the screaming starts. Every night. I go out, come back at a quarter past when it's over and close up."

"Screaming?"

"There was a mob massacre here in 1928. Always amazes me that the whole thing took less than fifteen minutes."

"It's haunted?!" Joe shivered. He was hearing the voices of the dead, right here, right now.

Richie shrugged. "Nah, I don't think so. They're just echoes. I knew some of those voices–knew them when they were alive–but I can't interact with them. They say the same things every night at the same times."

So what else can you hear?

"I heard that."

Can you answer me?

Joe frowned. *Ma numa-num,* he thought.

Ba deeba dee-beep! responded Richie, and smiled. *Actually, I can hear a lot from you.* Out loud: "You need to learn how to shut it down."

"How?"

Richie's eyes narrowed. "Imagine the inside of your head is lined with steel, like the inside of a submarine or something. Imagine the voice in your head bounces off of it, back at you. Like when you're in the shower."

Echo, echo, echo.

"No, not like you're on a mountain top in Switzerland. A small and close space."

This is the song that never ends....

Richie cocked his head as if listening, while Joe tried to keep the sound of his thoughts inside imaginary shower walls. Something must have been getting through because eventually Richie scowled. "Oh, not that. Do not put that into my head. Look, I like you. If you can come around some afternoons, I'd be willing to help you practice. If I can't convince you, that is, to get out while the getting's good."

I owe Evelyn a lot. And then something occurred to him. "Can Otto and Claude hear me? Can all vampires...?"

"Otto and me hear each other. That's how I let him know there was trouble the other night, and he alerted Miss Evelyn. Claude can hear, though I'm never sure how much, and I rarely catch anything from him that he's not purposely projecting. He pushes emotion, not thought. Well, you got a taste of that the other night."

"Yeah, it was weird, but I felt like he was an old friend. Until I saw you gaping like a fish. That snapped me out of it."

"Now, the Mater, you might as well have a glass skull when she's around. And the others on the council, they don't seem to hear or broadcast anything, except some of them that are bloodkin and can converse with each other. They may have other powers of one sort or another."

"Bloodkin?"

"Got their vampire blood from the same source. Litter mates," said Richie with a chuckle, "but don't tell anyone I called them that. Otto and I, we're bloodkin."

"You drank Otto's blood?" Joe had never imagined vampiric feeding to be anything other than sexy, and he couldn't quite imagine Richie and Otto together.

Richie shook his head. "We drank from the same woman. More like force fed," he muttered. "But Otto, he expired of, shall we say, blood loss, whereas I was lucky enough to survive. So, even though he's a member of that club and I am a bloodling, we are kin–bloodkin. That's why we can hear each other's thoughts."

"How can I protect myself from that?"

"Your mind is open. Close it." *This is song that never ends...* Richie started to send the song back at him.

Joe imagined his mind with a shiny metal roll-top lid, like on a buffet steam tray. He snapped it shut—and it worked! Suddenly the song stopped. He opened up again a little and Richie was sending the smell and taste and feeling of a cup of hot coffee. Joe opened and shut the clamshell.

Richie nodded. "You're a natural at that."

"You can tell?"

"It kind of bounces off and back at me when you close up. Did you have any of this ability before you drank Miss Evelyn's blood? I am guessing you can't transport like she can."

Joe sat up straight on his bar stool, surprised. "I haven't."

"What do you mean?"

"I mean I haven't. I haven't drunk Evelyn's blood. I am not a bloodling."

Richie stared. "You were born like this?"

"I guess so."

"Never met a breather quite so good at it."

Joe was flattered. They practiced some more. Joe alternately experienced Richie's breakfast and shut out the remembered sights, smells, and tastes of it.

And then the images he was getting changed. It was Joe on a bed and Evelyn on top of him and both of them naked. Joe was stunned for a moment and the clamshell didn't just not close, it opened wider, along with the pupils of his eyes.

"So," Richie leaned confidentially closer, "Evelyn and I, we had a delightful evening together once, but you know, you're pretty cute too."

"Ah...." Joe leaned back and wiped his suddenly sweaty palms on his jeans. Now Richie was in the picture, behind Evelyn.

"I think the three of us could have a good time together."

"I don't know if Evelyn would go for something like that." Joe tugged at his jeans to arrange things more comfortably. Richie peered over the bar to assess his impact.

"Well, then, just you and me." Joe's mind was suddenly flooded with the sound and image of Richie giving him a blowjob. Richie smiled slyly. *Miss Evelyn need never know. She's sleeping.*

An afternoon tryst with a bloodling who had offered to teach him psychic control in a haunted bar—no, Joe's life was never going to be normal.

Joe and Evelyn had never talked about fidelity, but he had been careful to keep his on-campus dalliances from following him home. This was something else.

Joe rubbed the back of his neck. His jeans were feeling uncomfortably restrictive, and he had no desire to shut out Richie's projected fantasies. He looked Richie straight in his chocolate brown eyes as he sent back some images of his own.

"Is this why you asked me here?"

Richie smiled broadly. "Not much point in immortal youth if you can't have fun, is there?"

The *Mater Omnium Lamia*

J oe and Evelyn spent Christmas quietly at home.
Evelyn had at first wanted to put up a large tree in the
front hall, all decorated in gold decorations, but Joe
had talked her into something homier in the games room,
where they spent most of their evenings anyway. Now the
room was pine-scented from a real tree–something Joe
had never had before, twinkling with colored lights and a
mishmash of decorations with no theme or color scheme.
They had simply picked out whatever caught their eye.

Over the holidays Joe had put aside his chemistry
textbooks for quantum physics. He was sitting in the
games room with Evelyn one night, trying to read *A Brief
History of Time*. It was difficult because odd images kept
popping into his head. Intersections of streets seen in the
dark. He would see the intersection and decide which way
to go in order to get home. It was like one part of his brain
was occupied with this seemingly pointless exercise while
the other part was trying to wrap itself around abstract
concepts of space and time. At first, the intersections
seemed random and then they seemed to be narrowing
down to places closer to home.

Metallica was mellowing into *Nothing Else
Matters* in his headphones when an image of their
darkened driveway popped unbidden into his head. Joe
looked up from his book.

What the hell?

Evelyn was reading too, with her legs curled under
her on the sofa. Joe pulled the headphones down around
his neck just as Evelyn looked up, head cocked to one
side, like she was listening.

"Did you lock the door?" she murmured.

135

Joe shut off the CD player and the faint strains of guitar stopped. There was a sound that might have been a footstep in the front hall, but the marble floor out there did not creak, and if someone was walking on it, they were treading as softly as a cat.

He saw, suddenly, the front hall. *Which door?* He chose the door of the room they were in automatically, without stopping to think that he shouldn't. Without thinking about it at all.

Evelyn rose from her seat, slowly and carefully, so as not to make a sound.

The only good weapons in the room were the fire tools. Forget being quiet, Joe wanted to be armed. He made a lunge for the fire poker and heard Evelyn's little gasp of surprise when she popped to the side of his chair and missed him.

"You're not all that big on security, are you?"

The intruder was not a monster—Claude was actually who Joe had been expecting. Instead, it was a stocky woman wearing scrubs and sneakers, her straight, blonde hair pulled back into a utilitarian ponytail.

Evelyn straightened and her back stiffened into the perfect posture she had acquired at school. "Tammi. How nice to see you again."

"I see you've managed to survive so far. And in style. This is quite the place."

Tammi? When Evelyn had described Tammi in her journals, the woman—vampire—who had rescued her from the morgue, she had sounded as far from Joe's idea of vampire glamor as possible. Seeing her in person, Joe was a little more impressed. Sure, she looked plain and harmless, but her eyes were glacially cold and hard, and she had just walked into their house uninvited.

"To what do we owe the pleasure?" Evelyn's voice was dead neutral.

Tammi smiled broadly, with her mouth. It didn't reach her eyes. "I'm looking for someone."

"Here I am. Here's my boyfriend Joe."

"Hi," said Joe, with a little wave. The fire tools were right behind him, within easy reach, and he didn't have any intention of moving away from them.

"The snack!" said Tammi with a grin, but then her eyes narrowed and the grin disappeared. "I think you know who I mean."

Joe couldn't see Evelyn's face, but her head tilted to the side and he could imagine the tiny frown lines between her brows. "I don't follow you."

Tammi's nostrils flared. Joe started reaching ever so slowly behind him while no one was paying attention.

"The Inquisitor."

Evelyn shook her head.

"I want him. I want to know where he is."

"I don't know who—"

"What are you going to do with that?" barked Tammi suddenly, pointing at Joe. "Show it to me."

Joe's arm lifted and held the ash shovel out in front of him without his brain being engaged in the action at all.

"Put it down."

Joe did as he was told. He *wanted* to put the shovel down. He couldn't remember what he had wanted it for anyway.

"You stop," Tammi ordered Evelyn, who was trying to move toward Joe. "Do you want to see him bash his brains out with that shovel?"

Evelyn stopped.

"In fact, move over there." Evelyn did as she was told, keeping her eyes on Tammi the whole while.

Joe thought Evelyn looked afraid, and he knew he probably should be afraid too, but he just couldn't feel it. Something was wrong. It was like his brain was wrapped in bubble wrap.

Tammi gestured with her hand and Joe found his chair looked irresistibly comfortable. As he settled himself into it his arms and legs became as heavy as wet sand.

"I don't know who the Inquisitor is. I only just heard about him last week at the council meeting." Evelyn sounded calm, but Joe could see the tendons standing out on the backs of her hands, which were balled into fists. He wanted to stand with her, but his limbs were so dead-weight relaxed that he didn't think he could move them.

"I think you do. A little bird told me you can transport."

Evelyn crossed her arms over her chest. "Some people seem to find that very upsetting."

"And you don't know why," mocked Tammi.

Evelyn's words were clipped and hard: "Enlighten me."

Joe felt like he was watching a play, but he had come in in the middle and didn't understand what was going on.

"Yes, alright, let's have a little lesson, shall we?" Tammi pulled the elastic out of her hair and remade the ponytail as she talked. "Bloodlines. Do you know what bloodlines are?"

"Like in horses or dogs?"

Tammi snorted. "I suppose. If I turn someone into a vampire by giving them my blood, they will have my abilities. More or less. If I can transport, they can. If I can read minds, they can."

Every time Joe tried to move or speak he felt the invisible bonds tighten on him. The experience had all the surreal feeling of a dream, made worse by the fact that he knew it was not a dream.

"But each time it gets passed on, it gets a little more diluted. Things get lost along the way. Lines diverge, just like evolution. There is no longer any line in existence that can transport. I am the only one who can do

138

it. Every vampire I made that could do it is gone. Except for one." She held up one finger.

"I can do it," said Evelyn.

"Show me."

Evelyn lifted her chin defiantly but before she could speak, Tammi pointed at Joe, and Joe raised both arms like there were marionette strings attached to them. He couldn't turn his head, but he was able to direct his eyes at Evelyn and he hoped that he looked like he was saying, *Please, do what she wants*. He still didn't know what was going on, but this was frightening him.

Evelyn blinked out of existence and reappeared in front of the console TV. Joe's arms fell down into his lap, where he could not move them.

You gotta get yourself out of this paralysis.

"Who made you?"

Evelyn was silent.

"When I met you, when I rescued you from the morgue, oh, I thought, an innocent little pampered lamb like you wouldn't live a year! Maybe not even the week!"

"You were wrong."

Joe had always admired Evelyn's I'm-not-taking-any-shit attitude, but he wished she would shelve it right now. He couldn't tell her. He couldn't even turn his head and give her a look.

Maybe if he didn't struggle, and Tammi's attention was elsewhere, the grip she had on him would loosen. Maybe he needed to do the opposite of fight against it.

"Did he send you to spy on me? Did he throw you in front of that bus to get you into my morgue?"

Joe picked a point across the room, a lapis lazuli vase with veins of gold, and stared at it, willing his mind blank. It wasn't easy with Evelyn and Tammi facing off like posturing cats, about to attack at any minute.

"No one sent me. The vampire who gave me this 'gift' wasn't around when—. You pulled me out of the morgue. You know this. The only help, the only instruction I got about being a vampire, was from you, and that was precious little. I am not a spy. I was invited to the council—I didn't go looking for it. It was only by chance I stumbled across Richie and Otto."

"So, this vampire who gave you the blood, you haven't seen him since?"

Evelyn huffed. "He did come back about a year later. He said you knew him, you just didn't remember. He said he was surprised that you let me go. He thought that was very funny."

"It was him, wasn't it? It was the Inquisitor. Oh, I don't care what name he used," Tammi growled when Evelyn started to object, "It had to be him."

"He told me I would be in danger if you knew who he was—if anyone knew who he was—because he was out of favor with the vampire community."

"Out of favor!" Tammi snorted and muttered something in another language, then, "What an understatement! Yes, he was right, if I had known then...." She pulled at her hair, ripped the ponytail holder out and then violently made it all into a lopsided pony tail again. "But now: deliver him to me and you have nothing to fear."

Joe's nose was itchy and he reached up and scratched it.

He could move. He leaned forward in the chair.

Tammi's attention turned to him immediately. Her eyes narrowed. "Well, aren't you a clever little witch."

Joe felt the force again, trying to weigh him down, and he just relaxed and let it slip off of him. Just be cool, go with the flow. He took a chance and tried to stand up.

It worked.

"You're talking about Simms," he said, before Tammi could redouble her efforts to bind him. "You have to be. He would throw someone in front of a bus."

140

Suddenly Joe seemed to lose control of his brain the same way he had lost control of his body. He was still able to view his thoughts, but not to control them. It was like someone was rifling through his memories, taking the various films and slides and throwing them up on to the screen of his mind then discarding them. And the memories weren't just images. They encompassed all five senses. He could see, feel, taste, hear and smell them with a clarity he didn't know any memory could have. There was a cricket he had tried to keep as a pet when he was seven. The smell of whiskey on his father's breath that made his stomach drop. The feel of chalk on his fingers. The first time he had kissed Evelyn. Joe stopped seeing the room. He was totally immersed in the memories that flickered on and off the stage of his mind.

Tammi was *in his head.*

Joe wanted to shout but he couldn't take control of his forebrain to form the words. It was occupied, like a defeated country. And worse, the invader was ransacking it carelessly. Joe was afraid Tammi would do damage. He had only just stopped willfully damaging that organ himself, and it was his most prized possession now.

And then she found what she was looking for. Joe was back in the bedroom of their apartment, confronted with Simms' snarling face, feeling Evelyn's cold, smooth back against him as she put herself between them, and smelling the new carpeting smell and....

Joe's fear built to panic that crested like a tsunami. He wanted to scream, but no sound came out, or if it did he was deaf to it like he was blind to his real surroundings. The panic blasted through the arena of his mind, pushing out the intruder.

And he was back in his chair, which he seemed to have fallen into.

Tammi stared at him wide-eyed.

"Get out!" Joe cried belatedly as the tsunami abated.

"That was him? Your piano teacher?" Tammi asked incredulously.

"Stay out of my head," croaked Joe.

Evelyn spread her hands helplessly. She had not been a party to the trip down memory lane.

"No, of course, you can't see anything, can you?" sneered Tammi. She turned to Joe. "Show him to me again." She spoke like she was talking to a child. "I won't invade. Just show me his face. Think of it. Call it up."

All Joe wanted was to run away, but he didn't dare. He was sure that Tammi would not let him.

Joe took a deep breath and thought about the last memory he had seen before he pushed Tammi out of his mind: Simms suddenly appearing in the bedroom of what they had thought was their hideaway. The sneer on his face. The way his eyes flashed with anger and possessiveness and madness. He pushed the thought out toward Tammi, the way Richie had taught him.

"That's Simms," said Joe.

"That," said Tammi in a slow whisper, "is the Inquisitor, Sebastien Arnaud."

"Simms was the Inquisitor?" asked Evelyn.

Tammi nodded. "And he made you."

Evelyn gave an indignant sniff. Joe nearly started to laugh. Here he was, terrified, his life and sanity on the line, in that order, and she was *indignant*.

"I already existed. He gave me a taste of his blood."

"Is he your master?"

"No."

Tammi nodded again, thoughtfully. "Oh, I wish I could get inside your head. It saves so much talking, and so much energy wasted on lies."

Evelyn's eyes flashed with anger. "I told you the truth the first time. I have told you the truth all along. He left me. I wasn't a vampire at the time. He left me, and he wasn't around when I became one."

"But he came back."

Evelyn didn't answer.

"Tell her," said Joe. "Tell her everything, or she'll just take it out of my head."

"I just need to know where he is," said Tammi, as if this was a perfectly reasonable request. Like all she wanted was to get together with Simms for lunch.

"And if we don't tell you?" asked Evelyn.

"Ev," chided Joe.

A breeze started to stir in the room. It lifted the untrimmed hair off the back of Joe's neck and he shivered.

"You give me what I want and I will go away and leave you in peace. I have no quarrel with you."

"If this is how you treat people you have no quarrel with, I am glad we're not enemies." Evelyn's voice was getting ragged. Joe had never seen her lose control before. Outside of the bedroom, anyway.

Tammi's eyes narrowed. "You know, when I had you in my apartment, I should have just drained you into a glass, and sucked the marrow out of your bones."

Evelyn's nostril's flared.

"Little upstart orphaned fledgling! Maybe I should do that now. Maybe I am holding the wrong one of you hostage." The breeze picked up. The pages of Evelyn's book riffled and her tasseled bookmark spun to the floor like a maple key.

"Look, look," said Joe, hands up in surrender to draw Tammi's attention away from Evelyn. "We can't give him to you. I mean, well, he's dead."

"Dead?" Tammi repeated the word in a near whisper that made Joe shiver. The breeze died and the room was suddenly quiet.

"Dead-dead," asserted Evelyn.

Joe swallowed hard. "You can see inside my head, right?"

Tammi nodded.

"Alright, well, let me show you what happened, only you stay out of my head and I'll, I'll project the thoughts at you."

Tammi turned around and gave the other wing chair a shove with her foot so it was facing Joe. She seated herself in it like a queen on a throne. With an imperious wave of her hand, she ordered silently: *Show me.*

Joe closed his eyes and remembered. He would never forget one detail of that day.

By the time Joe found the trunk it was late afternoon and his anger and energy were worn down enough that he was clumsy. The trunk was old, the wood darkened by years, and the steel bands that bound it were rusty. Joe wasn't sure if it was big enough to hold a body. There were things piled on top of it: boxes and old curtains and a yellowed painting of a ship at sea. When he had everything cleared off, and the hasp undone, he hesitated. A large part of him didn't want to find Simms. He told himself it would be empty like all the other places he had looked, but that wasn't comforting either. He lifted the lid, glimpsed a hand, and dropped it shut.

What if it wasn't Simms? What if there was some other dead body or some other vampire...?

He told his fears to shut the fuck up and opened the lid again. There was Simms, curled on his side, grey and still. Joe slammed the lid and hyperventilated.

He had a big butcher knife from the kitchen. His plan, when he found the sleeping vampire, was to stab him in the heart and then cut off his head. Just like in the movies.

Joe stood over the closed trunk, panting. The thought was terrifying. Just seeing Simms, even inert like that, made him want to run screaming. He looked out the dusty window and saw the sun shining on the snow, and the blue sky. How could all of that be so beautiful and this in here exist? He started to cry and snot bubbled out his nose.

And then he looked up again.

Sunlight.

The chest had a leather handle attached with metal brackets on either end, and Joe grabbed one and dragged the chest across the room. His energy and his anger were suddenly back. Simms was not going to win. If he wanted a fight to the death that was what he was going to get.

The trunk bumped down the stairs. Joe thought about just pushing it down the steps, but then Simms might tumble out and he would have to touch him to get him the rest of the way outside. That was a sobering thought.

He could not get the trunk outside fast enough.

Once he was on the marble floor of the front hall it was easier; a little jerk to get it over the lintel, and then it slid as smoothly across the snow as a sled.

Outside, in the golden sunlight, he opened the trunk and glimpsed Simms' face one more time, only for a second, because the body began to blacken and smoke immediately. It burst into bright flame with a hiss like a gas burner. Joe stumbled back from the heat and fell on his butt in the snow.

He didn't know how long Simms and the trunk burned. It seemed a very short time, and then there was nothing but twisted steel bands glowing like a sunset, and a smoking burn mark on the ground. The snow around it had not melted but evaporated. Joe sat in the snow and stared until darkness came and the cold forced him indoors again.

Joe let the winter scene dissolve and found himself slumped in his chair with Evelyn leaning over him from behind, one hand on his shoulder and the other stroking his hair. Tammi had promised to stay out of his head, but she had been in there, Joe had no doubt. The memory had been too clear and too enveloping.

The room was silent; the vampires weren't breathing.

Tammi's face twisted, and she began to giggle. "Three hundred years!" she whispered, and then jumped to her feet and shouted. "Three! Hundred! Years! And he's taken down by a boy. A boy!"

Evelyn leaned into Joe, and he grabbed hold of her hand, but Tammi wasn't making a move towards them. She threw her hands up in the air. "This is what comes of arrogance! I should find a cave in Tibet and meditate for the next century."

"So, as you can see, he's not here," ventured Evelyn.

Tammi chuckled. "Speaking of arrogance!"

"You don't, you didn't, like, want to find this guy to welcome him back into the family with open arms, right?" asked Joe. "I mean, if you've met him, you probably want to kill him."

Tammi snorted laughter. "Welcome him back into the family! Ha!"

"Who was he?" asked Joe.

Tammi chuckled wearily.

"Once upon a time, there was an Inquisitor, who took it into his head to hunt us down. We wanted to shut him down, and we wanted him to suffer. One of my princes...." Tammi faded off into reverie and sighed. "One of my princes made him into the thing he hated most. We figured he wouldn't make it through the first day."

"You made him a vampire?" said Evelyn.

146

Tammi nodded. Her mirth had given way to something else. She was white-lipped and looked suddenly old. "We thought he would kill himself if sunlight didn't get him, but," she pulled out her ponytail again and tossed the elastic away, "I miscalculated. I thought he was a zealot, but he was just a sadist who had found a Church-sanctioned way to indulge his appetites." She bit off the words individually. "It's a mistake I have been trying to remedy for the last three hundred years."

"That's a long time to carry a grudge," said Joe, just to fill up the silence.

Tammi grunted, staring into the middle distance. "No wonder he laughed at me, not recognizing you as my own kin. You are *sanguinem sanguine meo, autem genus.*"

"Blood of my blood," translated Evelyn slowly. "My...?"

"Tribe," finished Joe. He had images of countless other times Tammi had said this, to men and women, by gaslight, candlelight, firelight and the simple light of the moon. The words weren't always in Latin either. It was as if, spoken in his head, their meaning was transparent, even if he didn't know the language.

"But, what does that mean?" asked Evelyn.

"It means I recognize you as part of my family, my bloodline. We are kin. You are under my protection. The Inquisitor having been your maker means nothing." Tammi chuckled. "You're my great-grandchildren, of a sort."

"Are we protected from you?" asked Evelyn.

"You are so insolent!

"Are we protected from Claude?" asked Joe.

"Yes, yes, Claude does what I tell him. He has a healthy fear of me. But you don't even know who I am, do you? You think I'm just a morgue attendant."

"You are the *Mater Omnium Lamia*," answered Evelyn with a gravity Joe hoped Tammi would find appropriately reverential.

Tammi grinned with her fangs. "I am the Great Tamara, the *golodnykh dukhov*, the *Skoúro Theá*, *Imperata Noctis*, the *kančatkovaj carycy*, the *Zaharra*, and the *Mater Omnium Lamia*. Although I gave up all those titles decades ago and came to America to embrace democracy."

Suddenly she was in front of Joe, with a hand on top of his head like a priest giving a blessing.

"I dub you *Pueri Occidistis Inquisitor*–the Boy who Killed the Inquisitor. Everything is so much more impressive in Latin, don't you think?" Then she stepped back and looked him up and down. "You aren't even a bloodling, are you?"

"Um, I—"

She extended her arm, pale inside up, and drew a fingernail down the length of it, leaving a trail of bright red blood beading on the white skin. She said something that sounded like *pit-o-wits*.

Whatever language it was, Joe knew what it meant. He shook his head.

"Drink," she ordered in English.

Joe scrambled out of the chair and scurried to put it between himself and Tammi.

The Great Tamara laughed. "How can you turn this down? Immortality. Magic powers."

"I'm not ready to go there. I'm not ready to commit to that, uh, lifestyle."

"Lifestyle!" Tammi snorted. "You're funny." She licked her own arm and any evidence of a cut disappeared. "When you are ready, you come to me. My blood carries everything: all of the powers of all of the bloodlines. You will be first-generation."

148

"Um, yeah, thanks," said Joe. Far from wanting to become a vampire, he wanted to go crawl under the covers and hide.

"You will be one of us," she declared. She looked at them, clinging to each other, and smirked. "Romance never lasts," she said airily, and then to Evelyn, in a voice that was falsely lighthearted, "If at some time, you want to do Joe any harm: don't."

And then the *Mater Omnium Lamia* disappeared.

Joe leaned forward, over the back of the chair. He felt like barfing. Evelyn was clutching his back.

"I'm sorry. I'm sorry," she said.

"For what?"

"For... for ever dragging you into this."

Richie's voice echoed in Joe's head: *Are you out of your mind? She's in a dangerous business.* Tammi—*the Mater Omnium Lamia*—had just told him that he was safe from everyone, including Claude, but he didn't feel safer.

Evelyn dragged him to the couch and knelt next to him. "Are you okay?" She looked into his eyes like she was checking for a concussion.

"Yeah, I think so." *Codeine*, whispered his brain. *Valium.* "I am." He decided. He patted her hand that rested on his chest reassuringly. "I am. You?"

Evelyn nodded and threw her arms around him.

Oh, what I wouldn't give for my mother's medicine cabinet....

Thank God there's nothing like that here.

Joe Vampire

CLAUDE

Not Your Average Joe

Joe took a martini glass down from the rail above the bar and set it on the polished wood in front of him. He imagined an invisible hand sliding under the shallow cup, the stem between the second and third fingers, and lifting it.

The martini glass sat still.

Richie was freshening up. They'd had sex in Richie's office, like many other afternoons. When Richie and Joe had sex–standing, sitting, kneeling or bent over Richie's cluttered desk—there was never any cuddling before or after. Joe told himself that it was not an affair because of that, despite the fact that this had been going regularly for a couple of months now. It was just a repeated one—afternoon stand.

Joe concentrated, staring at the glass like his eyes were psychic lasers. Nothing. He shut his eyes and envisioned it, free of visual distractions. But when he peeked the glass was still sitting on the bar.

"What are you doing?" asked Richie as he came out of the back hallway.

"I'm trying to make it levitate."

Richie scoffed. "What are you, the Amazing Kreskin?"

Joe sat back. This was not working. Maybe this just wasn't one of his powers. Then instead of reaching out an imaginary hand to the glass, he tried pulling the glass into his head, reliving all the sensations he had ever had of a martini glass–the weight of it, the coldness of the glass—and he imagined the glass lifting all by itself.

The glass tipped just a little and rattled back into place like it had just experienced its own tiny earthquake.

"Shee—it!" said Richie. "How did you do that?"

"I just, instead of trying to lift the glass I, I don't know, I thought about the glass lifting itself."

"The glass lifting itself," Richie repeated.

"Um, yeah."

Richie took down a squat old fashioned glass. "Try this one."

"Why that one?"

"It's less likely to break."

Joe took a minute to get the glass in his mind. It was thick—bottomed, but the walls were thin at the top.

Up, he told it silently. *Up!*

The bottom lifted a little on one side and the glass rocked on the edge still on the counter.

Up! "Up!"

The glass began to tremble and Joe's concentration broke. The tumbler thumped gently back to the bar's surface.

"Damn!" said Richie.

Joe let out a breath and sat back.

The back door skreeled open and they both glanced down the hall to see Leroy in his ancient once—white dinner jacket and bowtie. He gave them a nod and went into the office to deposit his dinner in the fridge.

Richie checked his watch and Joe looked at the darkening sky beyond the dingy windows. "I got to turn on the neon," said Richie. There was already a customer at the door, who ambled up to the bar and ordered a mickey of rye whiskey. Leroy served it up and then set a glass of Coke in front of Joe without Joe asking.

It was a Wednesday night and Evelyn was not expecting him home. In fact, she would be in his dorm room soon, purchasing her weekly supplement from his roommate Carter. Joe chose to absent himself from those transactions. He would be back in the dorm to call her before he went to bed, while Carter watched Letterman.

A few more patrons came in while Joe continued to try and move the tumbler. They ordered a drink, or a bottle, and took it to a table where they sat alone, just the two of them, a man and his drink. Like Joe's father.

"I'm going to—" began Joe, but suddenly the building was on fire. Flames licked up the walls, they danced on the tabletops like someone had doused them in gasoline, and raced up chair backs to light the drinkers on fire. Richie's hair was burning. Flames ate holes in his jacket and strips of it peeled away from him.

Joe gave a cry and raised his arms to ward off the flames, and then stopped with his arms lifted half way. Richie was not doing the things you do when you are on fire, like screaming and flailing. Instead, he was giving Joe a *what—the—fuck—is—wrong—with—you?* look.

Joe lowered his arms and stared hard at Richie, who frowned back at him.

You are on fire.

"I am most definitely not on fire."

As Joe stared the flames faded away from Richie. Out of the corner of his eye, he saw Leroy, who had been standing behind the bar with a worried look on his face, also on fire/not on fire, suddenly step back.

Joe Vampire

Not on fire, Joe told himself. As he looked at it each part of the room returned to normal. There was no charring, no smoke. And as he turned to extinguish the front of the bar with his cleared—up gaze, he caught sight of what had made Leroy start: Claude was standing just inside the front door. Joe took a step back too and wondered if there was any point in bolting for the back door. Claude couldn't pop, but Joe imagined he had other tricks up his black leather sleeve.

Mater said you are safe from him.

"Not bad," said Claude.

"You did that?"

Claude, eyes hidden behind silver aviator shades, didn't answer. He walked up to the bar and leaned on it. As soon as Claude was clear of the door, the patrons scurried out one by one, leaving crumpled piles of cash and coins still spinning on the tables. The back door banged shut behind Leroy.

Joe kept his eyes on Claude, who leaned nonchalantly on the polished wood. His jeans, Harley T—shirt, and denim vest were dirty and his boots were scuffed but the mirrored shades were shiny.

"Always a pleasure to see you, Claude," said Richie loudly. "You do so much for my business."

"I do tend to have that effect on people." Claude grinned. He turned to Joe. "School is about to begin."

"What's going on, Joe?"

Joe saw his reflection in the mirrored lenses of Claude's glasses as he shook his head.

No idea. Run?

Predators pounce when prey runs, answered Richie.

Claude chuckled. "See, that's the sort of thing you need help with. Anyone with ears can hear you. And him," he gestured to Richie.

Joe swallowed.

154

"Don't you worry, boy, the Mater told me I'm not allowed to hurt you. Well, not seriously, anyway. Seems you're the golden child."

"I'm the *Pueri Occidistis Inquisitor,*" Joe said, just in case the Mater's warning was not enough.

The corner of Claude's lip twitched just a little in a suppressed sneer. "Whatever. Never did learn much Latin. Mater didn't say anything about not harming this bloodling here."

"Claude," began Richie in a warning tone, but be backed away from the vampire into the shelves behind him.

"So let's try some target practice, shall we? I am going to throw things at this breather you've been diddling around with, and you try to save him."

Joe opened his mouth to protest, but Richie began shuffling in place.

Hot coals!

Joe looked over the bar but he couldn't see any hot coals, only the floorboards blackened by time and dirt. Joe threw an imaginary, mental bucket of cold water on them. The imaginary coals hissed as the water put out their glow and Richie breathed a sigh of relief.

"Cute," said Claude. "But don't imagine it. Get into his head and see what he's seeing."

"I am not a puppet!" protested Richie. "I am not here for your entertainment!" He started and then folded his arms. "I am not on fire. You can't get me with that one. I know better."

"Get into his head," Claude told Joe.

"Look, there must be—"

"I know I am not on fire." Richie shook his head. Beads of sweat were standing out on his forehead.

"Better get going," Claude told him.

Richie was pulling at his shirt collar now.

Let me see what you see.

Richie obliged. It was not the whole bar engulfed in flames like before. Richie's shirt was smoldering and smoking.

Joe tried to douse him with water, but it disappeared in a puff of steam.

"Joe?" gasped Richie.

It's not real. Joe projected the image he saw of Richie, standing before him, sweating and fidgeting but not on fire. *It's not real. This is real.*

It's not real, Richie repeated like a Buddhist mantra.

Abruptly Richie gave an exhale of relief and Joe suddenly felt hot tongues of flame licking him. He turned to Claude.

It's. Not. Real.

Claude twitched and the sensation ceased.

"If you all don't mind—" Richie began, and then he jumped. "Jesus!"

Richie was looking at something on the bar that Joe could not see, so he peeked inside Richie's mind again.

Spider. There was a large black spider on the bar. It ran towards Richie's hand, and Richie backed away. And then Joe felt something crawling on the back of his neck. He swatted at it at the same time Richie swatted at the back of his neck.

He was feeling what Richie was feeling. He withdrew from Richie's mind and the sensation ceased. At least for him.

It's not real, he projected at Richie

"It's not real," murmured Richie. He stared Claude down, stiff and twitching, and the wings of Claude's bushy grey mustache went up in a smile.

It's not real, chanted Joe, *it's not real*. Richie was still twitching and had started to make a high humming noise. He sent Richie the image of himself as he saw him, spider—free, but it wasn't making any difference. Peeking inside Richie's mind again he saw a scorpion skitter by on the bar and Richie jumped back. The little bit of control he had managed broke and Joe was flooded with the sensations that Richie was feeling, of *things* crawling on him, under his clothes, biting and pinching.

"Stop it!" Richie hissed at Claude and began to swat at the imaginary insects.

This isn't real, insisted Joe, fighting the urge to swat at them himself. Calmness, he thought, he needed to project calmness into Richie, not just thought but emotion. He pulled out of Richie's mind and conjured up the periodic table in own. Joe began to recite the elements and their properties at Richie.

Richie's breathing was ragged and Joe heard Claude chuckle, but he didn't look at either one of them. He stared into the middle distance, intent on magnesium, and then potassium.

Suddenly Richie gave a cry and ran out from behind the bar. He crashed into a table and fell. "It's not real!" he shouted at whatever he was trying to ward off.

Joe dropped the periodic table and went into Richie's mind in time to see a giant praying mantis fade away.

Finally freed from Claude's illusions, Richie laid back on the floor, panting, and Joe felt a wave of revulsion for him. He was suddenly disgusted by his dark skin and pomaded hair, his sweaty fear and the way the whites of his eyes were showing like a frightened horse, and his unmanly prone position on the floor.

A frightened horse? Where is this coming from?

Laying there like that you could kick him in the kidneys easy.

Claude, of course. It was coming from that bastard, Claude. Just like the first time Joe met him, he was projecting an emotion onto Joe. Joe turned to face him and threw back the first thing that occurred to him, the opposite of revulsion: a shot of lust, with Richie as its object.

Claude's mustache dropped as his smile disappeared. From the expression on his face, it looked to Joe like his eyes widened behind the sunglasses.

"Damn!" exclaimed Richie from the floor.

Joe pulled back. The lust had served its purpose: it had cut off Claude's projection of racist revulsion, and he didn't want Claude lusting after Richie. That could not have a good outcome.

"Goddam faggot," muttered Claude.

"Take off those damn sunglasses," ordered Joe, out loud and mentally at the same time. Claude's arm raised half way, stopped and dropped to his side.

"Mater ought to just squash you like a bug," said Claude darkly, he grinned. "Well, that's enough lesson for now. I've worked up a powerful thirst." He sat on a bar stool. "You are an excellent pupil!" Claude grinned and reached out a hand to Joe.

Joe felt himself gravitating to him, carried on a wave of affection and approval. It was over, this test, and Claude was pleased. Claude was his buddy, his teacher, just a good old boy having some fun. He thought he heard Richie protesting, but it was faint and soon extinguished. Claude grabbed him in a bear hug, chuckling, and then sank his teeth into Joe's neck.

A quick vision from Claude about how his lifeblood would spray from his torn artery if he tried to pull away convinced Joe not to struggle. The good buddy feeling vanished, replaced by defeated fear. Joe was sure that was not coming from his gut, but he couldn't shake it. He held as still as a baby rabbit hiding in the grass.

"Claude, the Mater told you *not* to hurt him," insisted Richie.

Joe felt his heart picking up tempo. His knees buckled and Claude sealed his punctures with a slobbery lick and let Joe slip to the floor where he gasped for air. His vision had narrowed down to a small circle of what was right in front of him and the periphery disappeared into a fog.

"Mater never said I couldn't charge for my lessons," answered Claude. He slipped off the barstool and walked to the door. The bell jangled and he was gone into the night.

Richie arranged Joe on the floor on his back with his feet up against the front of the bar.

"He gone?" came Leroy's voice from the back.

"Yeah, yeah," answered Richie. "Get me a EpiPen. You still with me, Joe?"

Am I going to die?

"One would hope that a vampire as old as Claude knows when to stop. Hold still, I'm going to give you a shot."

Joe grunted as the needle stabbed into his leg.

"Epinephrine," explained Richie. "It'll keep your heart pumping."

Joe took a deep breath and his vision began to clear. Leroy brought a glass of ginger ale and a straw, and Richie lifted Joe's head just enough to drink. "It's not the best thing, but it's got sugar, and that will help."

"Gatorade," rasped Joe.

"I'll go get some," said Leroy.

"You think you can sit up without passing out?"

"No."

"Now, if you were a bloodling, I could give you a drink of my blood," said Richie. "As a human, though, you'd just get sick and throw it up, and you really don't need that right now."

The door jangled open and Richie started. Joe heard one of the earlier patrons say, "I just come back for this." He took whatever it was and skedaddled out the door.

Richie sighed and sat cross—legged on the floor beside Joe.

"You're strong, you know. When I resist Claude, well, you can see how well I do. Might as well be Fay Wray beating on King King's chest. But you hit him hard. You hit me like that, you going to knock me down. When you sent out that.... Jesus, I thought I was so sexy, I almost started playing with myself. I got wood."

Leroy came back with the bottle of Gatorade and a package of beef jerky. "Protein, that'll fix you up."

Joe struggled up to a sitting position. His vision spiraled down to nearly nothing and then gradually blossomed back out again. He didn't dare stand up and try to get up on a bar stool. It was better to stay where the floor wasn't too far away.

"So," said Joe to the floorboards. "This is what happens when you cross Claude?"

Richie snorted. "If you are the Mater's golden boy. Could have been a lot worse." Richie made a scoffing noise. "Fucking Claude!"

"What do you think I should do?"

"Do?" Richie was baffled by the question.

"Should I complain to the Mater? She said—"

"Mater doesn't have much tolerance for whiners."

"Whiner? I nearly passed out! I needed epinephrine! It's not like he stole my lunch money."

Richie stood up. "I told you it was a dangerous business. And Joe? I don't blame you for anything, but I don't want you in my bar anymore."

"Well, not after dark, right?" asked Joe.

Richie didn't look at him. "I think our lessons are over."

"You mean our lessons or...." Joe glanced up at Leroy.

160

I mean all of it, answered Richie. "I like you, Joe, don't get me wrong, but I don't want to be involved in any of this. I don't want Claude coming here looking for you. If I thought I could help you, I would, man, but there ain't nothing I can do for you."

Joe sighed.

Richie looked away from him and Joe caught some jumbled images of a woman by candlelight, but nothing clear, and then Richie closed off his mind.

There was silence for a while. Joe munched on the beef jerky, and he could hear Richie behind the bar, keeping busy rearranging glasses and bottles. Leroy's newspaper rustled once in a while. When he thought he was feeling strong enough, Joe pulled himself up using a barstool, stood bent over for a few minutes until he was sure he could straighten and stand on his own two feet.

Richie came to the bar but wouldn't look at Joe.

"I think I'm going to go. I think I'm okay to drive."

Richie still didn't say anything, so Joe turned towards the door.

"What was with the periodic table?" blurted Richie suddenly.

Joe turned back. "Everyone needs a happy place."

Fight or Flight

Joe cut classes and hid out at Evelyn's house. He did not want Claude doing to Carter—or anyone else— what he had done to Richie, who at least understood what was going on. Evelyn had tried calling the Mater, but she wasn't picking up. Joe wondered if she knew who was on the other end of the line.

He knew he had to go back to campus. Exams were coming up, he needed to be in class. The College, aka the American College of Clinical Pharmacists, not his *alma mater,* was making noise about requiring a Master's degree in order to be licensed and Joe wanted to get graduated and licensed as a pharmacist before that happened. It wasn't that he didn't like school—he did. He excelled at it. But he had had enough of being a student and wanted life to begin.

After a week of hiding out and no sign of Claude Joe packed up his things on a Sunday night to return to school.

"You know, I can pop you home every night," offered Evelyn.

Joe shook his head. "I can't live like that. I've got to figure out how to handle Claude."

"I called Otto."

"Yeah?"

"He was sympathetic, but he wasn't any help."

Joe slipped his jacket on and checked his pockets for keys and wallet. His fingertips encountered the pill bottle there. Asha's Auntie Louisa's tranquilizers. Joe had been using them to get to sleep. Once it was daylight.

"There's something you should take. For protection. For insurance."

"What—"

Evelyn bit into her own wrist.

"No."

"Just a taste."

"No."

"Just a lick."

"No!"

"Joe! It might keep you alive."

"No. No. You know, right now I don't want anything to do with vampires. Present company excepted. I certainly don't want to be one. I don't want to be part of that. Besides, what if he drinks my blood again? What if he gets your power to transport from it? That would be truly terrifying."

Evelyn considered that, her wrist still proffered and dripping blood onto the marble floor.

"What if my blood makes you stronger than him?"

Joe ran his hands through his hair. It seemed to him that it was getting thinner on top. "Mater told him not to hurt me."

Evelyn licked her wrist clean like a cat grooming itself. "I taste pretty good."

Joe laughed. "I'm sure you do, baby. I've got to go. I've got a long drive."

#

Joe had figured he was safe in a moving vehicle. Claude couldn't transport. But as he got off the interstate and headed towards campus Joe noticed that he was picking up a motorcycle escort. The first one pulled out of a parking lot into line behind him, and he could see in the rear-view mirror that it was not Claude, but when he looked again there were three bikes.

By the time he got into the neighborhood of the college there were more bikes behind him than he could count. Maybe he should just keep driving until sunrise. Were they all vampires, with Claude as their master, like some B horror film? Or were they real, live, human bikers, who could stand the sunlight? Joe wasn't sure which was more frightening. He looked at his gas gauge. He had less than half a tank, and it was three in the morning. Four hours yet till dawn.

Suddenly the bikes began to disappear. They peeled off to the left and right, down side streets and into parking lots, and the ones at the rear of the pack moved up, until there was only one left.

Run away!

Run where? He had to be on campus, he had to take his exams.

Like Simms, Claude had to be dealt with.

At a red light, Joe stopped and Claude pulled up into the lane beside him. He gestured to Joe to roll down his window. Joe did it. What the hell? A piece of glass wasn't going to keep him safe.

"It'd be a shame if you fell asleep at the wheel there, right in the middle of the road," drawled Claude.

All at once Joe felt an overwhelming fatigue. The stress of the last week had suddenly caught up with him. He could barely keep his eyes open and his hands on the wheel.

Claude is doing this.

Joe pictured the arena of his mind—the inside of a covered buffet table serving dish. Claude was smoke in the chamber. Joe conjured up a whirlwind and drove the smoke out. Then he slammed his mental shutters closed.

It worked. Joe's eyes popped open with surprise and sudden wakefulness just in time for the light to turn green.

As he started forward the darkness on either side of the road seemed suddenly deeper. Anything could be out there. Claude's pack of bikers. Any number of other vampires. Simms.

Keep going straight.

Joe turned right at the next possible place: the parking lot of a Whirlmart, full of bright lights on tall, numbered poles and cameras. There were about a dozen cars in the parking lot. Joe didn't wonder who shopped at Whirlmart at 3 am; he was often one of them.

Joe parked closer to the road than the store. Witnesses might be useful, but victims would not be.

Claude roared into the lot and skidded to a stop.

"That's the spirit!" he called. "We're going to do a little sparring, Joseph Junior."

"Don't call me that!"

Claude just laughed and dismounted from his bike.

"Well, have you drunk some of your little Brown Sugar's blood yet, or are you still purely a breather?"

"Is that what you're after?"

Claude grinned, fangs down. "That's the payoff. Can't catch that little bitch to get it from her, but I doubt a bloodling could transport, even with that blood. If you could you'd probably be in the yarn section of Whirlmart there knitting yourself a clean pair of drawers."

Joe suddenly pictured Claude in the yarn section of Whirlmart—how did he know they even had one, after all?—and started to laugh. He opened his mind the tiniest bit to send the image to Claude.

Judging by the way the ends of Claude's mustache fell, he didn't find it all that funny.

"Time to dance."

There was a dragging noise to Joe's left and he looked, cautious not to turn his head so far that Claude was out of his range of vision. Something was moving out there, coming around the cement base of a light pole. And then to the right, there was a moan. Joe turned to see a ragged cadaver lurching towards him.

"Brains," it hissed.

Just behind Claude was another one shuffling across the pavement, and a legless one dragging itself towards him.

Joe started to laugh. It was straight out of *Night of the Living Dead*.

"Do you think that's scary?" he bellowed at Claude. The volume and pitch of his voice sounded like it was on the verge of hysteria, but really, it was not the movie zombies that were frightening him. "I watched those movies as a kid. That's not scary." Joe's eyes narrowed. "This is scary."

The ground rumbled under their feet. Joe could not get into Claude's head to see what he saw, but he could tell by Claude's shift in stance that he felt it. The zombies disappeared. Again, there was a rumble, a distant impact. The footsteps of a hidden, stalking T—Rex.

Joe had always found that scene in *Jurassic Park* scarier than any monster you could see.

Take off those sunglasses.

Claude folded his arms over his chest, determined not to be impressed. Joe was just deciding where the T—Rex should come bursting from when he noticed discomfort in his lower belly. He had to pee. When had he last stopped to pee? The vibration of the ground, which he could feel even though he was making it up, made it worse. The pressure became intense. If he imagined that T—Rex bursting out from the trees on the edge of the lot with a roar, he would wet himself with the effort.

It was Claude, of course. But Joe couldn't shake the feeling. He wasn't even sure how to approach it.

Joe let go of his T—Rex.

"You want me to pee? Is that what you want?" It was annoying to have something as grand as a T—Rex going and then be derailed by something as banal as a bodily urge.

Joe unzipped his jeans and pulled out his penis, but he couldn't pee. The urge was painful, it was burning, but he could not make water.

Claude smirked, an expression that was entirely expressed by his mustache.

What am I doing with my dick out in a Whirlmart parking lot?

He visualized the Claude—smoke again, this time wrapped around his bladder instead of in his mind, and blew it away with a stiff breeze. He peed, gave it a shake, tucked himself in, and zipped up. He had hoped the cameras in the parking lot would offer some protection, but now he was afraid he was the one who might get arrested.

Don't let embarrassment get in the way.
Humiliation. That was a large part of Claude's arsenal.

He thought about the glass in Richie's bar. He hadn't been able to make it levitate, but it had moved. *Don't think about the hand lifting, think about the item moving itself.*

Could he push Claude? Just a little? No. Joe didn't even try. Instead, he pushed Claude's bike.

It took surprisingly little effort, and the big motorcycle toppled over with a crash.

Claude unfolded his arms. "That's dirty pool," he cried.

When Claude turned to the bike Joe did the thing he was best at: he hopped back in his car and sped off. He killed his lights and headed down some residential streets until he was lost. Claude did not appear in his rear-view mirror.

Once he found a major street and reoriented himself, Joe concentrated on keeping his mind shut and unfindable. He circled the campus once before pulling into his lot.

With the car off and his hands on the wheel, Joe leaned forward until his forehead rested on the backs of his fingers. He thought over what had happened. Claude in Whirlmart picking out yarn. Joe laughed until he cried, and then he cried until he felt empty. He turned the key in the ignition so that the dash lit up and he could read the time. Two more hours before he could safely take one of Auntie Louisa's tranqs and zone out.

Sunglasses at Night

For a while Joe had peace. Claude did not materialize in his life. Of course, Joe stayed mostly at home, venturing out for job interviews during the day. Even when the sun was up Joe couldn't relax. He kept his mind closed almost all the time. It got easier and easier. Now, as soon as he heard the psychic white noise that came from other people he was reminded to close his shutters. Before he had been so used to it that he didn't even notice it.

Graduation was coming up and Joe was working out how to go to the ceremony, celebrate with Carter, and still be safely home before dark. It irked him that Claude was hemming him in like this, restricting his movements. He vacillated between deciding to just say *fuck it* and meet Claude head on and being terrified to step out the door.

Graduation was only a week away, and Joe was eating dinner alone in the kitchen when he heard the door.

He got to the hall in time to hear Claude say, "Brown Sugar! How about you fetch Joe for me." Joe stretched his stride as long as it would go and picked up his pace.

"I didn't invite you in." Evelyn's creamy soft voice had an edge to it.

"That's a myth, you know. Vampires don't really need to be invited in."

"Get the fuck out," growled Joe as he entered the hall.

"You haven't been going to school, Joseph Junior, so school has come to you," answered Claude.

Take off the sunglasses.

Claude's hand rose towards his face but he caught himself in time and instead scratched his beard.

"How did you know where we live?" demanded Evelyn.

"You two are not that hard to track down, Brown Sugar. Now run along. Boys got business."

"Get out of my house," she growled. If Evelyn did have psychic powers Joe had no doubt that Claude would have been dead on the spot, vampire or no.

"I'll be fine," said Joe, trying to sound brave while totally not believing it. "You go, um...."

In the blink of an eye, she was gone.

Claude looked impressed for half a second before he turned to Joe with a grin and said, "You don't want her to see you humiliated, do you?"

Joe said nothing and closed his thoughts behind their steel shell like he was armoring up for battle.

"My apologies for being remiss in your education. Time flies when you're a vampire." Claude looked around. "Ain't got no one here to target with your little Brown Sugar gone, so I guess it will have to be you."

Take off the sunglasses.

Claude twitched, but he didn't do it.

Joe felt suddenly cold, like all the warmth had drained down his long legs and out his feet. He expected to see it in a puddle on the marble floor. Goosebumps prickled on his arms.

Get out! he pushed, and the cold withdrew.

That was easy.

Claude spread his hands wide. "Throw one at me. I want to see what you can do, breather."

Joe envisioned a snake, a big, pale python, no little garden snake. It oozed over Claude's right boot, tongue flicking as it tasted the air. Joe couldn't get inside his head, but Claude looked down at his foot. The snake lifted its head, aiming up now. It wound around Claude's leg, climbing him like a tree trunk.

"Good thing I ain't afraid of snakes," joked Claude, but he lifted his hands from his sides so that they wouldn't touch the imaginary serpent.

"No?" the snake's head was level with Claude's crotch and it opened its mouth wide.

"Heh." Claude took his eyes off the snake and pressed his lips together in concentration.

Holy fuck it's working!

The snake drew its head back, jaws unhinged and sharp teeth gleaming...

... and then Joe let the illusion collapse. He had the satisfaction of seeing Claude let out a sigh of relief.

Suddenly Joe's ankle twitched and he fell. It felt like he was tripping over his own feet even though he had been standing still. He landed face down on the marble, and while his arms kept him from smashing his face, it knocked the wind out of him and he felt electric sparks shoot down his forearm from his left elbow.

Claude snickered. "Sometimes you don't need the big guns. Sometimes all you need is a little push."

Joe looked at Claude's smug face and remembered the martini glass. Don't think about moving the glass; think about the glass moving. He concentrated on Claude's left hand. *Take. Off. The. Goddamned. Sunglasses.* Rather than giving an order to Claude, he gave the order to the hand, as if it was his own.

Claude's hand had just started to lift towards his glasses when Evelyn appeared in a blur of motion and Claude went sprawling on the floor with an *oof.* His sunglasses clattered across the marble and came to a stop several feet away.

"This is my house, Claude. My rules. If you knock Joe down, I will knock you down." In her hands she held a golf club.

Joe scrambled to his feet and realized immediately that he could not use his left arm.

When the adrenaline wears off that is going to hurt.

Claude rolled over half way to where he could see Evelyn and swore in French. "Goddamn you, girl, you could've broke my spine."

"Pity it didn't kill you," said Evelyn.

Claude sat up and reached for his sunglasses. "Listen, Brown Sugar, we are just having a little sparring match. No harm done. You need to leave this boy to his lessons, or there's going to be hell to pay."

Claude lifted the sunglasses towards his face and Joe projected, *put them down.*

The hand with the sunglasses lowered.

"Your tricks don't work on me," said Evelyn.

"True. But you don't have any of your own, do you, Brown Sugar?" Claude chuckled. "Psychic deaf mute—the Helen Keller of vampires."

Evelyn disappeared, reappeared behind Claude, and said sweetly, "I have one trick, and it's a good one."

Toss those sunglasses away.

"I am just following orders," huffed Claude, and threw the sunglasses behind him where they skated across the floor, then he turned and frowned at them.

Joe remembered how he had thrown that shot of lust at Claude, like a discus. *Beg for forgiveness,* he suggested, at the same time projecting a dog-like need for Evelyn's approval at the biker. He felt his emotional push hit the target and wrap around it.

He had done it. He had Claude lassoed.

Claude twisted around to face Evelyn. "It won't happen again. I'm just following orders."

"Whose orders?" asked Evelyn.

"The Mater. She told me to toughen him up. Get him to get that power of his under control. You know that.

I can't disobey the Mater. You understand, right, little girl?"

Joe and Evelyn looked at each other.

"Why?" asked Joe.

"Why? Repeated Claude. "You don't ask questions like that when the Mater gives you an order."

Evelyn turned back to Claude. "I don't care what your orders are. Joe doesn't belong to the Mater."

Beg, insisted Joe

"Don't be mad at me, Brown Sugar. I couldn't bear that. Forgive me, I'm only doing what I have to do, what the Mater told me to do." Claude shifted to his knees and dropped his head. "Have mercy, Joe," he pleaded.

"Are you making him do this?" asked Evelyn in wonder.

Joe nodded, afraid to talk in case it interfered with his hold on Claude.

Bow. Worship her. She is your goddess.

Claude stretched out his arms in front of him and touched his head to the floor. "Miss Evelyn, please forgive me."

If only Joe had that on film. If only Claude could show up on film.

"You'll treat Miss Evelyn with respect."

"Yes," agreed Claude from the floor. He hadn't moved.

Joe let Claude go. "You can get up."

The buckles on Claude's boots scraped the floor as he scurried back away from Evelyn before standing.

"I'm just doing what the Mater tells me. She said to see what you could do without the blood."

"By torturing Richie? Richie is my friend." *And if you say anything more about that in front of Evelyn you will be back on the floor licking it clean.*

Claude blinked "Richie and I go back a long way."

"Can you make him dance?" asked Evelyn.

Joe smiled at the notion but decided to opt for mercy, or at least a strategic retreat. He was exhausted and his arm's numbness was starting to worry him. "Naw, I can't even make me dance. We're done for the night, aren't we Claude?"

Claude spread his hands. "I believe you just graduated. If it's okay with you, I'll go."

Joe smiled magnanimously. "Yeah, sure, go."

Joe and Evelyn stood in the hall until Claude was out the door, which he shut gently behind himself, as if not to disturb the master and mistress of the house.

"You need blood," said Evelyn, looking at him critically.

"What? No, absolutely not."

"I mean food. Sorry."

"Yeah, easy to get those two mixed up. What I need, is a sling, and a trip to the ER." Maybe at the ER they would give him some nice, friendly painkillers.

Claude's motorcycle roared to life and faded off down the drive. Joe sank down onto the marble. It was cool and he felt feverish.

"I don't want this."

"*Father, if thou be willing, remove this cup from me.*"

"Quoting scripture? Don't they say that even the Devil can quote scripture?"

"Are you comparing me to the Devil?"

"No, no, of course not."

"Baby, this is a gift."

Joe had always thought of himself as a freak. The freaky kid who could hear what you were thinking, sometimes. It had been a passive thing that happened to him, not an active thing he could use.

Evelyn sat down beside him. "You can use it to protect yourself. Together, we can protect each other. From them, and from other people."

176

"Yeah. But baby? Right now I need ibuprofen and a ride to urgent care. Seriously."

While Evelyn got her car keys and purse, Joe went over and picked up Claude's sunglasses with his right hand and tucked them into the pocket of his shirt.

Joe Vampire

FROG

The Truth Shall Set You Free

Three weeks later Joe and Carter graduated. Joe managed *cum laude*, but Carter was *summa cum laude*. His elbow, which had been dislocated fighting Claude, was still tender, but at least he didn't have to wear a sling with his graduation gown.

Claude had not shown up since their showdown, and the longer he went without any trouble from Claude, the more secure Joe felt. He was not just the *Pueri Occidistis Inquisitor*, he was also *Et Puer Victus Claudii*. He had looked up the Latin translation on Babelfish.

Joe treated Carter and his mother to dinner. Evelyn arrived in time for a late dessert, which she declined, of course. The celebratory meal and the graduation ceremony itself felt inadequate for the joy that Joe felt. He'd made it. Once the poor kid with a drug habit learned early on, he had graduated from college. He had graduated! He would soon be licensed in his profession and on his way to financial independence.

All he needed now was a job.

So far he had only taken two of the three tests for licensing. His head was stuffed with symptoms and, drug properties and interactions. He obsessively scanned the job ads in pharmacy journals and the newspaper. He circled ones that appealed to him, ones that were close to home, but he didn't send out any applications. The pleasure was in anticipation.

Joe was sitting, on a Thursday night, long legs stretched out in front of him, on the leather couch in the games room reading the newspaper. He's finished the job ads and moved on to the personals. He'd been half watching the sunset, which had changed the sky from peach to rose to violet. It was getting too dark now to read and he reached up for the lamp behind him. His hand hadn't touched it yet when it clicked on.

"Huh? Jesus! Don't do that."

Evelyn chuckled behind him. "I just want to make sure you don't lapse into complacency," she said, running her fingertips up the back of his neck.

Joe would have purred like a cat if he could. "I shouldn't even tell you that Asha called."

"Asha called?" Her touch left his hair. *Damn.*

"Yeah, 'bout six o'clock." He shook his paper out straight.

Joe loved to listen to Evelyn's voice when she talked to Asha on the phone. When she was talking business, it was very even and formal; when she was seducing a meal, it was sexy, like velvet. With him, it was all over, depending on her mood, and with Asha, she was expressive too, but not as much. Her tone had the smoothness of her business voice and a cozy softness that made him think, *this is what family is supposed to feel like.*

They had visited Asha several times since her mother's death. Asha was slowly but surely moving on. She seemed to have found reserves of strength Joe hadn't suspected she had. But the days were getting longer and it was getting harder to explain why they couldn't show up before ten o'clock at night. So Joe was surprised when he heard Evelyn say, "Well, why don't you come down here for the weekend?"

Joe peeped over his paper but Evelyn wasn't looking his direction.

"Mm hm.... That's okay, you know we're both night owls.... Of course.... All right, I'll see you Friday, then."

She hung up the phone and turned to Joe.

"I'm going to do it. I'm going to tell her."

"What? Why?"

"She'll figure it out sooner or later."

"I'm not sure about that. It's going to be a long time before she notices that you aren't getting any older. Or, you know, older looking."

"I'm going to give her the choice. The same choice I gave you, but you've never given me an answer."

"Sure I have. Not yet. That's an answer."

Evelyn just stared at him.

"Do I need to give you an answer? You must know what it is by now." He raised his newspaper to hide behind it, but then he peeked out because he had another question. "Anyway, why now?"

"What's wrong with now?" asked Evelyn. "Who wants to spend eternity as an old person?"

"How do you think she'll live if you turn her? I mean, unlive. You know. She isn't rich, she has a job."

"She's on the graveyard shift anyway," answered Evelyn with a half-fanged grin.

#

"Can I get you something to drink?" asked Joe as he showed Asha and Frog into the games room. He'd decided he'd leave the house tour for Evelyn. "Coffee? Coke? Juice? Cough syrup?" he added as Frog noisily blew his nose.

"Ha ha," he rasped. "Honestly, I tried to stay healthy for this trip."

"Like there's anything you could do about it," chided Asha.

Joe had been dismayed to see Frog arrive with Asha. It seemed like every time they visited he made some excuse to come by. Joe wondered what his excuse was for getting into Asha's car and driving to Ohio with her.

Joe picked up the remote for the stereo but caught himself before hitting the button. "What do you like to listen to?"

"Country," answered Asha.

"Country?"

She shrugged. "That's what I like."

"Jazz," said Frog. "We try to be at opposite ends of the spectrum," he added, gesturing to himself and Asha.

"Yeah, we're night and day." Asha spread her dark-skinned hand toward Frog to show the contrast. "Go ahead, put on whatever you want, I don't mind," said Asha. "So, where is Evelyn?"

"Uh, well, not here yet. We weren't expecting you for another hour or so."

"Yeah? We were afraid we were going to be late. Evelyn said it takes three hours to drive."

"Three hours?" repeated Joe. It had never taken Evelyn three hours to make that drive.

"Well, maybe it takes a normal person three hours," said Frog. "If you drove any faster we'd have been airborne."

"Oh, stop whining, I'm not that bad."

"Must run in the family," commented Joe. "Can I get you guys anything?"

"Yeah, I wouldn't mind a Coke."

"Just water, please," said Frog.

Joe got ice water for Frog from the fridge door, then thought better of it and dumped it for plain tap water. Frog probably got migraines from ice or something. Maybe he ought to go upstairs and warn Evelyn that Asha and Frog were here already.

He was just handing them their drinks when he heard Evelyn in the front hall call, "Joe?" She appeared in the doorway and immediately lit up with a smile. "Oh! You're here!"

"Evelyn!" Asha ran over to hug her half-sister.

"Uh, I didn't know you were here," said Joe, trying to maintain his earlier lie. *Oh, what a tangled web we weave....*

"I was napping." Evelyn lied so smoothly Joe wanted to give her a thumbs up. "I didn't hear you come in."

"I hope you don't mind Frog came with me," said Asha.

"Oh, not at all," answered Evelyn. "There's plenty of room."

Asha and Evelyn took the couch and Frog and Joe ended up in the wing chairs, facing each other.

"Uh, can I get you anything, baby," asked Joe.

Evelyn smiled at him sweetly, "No, thank you, I'm fine."

"How come we never see you eat or drink anything?" asked Frog suddenly.

"Frog!" scolded Asha.

"I'm just asking a question."

"I'm on a very restricted diet," said Evelyn.

"And we never see you in the daylight."

Evelyn frowned at him.

"So, how did you get the nickname Frog," interrupted Joe.

Frog turned his oversized gaze slowly from Evelyn to Joe. "Me? Well, I wish I could tell you there was a funny story to go with it, but there isn't. I just look... amphibious, I guess," said Frog, making a face.

"We could call you Teddy if you want," suggested Asha.

"No, thanks, I'm used to Frog."

"Teddy?" asked Joe. Frog did not look like a 'Teddy' and certainly not like a teddy bear. 'Igor' or 'Erik' would have worked.

"Theodore Aloysius Markingham. Makes Frog sound a lot better, doesn't it?"

"It's impressive."

"Tell me about your job," invited Evelyn, touching Asha's arm.

While they talked Joe kept an eye on Frog. He was watching Evelyn with equal interest. Not surprising, Joe told himself. Frog was a guy, lots of guys stared at Evelyn. Even Asha kept sending shy smiles at Evelyn that made Joe wonder if she had a crush on her half-sister.

"Do you mind, uh, my asking," interrupted Frog, "what do you do all day?"

"Frog, why are you so rude?"

Joe was beginning to really not like Frog.

"I sleep," answered Evelyn with a smile that would have melted wax. "I sleep most of the day. I'm a night owl."

Frog stared at Evelyn and she stared back at him. Joe noticed she wasn't blinking or breathing but didn't know how to remind her.

184

"Something's not right," he said at last.

"Oh, Frog," moaned Asha.

"What?" asked Evelyn, raising one eyebrow.

Frog swallowed. He was breathing through his mouth and his lips were chapped and white. "You don't eat. You don't come out in daylight. You don't breathe and blink." He took a noisy breath. "I think you're a vampire."

"Really," said Evelyn, eyebrows raised. Then she blinked.

"Oh, Evelyn, I'm sorry," Asha said in a hurry. "Frog is determined to make an ass of himself." Asha glared at him.

"I'll prove it." Frog wriggled his fat hand down into his pocket and drew out a rosary with a big gold crucifix hanging on it. When Evelyn didn't react to it he came closer, dangling it from his hand. Evelyn reached out and grabbed the cross and Frog gave a sharp intake of breath and started to cough. Evelyn hung on to the cross for a few minutes, then let go and displayed her palm.

"See? No burn marks."

"Huh."

"Frog, sit down and behave yourself," scolded Asha.

"It's still true," said Frog, retreating to his chair. "You said it yourself: you never see her in daylight, you've never seen her eat, not even drink water."

"Frog...."

Knock it off, man.

Frog's head came up when Joe sent him the psychic message like he thought he had heard something but wasn't sure. It was a minute before he turned and looked in Joe's direction. Joe didn't meet his eyes. He was hoping a little confusion would derail Frog's train of inquiry.

Evelyn turned the conversation back to Asha, how she was doing on her own and how things were going with their father. Joe ordered food. He was just starting to relax when Frog broke into the conversation with, "Can I feel your pulse?"

"What?"

"Your pulse. Can I feel your pulse?"

"Oh, sweet Jesus!" Asha rolled her eyes heavenward.

Evelyn blinked at Frog. "No. You cannot."

"Why not?"

"Frog!"

"Dude, what is your problem?" asked Joe. He leaned forward a bit and clamped his hands on the ends of the chair's arms, ready to get up. He wasn't a violent person, but he was over six feet tall and he had found that if he made threatening motions, he got results without having to follow through.

"Frog...." Asha shook her head. "Evelyn, just let him feel your pulse. Maybe that'll shut him up about this."

Evelyn looked from Frog to Asha.

No. Why did she have to be psychically deaf?

"This wasn't the way I planned to do this," Evelyn looked down at her lap.

No! Joe did not want her to tell Asha, but something about Frog made him sure that she shouldn't tell him.

"Do what?" asked Asha.

"I am a vampire."

"Yeah, right!" laughed Asha.

Joe laughed along with her, louder and longer. He hoped Evelyn got the hint.

"I knew it!"

Evelyn was oblivious to Frog. "Asha...."

"I want proof," said Frog. "Asha still doesn't believe it."

"How you going to get proof?" challenged Asha.

"If she's a real vampire, she drinks blood." He thrust his hand into his other jean pocket and came out with a Swiss army knife.

"Will you please stop talking about me in the third person, as if I am not here?" admonished Evelyn.

Joe stood up. "Frog? Come on. Let's take a walk. Let me show you the grounds."

"In the dark?"

"Out here, away from the streetlights, you can really see the stars."

Frog gave him a doubtful look and turned back to Evelyn and Asha.

"What will you do if I cut myself? Will you drink it?"

"Frog? You're out of your mind!" declared Asha.

Evelyn turned away from Frog without answering him.

"Asha, you feel my pulse." Evelyn held her wrist out towards Asha.

Asha looked at Evelyn's pale wrist but didn't make a move to touch her sister.

"You're always so cold." She said at last. "Such cold hands, but you never feel it. You go out in the snow with no coat or anything."

"Go ahead," coaxed Evelyn.

"Sometimes you don't blink for a long time. Sometimes, I think you're not breathing." Asha's voice was a whisper.

Evelyn raised her wrist to her half-sister.

"I don't want to."

"I'll do it," said Frog.

"No," Evelyn pulled her arm back. The two stared at each other until Frog retreated into his chair.

"Asha," said Evelyn patiently. "What happened to your mother is never going to happen to me. I will always be here for you."

Asha frowned and shook her head like she had water in her ears.

"Asha, please—" Evelyn held out her wrist again.

"No! I don't want to feel your pulse. Stop trying to scare me."

Evelyn sat back in her chair. She hadn't anticipated this.

"You really are a vampire," said Frog, breathing audibly. Sweat stood out on his forehead and his upper lip.

"You think it's sexy, don't you?" sneered Evelyn.

"Sexy?" He shrugged. "I think it's fascinating."

"Why are you going on?" Asha got up and slapped at Frog, who covered his head with his arms. "She ain't a vampire. She ain't!"

"Asha."

Evelyn showed her fangs.

Joe wasn't prepared for a scream, but Asha let one out that rivaled any cheap horror film soundtrack. Frog pulled back, gasped, and started to cough violently.

"You ain't—you can't be—it ain't true!"

Frog looked like he very much wanted to say something, but he was still coughing and gasping for breath. Joe didn't have any sympathy for him. He had thought that this was a bad idea from the beginning, but Frog had only made things worse.

Evelyn was on her feet. "Asha, I've been a vampire as long as you've known me. Have I ever hurt you?"

"No, no, no, no...."

"I'm still your sister," said Evelyn.

"You ain't my sister," declared Asha with sudden vehemence. "You're a lie! My sister's dead, and you're the Devil!" accused Asha.

"Asha," croaked Frog, "come on, there's no devil."

"And Michael! That time you scared him. You really did show him those fangs, didn't you? What were you going to do to him?"

"Just give him a little fright," said Evelyn. "Make him show a little more respect."

Asha's eyes were wide and frightened. "Why are you telling me this!?" she demanded.

"Because I want you to know," said Evelyn calmly. "Because you are my sister."

"No! No, no, no, no!"

"Because I will never die and leave you, and I don't want you to die and leave me."

"You want—!" Asha started backing away from Evelyn, although she hadn't made a move. "Oh, no. No-no-no-no-no."

"Asha, look, there is nothing to be afraid of," said Frog.

Asha slapped at him again and Frog cowered under his arms.

"You're an atheist, you don't know nothing!"

"Stop hitting me!"

"Asha, please," pleaded Evelyn.

Asha grabbed Frog by the arm and dragged him to his feet. "We're leaving."

"Asha...." Joe tried to catch hold of her sleeve.

"Don't touch me!" she bellowed. Joe didn't know Asha could be so loud or so assertive.

"Asha...." Evelyn was nearly in tears.

"I'll talk to her," said Frog as Asha pulled him out the door behind her.

Joe Vampire

The Frog Prince

Two weeks later Frog called to say that Asha wanted to see her sister. Joe had just written his third licensing test, and he decided that this was a good omen. After he got off the phone he grinned to himself, imagining how happy this would make Evelyn.

Joe was waiting when darkness fell and Evelyn popped into the bedroom. He left the lights off.

"Boo," he said.

Evelyn just turned to where he was lounging back on his elbows on the bed. "Can't sneak up on a vampire," she said, "I heard you breathing."

Joe sat up. "One day I'll get you. Here."

"What's this?"

"Asha's new address. Frog called."

"Oh!"

"He says she wants to see you."

Evelyn turned the paper over. "Is there a phone number?"

"He didn't give me one. Maybe the phone isn't hooked up yet."

Evelyn frowned. "Maybe. But why have Frog call? And why during the day when I'm not available?"

"Um...." Joe's mood started to deflate. "You think he's going to be waiting with crosses and garlic?"

"I think something's up." Yesterday's skirt slid down over her hips and Evelyn stepped out of it.

"Do you think...? Could Claude have got to him?"

"Claude? Why would Claude be involved with Frog?"

"Yeah." Joe started running his hands through his hair but stopped himself. He was afraid this gesture of worry, which he did more and more often now, was making it fall out. "He makes me paranoid."

"I can't imagine how Claude could have gotten to Frog and made him set up this meeting."

"I can. I can imagine a million ways it could happen. All very unlikely, mind you."

Evelyn took him firmly by the upper arms. "Forget Claude. You've dealt with him twice and come out unscathed both times. He's just a nuisance."

Joe snorted. "I nearly passed out from blood loss the first time."

"But the second time you beat him."

"I ran away."

"Claude is not involved in this. I will stake my fangs on it. But still, something just isn't right."

"Yeah. I'm coming with you." Joe took the jade earring out of his ear and laid it on the bedside table.

"What are you doing?" asked Evelyn.

"Never go into a fight with an earring on."

"There won't be a fight," said Evelyn. "Why on earth would there be? And I thought you were opposed to violence."

"Yeah, but maybe Frog isn't, and I know how to be prepared."

She kissed him on the cheek. "And you were never a Boy Scout."

Evelyn looked at the address again. "You know, I don't think this is too far from Asha's old place. We can just pop into the parking lot, or the park, and walk from there."

"Give the drunks a scare? Yeah, I figured."

"You don't mind?"

"Naw, I knew you'd be in a hurry, baby." He kissed the top of her head, took her hand and—bang!— they were standing in Riverside Park.

Joe sat down on a picnic table and put his head between his knees. Some kids zipped by on bikes, laughing at him.

"God, I hope this doesn't happen when I'm a vampire," he said to the underside of the wooden seat.

Evelyn tugged on his arm. "Come on. The fresh air will straighten you out."

They walked to the end of the park, crossed a foot bridge and went up the steps to the street. The new apartment turned out to be over a drive-through beer store across from the university campus. As soon as he saw it Joe was suspicious. Asha had been talking about buying a house. But he followed Evelyn up dimly lit back stairs to a landing with two doors. Frog answered their knock.

"Hey, come on in," he invited.

The apartment smelled like a locker room with overtones of beer. A sagging couch and stained armchair that was missing one arm crowded around a cigarette burned coffee table.

Apparently, Evelyn picked up the same cues and stopped in the doorway. "Where's Asha?" she demanded in her no-nonsense business voice.

"At work," said Frog. "Have a seat. I lied, this isn't Asha's place." He sat himself down in the one-armed chair. "She'd kill me if I gave you her new address."

"When will she be here?" asked Evelyn, not budging.

Frog sighed. "You're going to make me confess everything at once? Okay, she doesn't know anything about this meeting. This place belongs to a friend of mine and he's letting me borrow it. I figured a vampire visiting me at home would freak out my mom."

"She's not coming!?" Joe didn't need to see Evelyn's face to know that her fangs were down. Frog scrambled backward and half rose from his chair.

"So what is it you want?" asked Joe, laying a restraining hand on Evelyn's shoulder. She jerked away from him.

Frog blinked at Evelyn, breathing noisily through his mouth.

"I want to find out about vampires. About becoming one, how it's done, what happens."

"You lied to me!" growled Evelyn.

"I knew you'd never come, otherwise. Look, I really did try. I tried logical argument, I tried appealing to her emotions, and I tried every angle I could think of. Asha won't change her mind and she says if I bring it up one more time our friendship is over."

Evelyn's shoulders drooped. "If she wasn't your friend I'd leave you drained," she said flatly.

"You're the only vampire I've ever met—this is probably my only chance—cut me some slack."

"Your only chance for what?" asked Joe.

"To find out—I need to know —" He stopped to construct his sentence. "I want to know if becoming a vampire would cure me. Make me healthy—well, I guess that word doesn't really apply. Not sick all the time, anyway. Normal."

"I don't think 'normal' applies either." Evelyn's voice was like ground glass.

"It might be better than my present existence. I want to find out." Evelyn's silence seemed to encourage him. "How is it done?"

"Frog," said Joe quietly, "Give up on this, 'cause it's not going to happen. Look, all the folklore, all the stuff you see in movies, it's made up shit. It doesn't get at what it means to be a vampire. Imagine yourself staying the same, and Asha getting older. You're in love with Asha, aren't you?"

"Yeah, well, I thought we were a perfect match, but, as it turns out, Asha doesn't like boys. So there's nothing holding me back there, is there? Are you going to do it?"

The question caught Joe off guard. "Um, well, It's different for me. Evelyn's all I've got."

"Yeah, well, in a hundred years it won't matter who I've got. In a hundred years Asha and my family will be gone, whether I'm a vampire or not. I'll be dead." He coughed into his handkerchief. "Likely won't take a hundred years."

"What is wrong with you?" demanded Joe.

"Everything. Nothing. Allergies. One walnut and I'm history. Asthma. Poor immune system—I catch everything. No sweat glands, so I overheat if I'm not careful." He blew his nose and stuffed the handkerchief into his pocket. "Being undead has got to be better." He looked past Joe to where Evelyn stood in the doorway, her arms wrapped around herself.

"You don't ever get sick?"

"I'm feeling sick right now," said Evelyn significantly. "Suicide would cure you," she hissed nastily.

"Yeah, but that's kind of a dead end."

Joe snorted at the unexpected joke. Evelyn didn't.

"But really, you don't get the flu or colds or cancer or anything?" Evelyn didn't answer. "Will you tell me how it's done? Please? Just that?"

"Tell me what Asha's afraid of. I have never hurt her. I never would."

Frog sighed. "Asha's not religious exactly. More superstitious. And vampires to her are, well, evil. She reads too many tabloids. I tried to reason with her. I'm in your corner, really. But like I said, but she won't listen. She gets like that." Frog settled down into the sagging chair. "So, will you at least tell me how it's done?"

Evelyn shook her head. "If you weren't her friend I might. I'd give you the blood and I'd leave you to figure it all out yourself." She shook her head in disgust. "I'm glad she doesn't love you, you little self-serving toad!"

She reached out for Joe's hand and he braced himself for the nauseating leap home.

"Wait!" Frog jumped up. "What do you want? I know this can't come free. I'll pay you. You want service? I'll be your henchman! Your chauffeur! Your butler! Anything to—"

The last he saw of Frog was his watery grey eyes and his open mouth. They popped back into the bedroom exactly where they had been twenty minutes ago.

"Bastard!" muttered Evelyn under her breath.

Beepbeepbeep. The phone rang. Evelyn reached for it, but Joe, sitting on the edge of the bed with his head between his knees was closer and grabbed it first.

"Hello?"

"Let me talk to her." It was Frog.

"I don't think so." Joe hung up.

"It was him?"

"Forget about him, baby. World's full of assholes."

Evelyn just gave a frustrated growl.

Beepbeepbeep. Joe snatched up the receiver. "Are you deaf, man? Stop it. This isn't going to do any good."

"But—"

Joe hung up the phone.

Beepbeepbeep.

"Frog? I'm going to call the phone company." He punched the off button with his thumb. Hanging up a cordless phone was not nearly as satisfying as slamming the receiver down used to be.

Evelyn was pacing, eyes unfocused. It was not a good sign. That's what she did when she was planning, and Joe didn't think any plan involving Frog could turn out well.

Beepbeepbeep.

"Let's go out," suggested Joe.

"I'll teach him to mess with a vampire," said Evelyn.

Beepbeepbeep.

"Baby, come on, I know he lied to you and you really wanted to see Asha—" *Beepbeepbeep* "—but you know, it's not his fault she won't see you."

Beepbeepbeep.

"Oh, answer it," she snapped.

Joe hit on and then off without putting it to his ear.

Beepbeepbeep.

"We're going to have to change our number," sighed Joe. What did Frog think he was accomplishing?

Beepbeepbeep.

Joe picked up the receiver. "Look, Frog—."

Evelyn disappeared right before his eyes.

"Evelyn!" he shouted into the receiver.

On the other end, Frog said, "How do you do that?" Then the phone thumped to the floor.

"Evelyn!" hollered Joe. He heard Frog gag, and then nothing.

"Evelyn, I know you can hear me!" he hollered as loud as he could. "What the hell do you think you're doing? What about Asha?"

The phone clicked and went dead.

Where was that paper with the address? Joe knew it didn't have a phone number on it, but he had to look. Just in case. Maybe he remembered wrong.

He didn't have it; Evelyn did.

Evelyn herself suddenly appeared in the center of the room. She had the healthy glow she got when she had drunk deeply. With her fingertips, she wiped a smear of blood from her lower lip.

"You didn't kill him, did you?" demanded Joe.

"No, but he'll be too weak to make any more phone calls tonight. And just for good measure, I ripped out the phone line."

"Shit. Are you sure? God knows he has breathing problems already."

Evelyn shrugged. "Tomorrow, will you call and have the number changed? To something unlisted."

Joe sat down on the bed. "Don't you think... when he tells Asha what happened...."

"You think he'll tell her? How he lied to me, tricked me, how his plan failed and he ended up a victim instead of a vampire? How he was wrong, and she was right, and I am a monster? I think he has too much ego for that."

"Sometimes you scare the shit outta me," said Joe quietly.

"I didn't kill him," she huffed, and stalked out of the room.

Joe let out a breath he didn't know he had been holding. He waited until Evelyn was out of earshot and used the last number redial to call Frog.

Busy signal.

#

Joe drove to Ypsilanti the next day and found the apartment over the liquor store again. A heavily bearded guy opened the door to a haze of pot smoke and Joe felt like he was being sucked into the room by it, but he resisted.

"Yeah?"

"I'm looking for Frog."

"Frog?" The guy turned to someone inside the apartment. "Did they send Frog home?"

"Yeah, yeah," a girl's voice answered. "The hospital sent him home."

"He went home," the guy repeated to Joe.

"Uh, do you know his address?"

Again the guy turned to the unseen girl inside.

"Blue house," she called, "corner of Adams & Catherine. Not right on the corner, but one in. You can't miss it."

"Thanks," said Joe.

The guy stuck his head out and looked up and down the hall. "You want to…?"

"No, I mean, yeah, but no, not right now. Gotta check on Frog first."

"Cool, man, come back anytime. Any friend of the Frogman…."

#

Vague though they had seemed, the girl's directions were correct. There was only one blue house near the corner of Adams & Catherine. Frog's mother answered the door and called him. She looked like a thinner and frailer version of her son.

"He's not feeling very well," she cautioned.

Joe thought, *when is he ever?* Frog's poor health was probably good cover for Evelyn's attack.

Frog appeared at the top of the stairs that ran up from the front door and just stared at Joe with his magnified eyes and lipless, unsmiling mouth.

"I came to see if you were okay," offered Joe as an olive branch.

"C'mon up." Frog turned away.

Joe assured Mrs. Frog, "I won't tire him out."

Frog ushered Joe into his bedroom. Sci-Fi movie posters were tacked to the paneled walls, and a green carpet Joe was not sure wasn't just moss covered the floor. Frog waved him to a rolling desk chair that leaned to the left and sat on the bed cross-legged. It felt a little like being back in high school.

"I'm sorry about what happened. I'm sorry about Evelyn. She does have a temper."

Frog waved it away. "I deserved it." His voice was more gravelly than usual.

"You seem to be okay."

"My friends came home and took me to the hospital. They thought it was an asthma attack. Turns out you treat a vampire bite pretty much the same way, I guess."

Joe nodded. A machine on the bedside table caught his eye. It was all tubes and something that looked like a face mask. "What is that?"

"A CPAP. It keeps me breathing at night. I have sleep apnea."

Joe nodded slowly. "About Asha—."

"Asha won't even speak to me. I've got no in with Asha." Frog sighed heavily, but then looked up at Joe with a sudden brightness.

"Joe, do you know any other vampires?"

"Uh...."

"Come on, you must."

"Yeah, I'm not sure they would be any nicer to you than Evelyn was. Maybe even worse."

"They don't even know me. It's usually only after people know me that they want to kill me."

Joe wondered if that was a joke or not.

"You owe me," added Frog.

"How do I owe you?"

"After what Evelyn did—."

"No, man, you brought that on yourself. And besides, I didn't do anything to you—that was Evelyn. I tried to warn you." The CPAP machine caught his eye. There was a litter of inhalers around it.

Frog fell sideways on the bed and rolled onto his back. "My quest for immortal good health has netted me two big zeroes: no health and I've lost Asha."

The room suddenly felt claustrophobic to Joe. He took a deep breath to dispel the feeling that his lungs weren't doing their job. It was suddenly dingier, and despite the bright sky outside the window, it felt like a prison. Joe stood up.

"I have to go."

"Yeah." Frog didn't move.

"I, um, look... Asha will come around."

No response.

"So, I'll see you," said Joe.

Frog's mother was nowhere to be seen and Joe let himself out the front door. He sat behind the wheel of the Beemer for a few minutes looking up at Frog's window on the second floor.

That feeling of claustrophobia, of not being able to breath was gone. He had been picking it up from Frog.

It sucked to be Frog.

Joe felt the back of his neck prickle and looked up. There was Frog's pale, dismal face at the window. Joe buzzed down his window and waved his arm. Frog struggled to open the window and had to hold the sash up in order to stick his head out.

"I'll ask around. I might have an idea," Joe called.

Frog brightened immediately. "Thanks, Joe," he croaked.

#

On Tuesday Joe picked a sniffling Frog up from the Greyhound station. Frog had been calling him nearly every day, asking if he had found a willing "blood donor" yet. Frog's misery was wearing him down.

When they walked into the Lazy Susan Leroy nudged Richie, who came up to his side of the bar to meet them with a scowl. Joe closed off his mind. He didn't want Richie reading it; he wanted more control over the whole interaction.

"I thought I asked you not to come in here anymore, Joe. I was serious about that," said Richie in a low voice.

Joe placed Claude's mirrored sunglasses on the bar.

Richie looked at them, back at Joe, and shrugged.

"They're Claude's. I made him take them off. I made his toss them away."

Joe was totally unprepared for Richie's response: "Dimestore sunglasses don't convince me."

Joe snatched up the sunglasses and folded them into his pocket. "Whatever, man. Look, it's broad daylight. And I'm not here for myself. Richie, this is Frog."

Richie nodded at Frog but said nothing.

Leroy appeared with two cokes on ice. Richie glared at him but the older man just shrugged and retreated to his stool and his newspaper.

"So, this is Frog," Joe began again. "And Frog is looking for some help."

"What kind of help?"

"I'm looking for a va—" began Frog.

"We don't use the V word in here," cut in Joe

Richie held up a hand, then turned his eyes to Joe. "What nonsense have you been telling this boy?" he asked pleasantly, like it was all a joke.

"He knows, Richie."

Richie's nostrils flared. "He shouldn't know, Joseph Junior."

"Do not call me that."

Joe and Richie stared each other down. Joe could tell by Richie's expression that he was trying to communicate mentally, but Joe kept his shutters down.

"Look, Frog is interested in joining *that club*. He knows about Evelyn."

"I had the pleasure of nearly being killed by her," sniffled Frog.

Richie snorted. "That's not exactly a recommendation. If Miss Evelyn don't like him, why are you helping him out?"

"Can I say something?" asked Frog. "Can I make my case?"

Richie gave him another long look. "Go ahead. Just watch your language."

"My—? Oh. Look, I have allergies, asthma, sleep apnea, and a deviated septum that my poor single mother never could afford to fix. I am sick 99% of the time, to some degree. I get infections, I have just about no immune system, I don't have an adequate number of sweat glands so I can't cool myself off and I overheat and pass out. I probably should have died of crib death, but I didn't, so here I am."

"So?" asked Richie.

"So, I know that a... that members of *that club* don't have these problems. They don't get sick. Being a member of *that club* would fix all these defects."

Richie looked from Frog to Joe and back to Frog again.

"Are you insane?"

"Wha—?"

"Being a member of *that club* just means trading one set of problems for another."

"You don't know what it's like to live like this," whined Frog.

"First off," began Richie, "your problems are not my responsibility. Sorry about your luck. Second, what are you thinking, Joe? You want to get him killed?"

"Come on, Richie, Otto would—."

"Otto!" Richie leaned forward and continued in an angry stage whisper. "You mean, Otto, the farmer, who knows all about culling the weak and defective ones from the herd? Otto, who runs a slaughterhouse where shiny stainless steel blades turn living creatures into pork chops and sausage? Otto, who has a rendering plant where he can dispose of any kind of carcass?"

Richie sent him a mental image of various unidentifiable body parts sliding down a metal chute, leaving a trail of gore, and both Joe and Frog winced.

"Uh...."

"You. Know. Nothing!"

"Richie, calm down. I'm sorry."

Richie turned away, muttering to himself, marched to one end of the bar and then back again. He leaned across the bar and pointed an admonishing finger at Frog. "Members of *that club* are dangerous. They will not pity you, they will not care about your problems."

Frog leaned forward so that Richie pulled back. "I don't expect them to care about me," he hissed. "I will pay for it."

"With what? You can't afford surgery for your nose."

"I will wait on them hand and foot. I will be their Renfield. Anything, as long as I can breathe."

"They don't breathe," said Joe. "Don't need to."

Frog threw his hands up in the air. "Even better!"

"Are you telling me Otto would hurt him?" asked Joe.

Richie sighed. "Yes, that is what I am telling you. I'm telling you—." Richie stopped and shook his head. "I don't want to have this conversation anymore."

"The members of *that club* are not monsters," objected Joe. "I can't believe Otto would—well, you know, in cold blood. Claude maybe, but...."

"I'm not going to argue with you, Joseph."

Joe was pushing his luck, and he knew it. He leaned on the bar. "Then don't. Give me Otto's number, we can argue with him."

Richie leaned forward in mocking imitation of Joe. "Y'all get your underage, lily-white asses out of my bar. This ain't no place for you."

"I'm not underage," Joe hissed back, but he grabbed Frog by the arm. "Come on."

"And Joe?" Richie called after them, "Don't come back here again."

In the car, Frog said, "Interesting accent he has."

"What?"

"He went from Detroit, to down south to I don't know what."

"Hm."

"You don't believe Otto kills people?"

Joe started the car. "If Richie says he does, I suppose he does."

"And what about this other guy? Claude?"

"No, no, no. Claude is this scary biker dude. You don't want anything to do with Claude. Look, I'll... I'll ask around some more. It might take a while."

Frog was quiet the rest of the way back to the Greyhound station.

Joe Vampire

Frog in a Blender

Joe stared at the ringing phone, but no matter how hard he tried, he couldn't tell who it was. There was no psychic connection between him and the person on the other end of the line. The electrical conveyance of their voice over wires didn't bring them any closer.

On the fifth ring, he gave up and picked it up. "Hello?"

"Joe? Is that you, Joe?" The voice was hushed and worn.

"Asha?" Joe sat up straighter. "Yeah, it's me, it's Joe."

"Joe, have you seen Frog?"

"Frog?"

"Frog gone missing. His mama don't know where he is, and he ain't been to class. We all been out looking places he liked to go, but he just ain't around. I figured it was worth giving you a call. I know he wanted...."

Yes, Joe knew what Frog wanted.

"I saw him a couple weeks ago, but not since."

"A couple weeks ago? When?"

"Uh, he came down the fifteenth. Went back the same day. I dropped him at the bus station."

"That was the last day his mama seen him. What did he come for?"

"He was looking for someone to... um...."

"And did he find someone?" Asha's voice had been flat, but now it curled up with a sarcastic edge.

"No. I mean, we went and talked to a friend of mine, who is not a vampire," he assured Asha, "but no."

"And Evelyn? I know she hurt him once."

"Evelyn didn't see him this time. This was during the day. She didn't even know he was here."

"You sure about that?"

"I made sure of that. I dropped him off at the bus station around three in the afternoon. What happened from there, I don't know. Is it possible he just took off?"

"To go where?" she demanded. "Frog ain't got no money."

"Asha, don't be mad at me, I don't know anything."

Asha sighed. "I ain't mad at you. I'm mad at Frog. Got everyone worried and looking for him 'cause he done something stupid."

"You don't know that."

"Yes, I do. Taking off and not telling people where he's going, that's the least stupid thing he done. And I'm worried that he's done something stupider than that. Or someone has done something to him," she added in a quieter voice. She sighed again. "Will you... ask her?"

"Ask Evelyn? If she's seen Frog?"

"Uh huh."

"Yeah, sure, but she doesn't even know he was down here."

"That you know of. I'll call you tomorrow."

"Asha, I wish you would talk to her. You're the only family she has. You know, the only family that she likes."

There was silence on the other end. Now it was Joe's turn to sigh.

"I'll ask. You take—" the phone clicked and the line went dead "—care."

When Joe had dropped him off at the Greyhound, Frog was all business. He had given up on trying to persuade Joe to introduce him to Otto. Joe hadn't thought that he was hatching some other plan to procure himself immortality, but now he wondered: what was Plan B?

Go back to the Lazy Susan and talk to Richie again? That seemed like guaranteed dead end. *No pun intended.* Buddy up with Leroy? Just hang out at the Lazy Susan and see who turned up? That seemed like a stupid and desperate plan to Joe, but he supposed it was entirely possible.

He had told Frog about the council, but he certainly hadn't told him that the Lazy Susan's back room was their council chambers. Had he? Had Frog put two and two together? Knowing Frog, he could probably put two and two together and come up with five.

Maybe whatever had happened to Frog had nothing to do with the Vampire Council of Ohio. There were other vampires. Maybe Frog had somehow made contact with one of them. Maybe his disappearance had nothing to do with vampires at all.

But Joe still had to check.

It was four o'clock on a Sunday. He called the Lazy Susan.

"Whassup, Joe?" Richie's voice was guarded.

"How are you? How're things at the Lazy Susan."

"Same." Richie's voice was leaden.

May as well get to it. "You remember Frog?"

"Mmm." Richie's tone was decidedly less friendly.

"You haven't seen him around, have you?"

"I don't know anything," said Richie.

"Uh...? All I want to know is if he came back after he and I left."

There was silence on the other end.

"Richie? He's disappeared."

More silence.

"Richie?"

"I gotta go help Leroy with a keg."

"Richie?" The dial tone buzzed in Joe's ear.

Joe clunked the receiver down and closed his eyes. He tried seeking out Richie's mind but the psychic buzz in his head, when he looked deeper into it, was a morass of thoughts and emotions and sensations. There was no way to find Richie in all of it. There were no roads and no signposts.

He was going to have to go to the Lazy Suzan in person. He checked his watch again. If he waited a couple of hours he could ask Evelyn to go with him. She didn't like Frog but he suspected that she would do anything to get back into her half-sister's good graces.

#

"I need a favor," said Joe when Evelyn came out of the shower.

"What kind of a favor?"

"The kind of a favor that being a vampire might be really helpful for."

"Oh?"

"But first, um, I did something that you aren't going to approve of."

She stopped and looked at him, waiting for more.

"I, uh, I went to see Frog a while back, to make sure that he was okay after you snacked on him."

Evelyn gave a little snort but said nothing.

"And he convinced me to try and find a vampire who would help him out."

"You didn't?"

"I did. I took pity on him. And really, I mean, why not? You want me to become one."

"I want to spend my immortality with you. I am not sure I want Frog in that universe. No, actually, I know I don't want Frog in that universe."

Joe watched her dressing. She was sexy even in her dress down clothes of blue jeans and a pink sweater.

Stick to business.

"Well, anyway, I thought, you know, Otto is a good guy, but I don't know how to get hold of him, so we went to the Lazy Susan to talk to Richie. And Richie got angry. He told me I didn't know what I was doing and kicked us out. He said Otto would slaughter Frog like one of his pigs."

"Otto is a nice guy," said Evelyn. "I wouldn't call him a psychopath or anything. Only for him, vampires are his species, and humans, breathers, they might as well be swine. In fact, I think he has more regard for his pigs."

"You think Otto would kill Frog, if he got a chance, knowing he's my friend?"

"Remember, Joe, you're just a snack to Otto. And that's not just a cute little euphemism. If Otto was offered a free drink, he might very well make an end of Frog."

Joe blinked at her.

"It's nice to drink your fill," she added.

"*Nice?*"

Evelyn shrugged.

Maybe Richie was right, maybe being a member of *that club* did change people.

"Well, anyway, as far as I know, Frog never connected with Otto, or anyone else. I took Frog back to the bus station and I thought that was the end of it."

Evelyn sat down on the bed where Joe was lounging. "I'm not going to change my mind."

"No, no, I'm not asking that. That's not the favor. Asha called. He's been missing since then. He never went home, apparently. She figured it was a long shot, she didn't know he'd been here."

Evelyn thought for a minute. "Did you tell her?"

"Yeah."

"If he's been reported missing the police are going to want to talk to you."

"Well, I'll tell them what I just told you, only I'll leave out the vampire stuff. But, there's more. I called

Richie and he just stonewalled me. He knows something. I need to talk to him in person. I think I can get into his head."

"If Richie won't talk to you.... Don't you think no news is probably bad news?"

Joe sighed. "Probably." He had been mulling over how bad the news might be for the last 2 hours. "But maybe... I don't know, maybe Richie has other reasons to keep secrets."

"Hm."

"I have to know. I have to tell Asha something."

"Whatever we find out, we need to agree on what to tell Asha. One thing I have learned about this council is that as much as they rub each other the wrong way, as much as they may even hate each other, they work together. They keep each other safe because each other is all they have. I'm part of that now."

"What about Frog?"

Evelyn made a face. "What about him?"

"And Asha? You didn't hear her on the phone. First her mother, now Frog."

"Look, I'll go with you, but no matter what we find out, we will not be telling Asha? We will have to figure out what to say to her."

"Yeah, yeah, okay. Do you want to drive or—"

"Oh, no, we're going the easy way."

Evelyn took his hand and next thing he knew Joe was in a small paneled room. It was mostly filled by a scarred and cigarette-burned table and assorted chairs. Joe reeled and steadied himself on the back of a chrome and black vinyl chair.

"Where are we?"

"Back room of the Lazy Susan."

Joe shuttered his mind immediately. "Where the council meets?"

"Mm hm. Pretty impressive, isn't it?"

"Well, I wasn't expecting it to be like the Ritz or anything back here based on the rest of the place. Hey, you've even got a flag. Do you start meetings with the Pledge of Allegiance?"

"No. So, can you, I don't know, *see* into Richie's head from here?"

Joe felt around. There were all the ghosts talking and laughing and clinking their teacups of bathtub gin. A sax started up and suddenly a whole world opened up to Joe. The bar was full. Men in suits and hats and women in beaded dresses and feathers. There was a woman on stage singing, and Richie was playing the sax. Joe could feel the reed that gave the instrument its sound vibrating against his lip and the tip of his tongue. He felt the music too, and he couldn't distinguish between hearing it with Richie's ears, or his own.

Richie didn't just hear the ghosts like Joe did. He went back there, back to the 20s. No wonder he kept the place alive.

Evelyn put a hand on his arm and the touch pulled Joe out of Richie's mind.

"He's playing sax," said Joe.

"Yes, I can hear him."

"Right." The music was a bit muffled through the walls, but it was loud enough. Only Richie was really playing to a near-empty room.

"I have a plan," said Evelyn. "Richie will shut down if you go to talk to him, right?"

"Probably."

"So I will go and ask him about Frog and you stay here and mentally eavesdrop."

Joe nodded. It sounded like a good plan to him. He sat down in one of the chairs and followed the sound of the sax back into Richie's mind. He didn't know how to rifle through it like the Mater had his, and he didn't want to alert Richie that he was nearby, so he just sat back and watched/listened/tasted/felt. Through Richie's eyes, he saw Evelyn stroll into the room and take a table. She rested her chin on her hand and smiled at him dreamily.

When Richie had finished the piece, he said, "This next one is for Miss Evelyn."

"Come on, Richie," muttered Joe under his breath. He liked Richie's playing, but he didn't want to have to sit through a whole set before he started to get some information. He had waited long enough in waiting for sunset.

But while he played, some serious sex was going on in Richie's head. Him and Evelyn in a car. Joe adjusted himself.

In the background, distinct from the memories, the Prohibition-era bar crowd carried on.

And then it was fantasy stuff, less sharp-edged, about him and Richie and Evelyn in between them.

He knew. Richie knew he was here.

"Where's Frog?" Joe asked out loud. He pulled up an image of Frog in his mind, and in Richie's too. The sax squeaked.

"Excuse me, ladies and gents," Richie coughed. "I seem to have a frog in my throat."

The images changed to a vision of Richie punching Joe out. And then nothing: Richie closed his mind.

"Goddamn," muttered Joe, and headed for the door. He opened it to find Richie striding down the hall towards him. Evelyn was at his heels. Once they were both in the room Richie slammed the door.

"I told you never to come back here!" Richie shouted.

"I'm looking for Frog. He's disappeared. People are worried about him."

Richie gave a sharp bark of derisive laughter. "I can't help you."

"Yes, you can. You know something," insisted Joe. "Look, boy—"

Evelyn put a gentle hand on Richie's arm. "What is it you're afraid of?"

Richie turned away, his mouth clamped shut, but Joe caught a snatch of an image. A biker in an American flag bandanna and sunglasses.

"Claude has Frog?" asked Joe.

"Claude? Not Otto?" asked Evelyn.

Suddenly Richie was in Joe's face, a handful of Joe's shirt in his fist. "Get the fuck out of my head, boy! Leave it alone. You are going to get one or all of us killed."

Joe had his butt perched on the edge of the table, and he stood up now, to his full height, forcing Richie to look up at him and to step back. Richie did not let go of Joe's shirt.

"Did Claude kill Frog? That's all we want to know," said Evelyn. She sounded so calm and reasonable.

Richie kept his eyes locked on Joe's, but he snorted and answered Evelyn: "If he's lucky."

"Meaning," said Joe, "that you don't know."

Richie finally let go of Joe's shirt. "No, I don't. Here's what I know: your amphibious friend kept hanging around here till I got tired of throwing him out. And then one night Claude showed up and they left together. I haven't seen Frog since. There! Are you happy? Now, if you run off and pester Claude, I'm going to get my ass whipped. You've seen what he will do to me when he isn't even mad."

Evelyn frowned. "How did Claude know he was here?"

"Did you *ask* him to get rid of Frog?" asked Joe, incredulous.

"No, I didn't ask him! I don't ask Claude for anything. I don't talk to him, I don't hang with him. I keep

215

out of his way as much as possible. But here's the thing, Otto and I, we are Claude's bloodline, and that enables him to tap into our little psychic network. He's good. I can't tell when he's listening in or not. Not like you, Cheney. You got all the subtlety of a neon sign."

"I'll have to work on that," said Joe flatly.

Richie ignored him. "Claude might be listening in now, I don't know. But I do know if you go and ask him about Frog, however politely, he is going to know where you got that information."

"You want me to abandon Frog to Claude?"

"Damn straight! That boy came in here looking for trouble. He was warned. Kept coming back anyway. He got his just desserts."

"Richie, no one deserves Claude," scorned Joe. "If Claude hasn't killed him already—"

"No, no, no—" said Richie.

"—we have to rescue him."

"—no, no, no! You got to stay away from him and keep your hide on your backside. Evelyn, talk some sense into him."

"I'm the *Pueri Occidistis Inquisitor*," Joe reminded Richie.

"Then you got to leave him alone so I can keep my hide on my backside."

Joe looked at Evelyn. "What do you think?"

"Claude isn't going to tell us anything. Can you *make* him tell us?"

"Yeah. Probably. Maybe."

Richie, who had been pacing back and forth in the three feet between the table and the wall, stopped. "You got that kind of power?"

Joe lifted his chin. "Yeah. I made him beg for Evelyn's forgiveness. I made him call her Miss Evelyn, like you do, instead of Brown Sugar," he bragged. "I even made him take off his sunglasses."

Richie didn't look impressed. "You're playing a dangerous game, Cheney."

"Joe, are you sure you want to pursue this?" asked Evelyn. "I know what you did before, but Claude is dangerous, and not just because he has psychic powers. He has a network. He has people who can operate during the day."

"He's mean as a snake," added Richie. "If I had a choice between Claude and a hungry anaconda, I would pick the anaconda."

"Besides, Frog is probably dead," said Evelyn quite reasonably. "Claude probably drained him and dumped him somewhere."

"I agree with Miss Evelyn. I can't imagine any reason Claude would keep him alive. It's not like he's got a sparkling personality or something."

"But what if he's not?" asked Joe "I mean, I know you don't like him, but do you really want to leave him to Claude?"

Richie turned away, shaking his head.

"He's a human being, Richie! Or have you been too close to *that club* for too long?"

Richie looked like he was ready to punch Joe. "I'm a human being too. And I wasn't the one who went out looking for trouble like an idiot. What about me?"

Joe put his hands on his hips. "If Claude is so dangerous to you, why hasn't he killed you already? How have you managed to escape his wrath for two hundred years?"

"Because if he kills me then I am a member of *that club*, and Claude doesn't think my black ass is worthy of that. Besides, Claude like to torture people. He likes me being afraid of him."

"So Claude is probably torturing Frog?" asked Joe.

Richie waved his hands as if to erase that part of the conversation from the air. "What I am saying is, better Frog than me."

Joe ran his hands through his hair and tightened his mental shutters before he said, "All right, we won't go to Claude. You are probably right, and Frog is dead, or as good as." He reached out a hand to Evelyn. "Let's go." He could feel Richie's eyes boring into him and Richie might have had his mouth open to rage against him some more, but they were back in the front hall at home before he got any words out.

Joe leaned on the hall table and breathed slow and deep to fight off his nausea.

Evelyn chuckled in a way that Joe thought of as somewhere between mischievous and evil. "You're not ready to give up, are you?"

"No."

"If Frog isn't dead already he will be soon enough. We could just tell Asha that he's dead. Only...."

"Only... you don't want to lie to her?"

"I don't want her to be so sad. I don't want her to grieve."

"So!" Joe interlaced his fingers and bent them backward to crack them. "This is a rescue operation then."

Evelyn smiled. "I think we make a pretty good team."

"But how do we find Claude?"

"We could wait for the next council meeting, but I think that greatly improves the chances of Frog being dead. Why don't we ask the Mater? I have her phone number." Evelyn got her address book from her desk in the morning room. "You call. She never answers if it's me." She flipped through to the T's. There was no last name.

Joe shuttered his mind as tightly as he could and dialed the Great Tamara's number. It rang three times and then there was a click and Tammi said, "If *you're* calling *me*, you must be in trouble."

Evelyn pressed her ear to the back of the receiver.

"Uh, no, no. I'm fine. We're fine. I just wanted to ask—I need to get in touch with Claude. Do you have a number for him?"

There was silence for a second and Joe tightened down his mental shutters as he felt the Mater probing them. Apparently, distance and phone lines were not obstacles to her.

"I think it's safe to say that no one has ever asked me that before. What do you want to talk to Claude about?"

"It's, um...." *Do I tell her?* He mouthed at Evelyn.

"Well?" Tammi was suddenly in front of them. Joe jumped, and in his surprise lost his grip on the phone and his shutters. He felt Tammi reach into his brain, like a greedy kid into a candy dish, and scoop out a handful of information.

"So, you want my help to keep Richie safe and to rescue... *Frog*." She gave a derisive snort.

Joe swallowed. "That would be great."

Tammi folded her arms over her chest. "Why should I help you?"

"Because we're family? Bloodlines, and all that?"

"Hm. If this Frog isn't dead, then what?"

"Then...."

Tammi chuckled.

"You want to mount a rescue operation, like a couple of superheroes in capes."

"Not me," said Evelyn, "I just want to beat up Claude."

"Ha! Be careful what you wish for." Tammi barrelled on: "All right, kiddies, take my hands, we're going on a field trip." She rubbed her palms against the thighs of her jeans like they needed cleaning off and held them out to Joe and Evelyn.

Evelyn raised one eyebrow. "Where?"

"You want to know where Frog is? I'll show you where Frog is." She smirked.

Joe reached for her hand, and Evelyn grabbed his other one tightly and gave him a sharp look. *We stick together*, it said. He nodded.

"I'm not hanging around," Tammi warned them. "What you do after I leave you is between you and Claude."

And then they were outside, in the muggy summer night. Bugs swarmed around the square spotlights on the corners of a small cement block building that illuminated a gravel parking lot and a row of Harleys. Joe tried to breathe slowly and not be nauseous.

A metal door banged open and Claude came out and stood about ten feet away, his thumbs tucked into his belt loops.

The Mater had called him, and Joe hadn't heard a thing.

"More lessons." Claude's voice was completely neutral.

"I want them to see your operation."

Claude looked down and poked at the dirt with the chrome toe of his boot. Even in the dark, he wore his sunglasses.

Joe strained to overhear the silent conversation they must be having, and he got some things from Claude, but they were jumbled flashes of image and sensation like someone was flipping through channels on a mental radio.

After a few minutes, Claude said, "Yeah, okay."

Tammi turned to them. "This is a lesson, you two lambs. Claude has promised not to hurt you." She slid her eyes sideways at Claude, conspiratorially, and he made a guffaw. Joe didn't take it seriously. It was too obviously theatrics designed to unsettle them.

"What are we going to learn, Professor?" asked Evelyn.

"How things are," answered Tammi, and was gone.

"Alright, come on," said Claude and turned towards the back of the parking lot.

Claude led them across a field. There was a little footpath worn into the long grass. On the other side of the field, Joe could just make out a single, feeble light on the side of a large building, like a factory or a warehouse. Some of the panes in its upper windows glittered back a reflection of the lights on the motorcycle clubhouse behind them, and some were simply black.

Before they were out of the field, Claude stopped.

"This is one of my operations; I have more. So if you get any high and mighty ideas about putting me out of business, can 'em. There are plenty more girls, plenty more places like this."

"Why does the Mater want us to see this?" asked Evelyn.

"Damned if I know," answered Claude, and spit into the weeds. "I don't question the Mater." He turned and walked away, announcing, like a ride operator, "Please fasten your seatbelts and keep your hands inside the vehicle at all times."

They walked through an open loading dock into a vast empty space. Near the door, a single bulb on a wire hung low over a table where four guys sat playing cards. They were dressed in leather and denim. One was a skinhead with some kind of tattoo on his scalp that Joe couldn't make out in the gloom, and the others had long hair and beards. One had a handlebar mustache waxed up into curling points.

"Hey boss," one of them greeted Claude, and they all chucked in their hands and turned, ready for orders.

"Just bringing a couple of sightseers through on a tour," said Claude airily. "At ease."

"New girl?" asked one of them, eyeing Evelyn.

"Two new girls," snickered the skinhead. He was tipping his chair back on two legs and Joe gave him a little mental push that sent him crashing backward. His feet hit the card table, and cards and paper money scattered.

Claude turned and gave Joe a *will you behave* frown.

"Any customers tonight?"

"Not tonight. They're hungry."

"Well, that always makes things more interesting. Come on, kiddies."

The light from the single bulb made their shadows monstrous. Claude led them to a caged-in elevator shaft. He used a key to call the elevator up, and once they were in, used it to take them down. Two or three floors, Joe figured. There were no numbers, no buttons, and only a dim light overhead, behind a yellowed plastic square, that flickered in tempo with every hitch and jerk of the elevator.

Joe's hand was sweaty in Evelyn's, but he didn't dare let go.

Another single bulb and another four men at a table. These said nothing. They didn't look like bikers; they looked like vampires: pale faces, black clothes, and dark hair. No beards. It was as if they had been selected for their looks.

"They were," said Claude, then he leaned towards the two of them conspiratorially and said quietly, "and don't think they're just window dressing."

"*Ouvrez!*" he ordered, and one of the men swung open a heavy metal door. It was wide enough for a forklift to drive through.

The room beyond seemed bright compared to the rest of the place, but the first thing that hit Joe was the smell. It was more than stale and damp: it was an animal smell, like a house with too many dogs, and under that a whiff of something that had gone bad.

As they stepped through the door behind Claude, a voice called out: "Welcome to Hell!"

Evelyn gripped Joe's hand even harder.

In front of them stood Frog, his arms spread in a showman's flourish. There was a top hat perched on his head and a cane in his hand. He had lost weight. His clothes were dirty and stained and his feet were bare. Smudgy glasses winked back the light. One lens was cracked. A chain was padlocked around Frog's left ankle.

"Oh my god," breathed Evelyn.

Seeing them, Frog giggled. "Welcome to Hell," he repeated, "where your darkest desires can be fulfilled. Look at these lovely ladies. You can have any one you like."

He swept his arms wide, indicating the cages that lined the room. Each one was large enough to hold a mattress, no bedding, and a naked woman. The occupants came to the bars, dragging their own clinking chains. Their eyes were dark and hungry. All but one. Frog shuffled over to her cage, his chain scraping against the cement floor, and rattled the door.

"Get up!" he ordered. "Get up, bitch!"

A woman in one of the closest cages reached out through the bars towards Joe. "Come here, Ginger. What is it you want? I can give it to you." Her pupils were blacked out by her dilated irises and her fangs flashed in the fluorescent lights that buzzed and flickered overhead.

Joe felt a tingling of lust and shut his mind again more firmly.

"Get up!" screamed Frog.

The woman lay on her side on the mattress, face hidden by long, matted hair. She lay motionless like only the dead can.

Frog unlocked her cage, grabbed her by the scruff of the neck, and dragged her to her feet. She didn't fight or protest. Her eyes were not dilated, but they were unfocused. The light had gone out in them: there was no one home.

"Frog here has traded his immortal soul to be my madame, haven't you Frog?" said Claude. "He looks after the girls down here."

"This can't be," whispered Evelyn.

"There's a certain market for the vampire whore. People come from all over. They pay a lot of money to get.... sucked on." Claude chuckled.

"Come on Ginger, come over here. You can put your dick wherever you like."

The women all shared one thing: they were young and beautiful. It showed even through the grime on their skins and their tangled hair.

Frog let go of the inanimate woman and she dropped to her hands and knees and stayed there, immobile, head down.

"Get up!" he screamed. He cracked the cane over her backside. Its passage was followed by a red welt and a trickle of blood down her hip. The woman did not react. The other women seemed oblivious to their sister's condition or her treatment.

"I'll do the girl," one of them offered.

Evelyn turned and bared her fangs at the woman and the caged vampire hissed back at her like a cat.

"Claude, I can't do anything with her," whined Frog. His voice was like a rusty saw in Joe's brain.

Tell me again why we wanted to rescue him?

Claude walked over and casually kicked the woman in the face. She rolled over, her broken nose spouting blood, and simply lay still on her back. "Put her back," said Claude. "I'll take care of her later. So," he turned back to Joe and Evelyn, rubbing his hands together. "This is my operation. I keep a whorehouse for people with certain appetites." He chuckled. "You two know what I'm talking about. Care to partake, Joseph? Any one of these ladies will oblige you. Anything you want, your wildest fantasies—in return for a little blood."

Without letting go of Joe, Evelyn took a step forward. "How much to buy him," she asked indicating Frog with a nod of her head.

Frog locked the cage of the uncooperative captive and retreated to the post that he was tethered to.

"Why, Brown Sugar, I mean, Miss Evelyn, if you want to tussle with Frog, you can have him for free. Call it a professional courtesy. I don't know that you'd get much out of it, though. I'm not even sure he has a dick."

Frog didn't say anything. He was still breathing, but it was easy now, no wheezing or coughing.

"I don't mean for the night," persisted Evelyn, her voice like stainless steel. "I mean to purchase him. Buy out his contract."

"Ha! More money than you've got."

Evelyn's chin tilted up. "Name a price."

"You know, I can get a thousand dollars for one of these bitches just to bite some guy on the neck and play with his wiener. You want to flay the skin off of one of them with a cat 'o nine tails? Five thousand. But for Frog, well now, Frog is special, wiener or no."

Evelyn cocked her head to one side. "A hundred thousand dollars," she said.

A sharp inhale of breath betrayed Claude's surprise or greed or both, but then he rubbed his stubbly chin and pretended to consider the offer.

"Well, wouldn't that be ironic, you buying a white boy."

Frog giggled, but it didn't sound cheerful. "If you prick us, do we not bleed? If you tickle us, do we not laugh? If you poison us—"

"Shut up," ordered Claude. "If you're really serious, come back with cash," said Claude. "Need I add, non-sequential, small denomination bills?"

"How will I find you?" asked Evelyn.

"Go to the same place you started at earlier tonight. And say hi to Richie for me."

"Leave Richie alone," said Joe. "That's part of the deal."

Claude shrugged. "Whatever."

Evelyn turned to Joe, but he held a hand up to stop her from popping them home.

"What are you going to do with her?" he asked about the woman Claude had kicked. Her face had stopped bleeding and her nose was reconstructing itself. She made no sound and didn't move.

"I'm going to drain her dry and toss her body out where the sun will take care of her. Why? You want her, Joseph Junior? Does that appeal to you? Are you into necrophilia?" taunted Claude.

"Joe?" Evelyn looked a question at him.

"You want her?" Claude gestured to Frog, who jumped to obey the order. He unlocked the cage and picked up the woman's shackled ankle so Claude could more easily unlock the chain.

"There you go. Take her. As a sign of good faith on our deal about Frog." He removed the ring from her ankle. "You go ahead."

Joe took a step but Evelyn held him back.

Claude laughed. "Too scared to let go of your girlfriend's hand, huh?"

Joe looked at Evelyn. He was not going to be bullied or shamed into letting go of her. She was his safe passage out of this nightmare.

This time Evelyn came with him. She crouched down and took the woman's limp hand.

"See you." Joe said the first word in Claude's house of horrors and the second in the front hall of their house.

With Evelyn's help, Joe got the woman into the bathtub in the blue room's ensuite.

"Will you, um...?"

Evelyn shook her head. "I.... You take care of her. I...." She shook her head. "No."

The woman was pliant and vacant. At first, Joe was shy about washing her but after a while, it was just like handling a large doll. He had to cut most of her matted hair off, for which he apologized, but there was no reaction on her part.

While Joe bathed the vacant woman, aluminum foil was unfurled and duct tape ripped off the roll as Evelyn prepared the room for a vampire's daytime sleep.

They put one of Joe's T-shirts on her, put her to bed, and closed the door. Throughout his caretaking, she never made a sound, made eye contact, or even twitched. Pale as she was—her skin was almost translucent—she never tried to bite.

"What are you going to do with her?" asked Evelyn, in the hushed voice of a parent who has just settled a toddler down for the night.

"I don't know, but I couldn't leave her there. I mean...."

"Letting him kill her might have been a mercy," suggested Evelyn.

"Nothing about Claude is a mercy."

Evelyn slipped her arms around his waist and snuggled up to his chest. Joe was happy to hold her. The smell of Claude's dungeon was still in his nostrils.

"What do you suppose Tammi wanted us to learn?" he asked as he breathed in the scent of her shampoo.

"When she called us lambs," said Evelyn her cheek pressed against his chest, "I thought, you have no idea what I have been through, what *we* went through, with Simms. And then when I saw that place...." She shuddered.

"Yeah," agreed Joe. "That was... an education, I guess."

"When I first met Claude he offered me a job."

"Yeah?"

"Mm hm. All the men I could ever want to dine on, he said. Delivered right to me. *That* was what he had in mind."

"He could never hold you in a cage," Joe reminded her, then he said, "Somebody has to stop him."

Evelyn pulled away enough to look up at him. "We are not those people."

"But—"

"No. It would start a war. It would be like Simms all over again. Worse."

Joe pulled her close again. He knew better than to argue with that voice, and she was right, of course. But still....

"It will take a few days to get the money," Evelyn said. "Krause Junior will want to know what I want it for."

"Tell him you're going on a shopping spree."

Evelyn gave a tired chuckle.

#

The next morning Joe wanted to check on the girl, but sunlight was streaming through the skylights at a dangerously close angle to her door, and he didn't want to take the chance of any of it hitting her. He listened at the door and heard nothing, of course.

Asha called and Joe did not pick up. He waited. The little red light on the answering machine lit up. When it changed to blinking Joe listened to the message, but all there was, was a hang-up click. That was okay. Evelyn's fancy answering machine had recorded the caller's phone number. No psychic sense told him that it was Asha, but it was the same time as she had called the day before. He wrote the number down, with her name, and left it by the phone.

As Joe backed out of the garage on his way to work, his first clue that something was not right was the scorch mark on the lawn. Joe put the car into park and ran over to the spot. The burnt grass was a familiar sight. There was a twisted window screen not far from it.

Above him a window was open, blue curtains visible, and beyond them, shreds of aluminum foil danced and flashed in the breeze. Joe looked at the ground again. There was nothing but scorched earth. Not a bone remained. He went back into the house and up to the blue room with a heavy tread and a heavy heart.

The room was empty. The aluminum foil was torn from the window and hanging in strips. Other than the rumpled covers it was as if the girl had never been there.

She must have jumped from the window sometime before dawn. While they were whispering in the hall? If he had only stayed with her and kept an eye on her until sunrise....

Joe closed the door to the blue room. After debating for a while, he just scrawled, *Ev, call me* on a piece of paper and stuck it on the door. Then he hurried off to work. There was nothing else to do, not even a body to bury. Whoever she had been, she was no longer suffering.

At least she got to make the choice and end it herself, instead of living and dying at Claude's hands.

#

At work, Joe found himself in front of the bottles of Adderall. He needed a pick-me-up. He had dreamed about cages, in the few hours of sleep he had gotten, but he wasn't sure if it was Evelyn or him on the inside, just that there were bars between them. Every time he thought about the dungeon he could smell it.

Instead of Adderall, he helped himself to a couple of caffeine tablets.

Throughout the day he thought about the dungeon. Where did Frog sleep? On the concrete? Where did he take a leak? That explained some of the smell. They must have been feeding him, but not much. Frog had keys to the cages. Did he...?

The caffeine left him jittery, and Joe pocketed a few Valium. He took one in the car on his way home and kept the others in case he needed help sleeping.

#

"We're looking for him," said Joe when Asha called the next day.

"What do you mean you're looking for him? Looking where?"

"We've got someone who thinks he saw Frog with someone else we sort of know," Joe cringed inwardly at the clumsiness of his lie, "and we're trying to find that guy, to see if he knows anything."

"Who? Tell me who. I'll tell the police and they can track that guy down faster than you."

"I, uh, I don't have a name to give you. Just a guy. I've seen him around."

"Joe! Stop messing around. I need to find Frog."

"Just a couple more days, Asha. Trust me."

He heard a long cigarette smoke exhale on the other end. "Is Frog in any danger?"

Joe wiped his lips with the back of his hand. "No. He's fine, I'm sure. He's just...." *Chained up in a dungeon.* "Uh, involved with some... people."

"He's so involved he can't call his mama or let anyone know where he is? Has he joined a cult?"

"Um, well, you could sort of look at it that way...."

"Joe! For chrissakes!"

Joe jumped. His sleep had been muddled with nightmares, and now Asha was yelling at him when he was trying to help her. He was going to need those Valium. Just one. He could take it when he left the house and it would kick in just after he got to work and make for smooth sailing through his day.

"Look, just give me a couple more days, Asha. I swear I will get Frog back to you."

"If Frog don't call me in two days, I'm calling the police and telling them to look in your neighborhood."

Joe closed his eyes. "We'll find him, Asha."

The phone clicked and the dial tone buzzed in his ear.

#

The next night when he got home from work Evelyn showed Joe a fat envelope, wrapped in packing tape.

"That's a hundred thousand dollars?" he asked, weighing it in his hand.

"I didn't count it."

"So, we go to the Lazy Susan and wait for Claude to show up?" Joe checked his watch. "It must be nearly closing time."

"I have a better idea," she smiled. "I've been to Claude's 'establishment', I've seen it, I can pop there directly. We go, we take Frog, and we leave this behind. Claude can have no objection. All he wants is the money."

"I guess. I don't feel the need to see Claude again. Can you pop Frog out of that chain?"

Evelyn thought about it. "I don't pop you out of your clothes."

"Damn good thing! So, what would happen?"

"I don't know."

"Okay, well, maybe we should bring something to get him out of that thing then."

"Like what?"

"A saw? Bolt cutters? I don't know. I'll go see what there is in the shed."

Evelyn grabbed his hand and they were suddenly in the shed.

"Don't do that!" cried Joe.

"It saves time."

"I like walking. Walking is not nauseating."

Evelyn flicked on the lights. The shed was as they had left it, still heaped with dead flies raised in the nursery of Clara's corpse.

"Shit," muttered Joe.

"What about this?" asked Evelyn. She had a long-handled branch trimmer.

"Uh... I don't know. Bring it, I guess. Aha, here's a hacksaw. Um..." Joe looked around. "There's a chainsaw."

"Will a chainsaw work?"

"I don't know. I've never had to cut through a chain to free someone before," Joe snapped. He wanted another Valium, but really, he needed to be alert. He was going to need his adrenaline. He wished he had grabbed some more caffeine tabs.

Joe strode over and grabbed the chainsaw down off the wall. "I think that's everything useful. Okay. I guess I'm—"

Evelyn touched him and the shed disappeared and became Claude's dungeon establishment. Joe recognized it by the smell alone. It was totally dark and silent.

"There's no one here!" cried Evelyn. "The cages are gone."

"Can you see well enough?" asked Joe. He reached out psychically and got nothing.

"Yes, yes. He's moved his operation!"

"Huh. Guess he doesn't trust us. So, the—" Joe blinked in the comparatively bright fluorescent light of the Lazy Susan's back room. Leroy, who must have been on a break, jumped out of his chair, and his lit cigarette flew across the room.

"I am going to barf." Joe sat down in one of the chairs and put his head between his knees.

Evelyn stamped out Leroy's cigarette. "Would you tell Richie that we're here?"

"Is Claude here?" asked Joe from between his knees.

"I certainly hope not," whispered Leroy, and shuffled out of the room as fast as his old legs would carry him.

A minute later Richie burst in. "What in the nine circles of Hell are you doing back here again?" His voice broke high.

"Claude told us to look for him here," said Evelyn.

"Claude! And he told you to bring implements of destruction?" asked Richie, eyeing the chainsaw at Joe's feet.

"Rescue operation," answered Joe. He breathed as calmly and deeply as he could through his mouth. He wished that there was a window he could open for some cool air.

Richie swore long and elaborately.

"Such language," admonished Evelyn, with a long, slow bat of her lashes.

"Miss Evelyn, I have always treated you as a lady, but—"

"And you'll keep it up," ordered Joe, though he didn't feel like he was in any shape to enforce it. "Can you call Claude?"

"Can I what?" Richie's voice jumped two octaves.

"Psychically."

"Oddly enough, I don't know because I have never tried! Are you two insane? We've been over this! You are going to get us all killed."

"You want to know where we found Frog?" Joe straightened up. "He was chained up in a dungeon where his job, ostensibly, was to look after a bunch of women in cages. Vampire whores, Claude called them. He—"

"Joe," said Richie quietly. "I know what Claude's business is. I've worked for him. I know how he operates. I know what he is capable of." And then he shouted. "That is why I am so afraid of him! Jesus Christ, boy!" then he stopped. "How did you find him? How did you even get in there?"

"Mater took us," answered Evelyn.

"She... she...?" Richie shook his head like he would never understand.

"She said she wanted to educate us on the way things are," said Evelyn.

Richie gave a low, despondent laugh. "Well, I guess you two are educated now. But maybe not well enough. You planning on going back with a chainsaw to rescue everybody?"

"We made a deal with him. To buy Frog."

"I hope you got a bargain. So why the chainsaw?"

"We thought we might take a short cut," said Joe. He was embarrassed to admit it. He knew what Richie was going to say next.

"You were going to cheat Claude? Oh, no, no, no! You two are going to start a blood war."

"We weren't going to cheat him." Evelyn held up the taped envelope of cash. "We were just hoping to expedite matters. We didn't want to meet him here, Richie. But Claude was one step ahead of us, so now we need to do it his way, I guess."

"I don't want you waiting for him here. I don't want Claude coming here. Dammit, this is *my* bar! This is *my* property!"

Evelyn shrugged. "We don't have a choice. Unless you can call him."

Joe suddenly had the feeling he had forgotten something and needed to check on it. He frowned.

Check on what?

The answer was an image of the front of the Lazy Susan. The gaze turned away from it, across the street, to a red, windowless van.

Joe stood up. "He's here. Outside."

"Good! Take your business outside. Keep it outside! And," warned Richie in a low voice, as if Claude might be listening in at the door, "beware of ambush."

#

They left the implements of destruction in Richie's back room and Evelyn held Joe's hand with her left, and the packet of money with her right. Through the glass and grille of the Lazy Susan's door, they could see the red van parked across the street. Claude was leaning against it, projecting good ol' boy bonhomie.

"Beware of ambush," muttered Joe.

He opened the door with his free hand, and as they stepped out there was a flap of dark movement at the corner of Joe's vision. Before he had time to turn the perspective changed and they were in the middle of the street, thirty feet or more from the van. Joe gulped cool air and tried to maintain his equilibrium.

"That's not playing fair," called Evelyn.

Claude startled but recovered. "Neither is going to my establishment with a chainsaw. A chainsaw! You know they don't call them that because they're for cutting chains."

"Then we're even," answered Evelyn. "So let's make this trade. I have the money. Where is Frog?"

There was a ratchet sound, just like in the movies, that sound that alerts the hero, to a gun being cocked. Joe saw the gun in the hand of one of the men (vampires?) who had tried to jump them.

Put it down.

He was a lot easier than Claude, or even an inanimate glass. The man lowered his arm and put the gun on the ground by his feet. Then he looked at Claude, confused.

Claude snorted and knocked on the side of the van. The back door opened and Frog tumbled out onto the pavement with a groan. He was bound and gagged.

"Are you sure you even want this amphibian?"

"No," answered Evelyn smoothly, "but my sister is fond of him."

"Can't imagine why," said Claude.

Evelyn moved towards Frog with Joe in tow, and Claude hurried forwards.

"My money!"

Evelyn tossed him the package, and Claude scrambled for it and tore it open.

So this is what makes Claude tick.

Money makes the world go round, answered Claude in Joe's head.

Evelyn did no more than touch Frog with her foot and suddenly they were in the green bedroom. Joe collapsed on the bed with a groan while Evelyn turned on the lamps. Then she looked down at Frog, motionless on the floor. "Hm."

"He's not dead, is he?"

Frog was struggling to breathe and Evelyn crouched down and pulled the gag from his mouth daintily, with the tips of two fingers, like she didn't want to touch him.

Frog made a sound between a sob and laugh. "Dead? No. They'd never kill me," he whispered. "That would be too kind. I can be bled again and again, and I'll live."

Joe found scissors and cut the zip ties binding Frog's hands and ankles. Frog didn't make a move to get up, he just sagged on the floor. There were twin holes in his neck, crusted over with dark red. Evelyn licked her fingers and wiped the holes with her blood to heal them.

"It's okay, Frog, you're safe now," Joe assured him.

"Safe?" Frog laughed.

Joe looked at Evelyn. "Do you think you could go get an EpiPen?"

"At this time of night?"

Joe knew exactly where they were at work, but Evelyn had never been there. He ought to liberate a few, he supposed, and keep them on hand.

"Richie has some at the Lazy Susan. If he won't give you one, ask Leroy. He's probably more afraid of you than of Richie. And some Gatorade."

"No!" crowed Frog. "No Gatorade! God, no. I've had so much fucking Gatorade...."

"Something sugary," said Joe.

Evelyn disappeared mid nod.

"I'm going to help you onto the bed, okay?"

Frog didn't answer, but he managed to climb onto the bed with Joe's help. He stunk worse, close up, but Joe didn't fancy bathing him. That could wait until Frog could take care of himself.

Frog settled into a drowse. His breathing was rough, and every now and then he would gasp in a way that made Joe worry he was about to die. His mind was all a jumble, but fear flowed steadily off of him, like mist out of a container of dry ice.

"Not going to die," Frog muttered at one point, and Joe reminded himself to keep his mind shuttered.

Evelyn was back in ten minutes with the EpiPen in one hand and a plastic shopping bag in the other.

"Claude and his goons got back in their van and left after we did, but Richie had already taken off. Leroy was very helpful."

"Cause he was scared shitless?"

"No, I don't think that was it. I think Leroy has some of the compassion that his employer is lacking."

Evelyn handed Joe the EpiPen, and he pulled the cap off and plunged it into Frog's thigh. Frog gave a cry and Joe flinched.

Frog took a deeper, easier breath.

"Frog? Can you sit up and drink something?"

"Blood?" whispered Frog.

"No, not blood. Sunny Delight or Pepsi?"

Frog giggled. "Sunny...."

Joe propped him into a sitting position and Evelyn opened the plastic bottle and inserted a straw.

"... yesterday my life was filled with rain..." whispered Frog.

"Should we call Asha?" wondered Evelyn out loud.

"Maybe wait until he's a little more, um...."

238

"... you smiled at me and really, really eased my pain...."

"Sane?" suggested Evelyn. She put the straw between Frog's lips, and he closed his eyes and greedily sucked down the orange drink.

"I was going to say recovered. An IV would hydrate him faster, but I don't think we should take him to the hospital like this."

"Absolutely not."

"Tammi works in the morgue, do you think she knows how to set up an IV?"

"I don't think I want to ask the Mater for any more favors, do you?"

Frog finished his drink with a sigh of satisfaction and laid back down on the bed. Evelyn cracked open the Pepsi, but Frog turned away.

"Lemme sleep," he whined.

Out in the hall, Joe stopped and said, "I think maybe we should keep an eye on him."

Evelyn looked back at the half-closed door. "I'm going to call Asha."

"Yeah?"

Evelyn disappeared. Joe went to the railing to look down at the front hall and the doorway to the morning room. He wanted to go down and listen in, but he wanted to keep an eye on Frog too. He couldn't kill himself with sunlight, but he could jump from the window. What worried Joe more than Frog killing himself, is that he would run off, and then they would have to look for him all over again.

From the railing, Joe could just hear Evelyn's voice murmuring. He went back to Frog's door and peeked in. Frog was muttering in his sleep. Joe went in and folded the coverlet over him. Frog's glasses lay beside him. They were smudged and dirty. One lens was cracked and the arms looked like they had been bent out of shape and straightened a few times.

I can be bled again and again, and I'll live.

Joe shivered.

When he turned around Evelyn was in the hall. She was looking down at the carpet.

"How did it go with Asha?" Joe asked.

Evelyn gave a little shrug with one shoulder.

"Was she happy we got Frog?"

"Happy isn't really the word. Angry. Not that we found him—just angry. She asked me a lot of questions that I declined to answer, and she wanted to come get him, but I said he needed a few days to recover before he would be fit for travel."

"And what did she say to that?"

"She hung up." Evelyn sighed and looked away. "She used to be so demure."

"Yeah, well under all that shyness I think she's got that same steel backbone you got."

Evelyn made a wan attempt at a smile and Joe went and put his arms around her. "She'll come around, baby. She's mad at Frog for putting her through this, and it's just spilling over."

"I hope so."

"So, will you keep an eye on him while I get some sleep? Wake me before sunrise and I'll take over."

Evelyn nodded. "Just let me get my book."

#

Joe dozed in the green armchair by Frog's bed and was awoken by the sound of water running in the bathroom. *Great guard I am. He could have jumped from the window. Or been out the door.*

Frog shuffled back into the room, collapsed on the bed and curled himself into a ball.

"You hungry?"

"Mm."

"How about I go get you something to eat?"

There was no response and Joe got up from the chair. When he opened the door Frog cried "Don't leave me!"

"Well, the kitchen's downstairs. If you want me to get you something to eat, you'll have to come with me. And you need to eat."

And after you eat, you need to shower.

Frog dragged himself off the bed and followed Joe. He was leaning on the wall for support by the time they got to the kitchen and he slumped into the banquette.

Joe whizzed Frog up a milkshake with strawberries, bananas, and chocolate ice cream, then fried up two burgers for Frog and one for himself. When he brought them to the table, the glass was empty and Frog's head was on his arms, but his eyes glittered under half-closed lids.

"Here. Protein. That will help you feel better."

Frog lifted his head and poked at one of the burgers.

"Who is it?" he asked.

"Who's what?"

Frog lifted the bun and peered at the meat. "Who is it?"

"It's a burger. Beef. From a cow. Shit, what have they been feeding you?"

Frog lifted the burger and sniffed it suspiciously. "Doesn't matter," he muttered and bit into it.

"Slow down. You're going to choke."

Frog laughed. "Don't matter," he said around a mouthful of burger. "I'm immortal now."

"You're a bloodling?"

"That was the deal. Drink his blood and be his slave." Frog shuddered.

"And did it work? Are you... healthier?"

For the first time Frog looked up at him, his eyes distorted and pale through his glasses. "I can breathe."

"You're still wearing glasses."

"My eyesight did not improve."

Was it worth it? Joe didn't ask. He figured he could judge that answer for himself.

"How long till sunset?" asked Frog suddenly.

Joe checked his watch. "Four or five hours."

"Sunset," said Frog. "That's when the fun begins."

"Frog, you are safe. We rescued you. No more Claude, no more cages, no more chain."

"Evelyn owns me now." Frog was onto his second burger.

"Evelyn doesn't want you to do anything for her. She bought you to set you free. Asha called—"

"Asha!" squeaked Frog.

"Asha called," continued Joe in a calm voice and soothing voice. "She said you had been missing for some time."

"Claude will come."

"No, he won't."

Frog shuddered. "Claude will come take me back." He looked up at Joe. "He'll probably kill you. He'll put Evelyn in a cage." Frog giggled. "I wouldn't mind that. Evelyn in a cage. Miss High and Mighty."

"Evelyn just paid a hundred thousand dollars to rescue you." Joe reminded him.

Frog shrugged.

"And Asha wouldn't like that, I imagine."

Frog frowned. "No cage for Asha. No, no. no." He shook his head vigorously.

"You've snapped."

A giggle burbled out of Frog, then a laugh, and then hamburger tumbled out of his mouth. He shook with uncontrollable mirth. Joe sat back. It was freaky to watch.

When Frog was done and had caught his breath, he said darkly, "You would too."

"You just need some time," said Joe, hoping that it was true. "Some sleep and good food and get you back home, and—"

"Home," said Frog suddenly. It was a mournful sound, like a distant train.

"Yeah, home."

"I can't go there."

"Why not?"

"I'm... I don't... I don't belong.... I'm a monster," Frog whispered.

"Jesus, what did they do to you?"

Frog looked at him and giggled again, and Joe didn't pursue an answer. He really wished that Evelyn was awake and available to help him figure out what to do. Should he call Asha and say, *come take this crazy friend of yours away?* Should he check Frog into a hospital? Should they try to look after him for a while until he was himself again? Or would he ever be himself again? Should he even have Frog talk to Asha in this state?

Frog's head was drooping over his empty plate.

"Why don't you go sleep some more."

"Sleep, that knits up the raveled sleeve of care."

"Uh huh. Come on." Joe led him back upstairs and Frog collapsed on the bed and was snoring before Joe left the room.

He called work and told them he would be late. "I've got a friend who needs babysitting. Withdrawals." He was banking on John having been in the same place at some point in his life. "There's no one else to do it until eight," he told John.

"Aw shit."

"I'm sorry for the late notice...."

"You look after your friend. We'll manage. But you'll be able to come in at eight?"

Got to restock, thought Joe. *And maybe get some antipsychotics for Frog,* but out loud he just said, "Yes, absolutely."

Joe checked on Frog again, who had not moved, and went down the hall to his own room and turned on the TV. He didn't even realize he had fallen asleep until he heard the doorbell and someone pounding on the door. It was two in the afternoon.

He hesitated on the stairs when he thought that it might be some of Claude's henchmen, but they probably wouldn't knock. A peek through the light beside the door showed him that it was Asha.

She had aged since he had seen her last. Her face was leaner and harder and she wasn't afraid to look him in the eye. She didn't bother with any niceties, just demanded, "Where's Frog?"

"He's sleeping upstairs."

Asha bustled in and looked up at the railing and the rooms above. "Frog?" she called, as she headed towards the stairs.

"Second room on the left," said Joe.

"Frog? Where you at?"

Joe followed her, but he didn't rush. There was no point—Asha was a woman on a mission. He was not going to be able to shelter her from Frog's condition.

When he got to the top of the stairs Asha was just coming out of the green room. "Where is he?" she demanded.

"In there. I left him sleeping a couple hours ago." Joe hurried past her and looked. Frog was not on the bed. The window was shut.

"He's under the bed," said Asha, pointing. She bent down and lifted the covers. "Frog, what the hell are you doing? Come out of there."

"No." came the reply. Joe couldn't tell if it was sulky or frightened.

"Frog!"

"Go away!"

Asha looked at Joe. "What in the hell is wrong with him?"

Joe spread his hands, and Frog's pale face appeared under the edge of the dust ruffle.

"Asha, go home. Go away. Stay away from me."

"Frog, get your ass out here. What is wrong with you?"

"No!" Frog disappeared into the darkness under the bed again.

Joe wished he had a syringe full of Klonopin handy. If Asha wanted him, Asha could have him.

"What are you, five years old? Frog, I drove all the way up here to take you home. I am running on Red Bull and determination. Now get out here."

No answer.

Asha looked at Joe. "You go round that side and push. I'll pull."

Joe crawled part way under the bed. "Go, Frog."

"No!"

Joe grabbed his feet and Frog started to kick.

"Frog, get yourself out here!"

Asha wasn't very tall, but she was strong. She got hold of Frog's arm and dragged him half way out from under the bed. Joe gave up on pushing and came around to help her pull. They got Frog into a sitting position on the floor halfway across the room. Frog gave up and just sat and cried.

"What in the name of God is wrong with you?"

"I'm one of them, Asha. I can't go home."

"One of who?"

"I'm a—"

"Don't you say vampire."

"I am."

"Look," Asha pointed at the window, her arm trembling with anger or fatigue or both. "There's the sun, and you okay. You ain't no vampire."

Frog was weeping into his hands.

"He's a bloodling." said Joe.

"I'm taking him home!" Asha took a step toward him and Joe backed up. He had never seen her like this. "Whatever is wrong with him, we'll fix it."

Frog wiped snot from his nose on the back of his hand. "It's true. I met the Devil, Asha. I drank his blood. He made me... do horrible things. I'm not fit to—"

"Joe, help me get him up."

"He beat me, and he let me heal," said Frog. He got to his feet when they lifted him by the upper arms and walked as Asha led him, his arm around her shoulder, as if in a trance now.

"Beat me, and let me heal. Over and over again. With whips, with chains, with his fists. Kicked me...."

"Come on Frog," said Asha, "we going to take you home. Take you to a doctor, get you fixed up."

But Frog seemed oblivious. Joe helped them along, opened the front door and the passenger door of Asha's little hatchback.

When Frog was tucked inside and belted in Joe turned to Asha.

"Evelyn paid a hundred thousand dollars to buy him out of slavery."

Asha frowned.

"Seriously. This guy had him chained up in an empty warehouse."

Asha gave him a long hard look. "You stay away from Frog, you and Evelyn." There was the same steel in her voice that Joe sometimes heard in her sister's.

"Asha...."

Joe followed her around to the driver's side and Asha got into her car. She would not roll down her window or look at him.

"Asha!"

She revved the car's engine to warn him before she put it in gear, and then she took off, faster, Joe thought, than was safe.

Joe Vampire

COMMITMENT

The Engagement

Joe waded through impatient patrons at the entrance of Paesano's. He hadn't anticipated a bus tour when he'd arranged to meet Carter and his girlfriend for dinner. Now the tastefully dim lobby with its imported Italian tiles and original artwork was packed with senior citizens in sensible shoes.

The diminutive hostess smiled broadly at him as he approached her podium. She was barely tall enough to see over it.

"You have a reservation?" She spoke slowly and carefully, and with a Chinese accent.

"Yeah, Cheney, for seven o'clock?"

"Afraid we running a little behind," she said with an apologetic smile. Did she know how cute she was? He wondered what time she got off work, and a gentle push of the question towards her head returned a vision of her taking off her shoes and putting her feet up.

He hadn't quite got the hang of fishing information out of other people's brains. It was a delicate business. Push too hard and people got this frown like they knew something was happening, but they didn't know what, and Joe didn't want to scare anyone. He wanted to use his powers for good, or at least, to do no harm. Also, he wanted to be as subtle as Claude.

"It might be... seven thirty?"

"Seven thirty?" Joe echoed.

"Sorry. You can wait at the bar," she offered.

Joe tried again to find out when she got off work, but now she was thinking about her shoes, and all he got back was that her toothy smile was an attempt to mask the pain they were causing her, and she should never have bought the stupid things in the first place, no matter how sexy they looked.

"I like your shoes," he said before he turned away.

Stools sprouted like mushrooms around bigger, or at least taller, mushrooms that were tables, in front of the polished pine bar. Joe snagged a seat as a group was called for their table. He could easily see the door from here.

True to form, Carter was right on time. He wove his way through the seniors, new girlfriend in tow. Joe's first impression of her was that she was some kind of professional–sales, upper management, talent agent–something like that. She was wearing a pale pink linen suit with a narrow skirt that ended decorously just above the knee. Her hair was straightened, streaked with bronze and swept up into a perfect French roll. As she got closer he noticed her high heeled pumps matched her outfit. What had Carter told him she did for a living?

"Joey! My man!"

Carter had blossomed, if you could apply that to a man, from a skinny, geeky brown-nosing student into a self-confident, slightly arrogant, chemical engineer.

"That's not my name," Joe growled back but grinned broadly.

"Lisa, I'd like you to meet Joe Cheney. Joe, this is Lisa Trembley."

"Pleasure to meet you," she said. "Joe—my Joe—has told me a lot about you."

"None of it is true, except the part about me being handsome and intelligent and a terrific roommate." Joe straightened his tie as he stood. "Please, have my seat," he offered. "They said our table might be late."

"What a gentleman," she commented sweetly and slid up onto the stool, knees primly together. They were nice legs, thought Joe. Carter caught him looking and cleared his throat.

"So, you lose a bet?" asked Carter.

"What?"

"Last time I saw him, he had a ponytail," Carter told Lisa, slipping his arm around her waist as casually as he could. Carter looked like this relationship was as new to him as his grey suit and tie.

"Oh, yeah," Joe self-consciously ran his hand over the top of his now very short hair. It had proven to be a lot thinner than he remembered. "Well, you know I figured I'd better go for a different image if I want to get a job."

"Some companies are very particular about that," commented Lisa.

"But it paid off, right?"

A table was called and Joe had to squeeze up against the bar to let people pass. He breathed in Lisa's perfume. It was nice. Perfume didn't really work on Evelyn—she had no body heat to make it evaporate into the air, and no human musk of her own to mix with it. It smelled on her exactly like it smelled in the bottle.

Joe laughed. "Yeah, I got in at that place I was telling you about, Semple's Pharmacy. But I don't know if the haircut helped. The owner has a ponytail himself."

"You work in a drug store?" asked Lisa in a carefully neutral voice.

Joe decided then and there that he didn't like her.

"Yeah, I'm a pharmacist."

"That must be interesting," she said with a practiced smile. Joe gave her the same kind back. He could hardly keep the challenge out of his voice as he asked, "So, what do you do?"

"I'm head of personnel at Hybrid Foods. And... are you going to tell him?" she asked Carter, grinning with big white teeth.

"I was going to wait until we were at the table," said Carter, "but now that you've brought it up...." He lifted Lisa's hand to display her engagement ring.

"Wow," popped right out of Joe's mouth. The diamond was at least a carat. "Congratulations. But I have to warn you, Lisa: he snores. Like a truck dumping gravel."

"I know," she said coyly, leaning closer to Carter. She gazed at him with syrupy sweetness. "I just tell him to roll over."

"I just moved into Lisa's place," explained Carter, blushing.

More people pushed past. The crowd was starting to thin.

"What does your mama say about that?" Joe had to ask.

"Mama Carter likes me," answered Lisa a bit defensively before Carter could say anything.

Joe smiled and drank his Coke. It was true what they said about guys looking for women who were like their mothers. He'd always known Carter would end up with a girl who told him what to do and how to do it. Thank God he had had therapy.

"Evelyn coming to join us?" asked Carter, to change the subject. Joe caught him checking to see how much daylight was left.

"Naw, she's off checking out properties in Mexico. And I gotta work," he grumbled.

"When are you going to marry her?" Mischief sparkled in Carter's eyes.

"Oh, I don't know...."

"They've been living together for four years now," he told Lisa.

"Yes? What does *your* mama think about that?" she asked.

Joe kept the smile from falling off his face. "My folks are dead."

"Oh! Oh, I'm sorry."

"It's okay," said Joe with a shrug.

"Cheney, party of four," came a man's voice over the speakers at the bar. They made their way to the hostess' podium, now attended by a balding man with bushy eyebrows that matched his bushy mustache.

He led them to a booth by the window. The window was mirror coated on the outside, so from the inside, the brilliant summer sun was muted and the colors of the street were faded, like a photo from the 70's.

Lisa wriggled up close to Carter with a smile and he put his arm around her. Joe felt suddenly lonely on his side of the table.

"So what is your girlfriend looking for down in Mexico?" asked Lisa.

"Oh, looking for a vacation place."

"You know, some people have a cottage," explained Carter, "Evelyn's have, like, four bedrooms and they aren't in the woods."

"And you have to work," said Lisa. It was just on the line between commiseration and sarcasm.

"Well if I'd gone I wouldn't have gotten to meet you," said Joe, toasting her with his water glass.

"You ready to order?" Their waitress was the pretty woman from the hostess stand. Joe couldn't help poking into her mind but all he found out was that she had changed her shoes and gone back to waiting tables after all the seniors were seated. He still didn't know when she got off work.

Joe didn't want to flirt with her in front of Carter and Lisa. Carter disapproved. He had been known to tell girls that Joe was chatting up that he had a girlfriend.

The waitress had other ideas. Joe caught a clear flash of an image of him bending to kiss her. It was so vivid he could almost feel her lips. He looked up from his menu in surprise and she blinked in confusion and blushed.

"I think we need a few minutes," answered Carter.

"I be right back," she assured them.

"I'm going to the little girl's room," announced Lisa, folding her menu. "If she comes back while I'm gone, will you order me the pear gorgonzola salad and the fettuccine?"

"Sure," answered Carter.

"But no capers."

"No capers," repeated Carter. As soon as she was out of earshot he leaned toward Joe. "So what do you think?"

"I don't like capers either. What exactly are they?"

Carter scowled. "No, man, about Lisa."

She's a stuck up bitch.

"She's fine. If you had gone to the john I'd be over there in your seat in a sec,"

"Yeah, you would, too. Despite that fact, I want you to be my best man."

Joe couldn't help but notice that Carter waited until the bride-to-be was gone to ask him. "Yeah? Well, thanks. Sure, I'd be honored. When's the wedding?"

"This fall. November 24th."

"This is... kinda sudden, isn't it?" Three months ago when they'd packed up and left their dorm room Carter hadn't even been dating anyone.

"Love at first sight," Carter explained. "And Mama does like her, so, you know, she's the one I got to marry."

"She's the one?" teased Joe. "Like you got a whole harem to choose from."

"No, I don't have your charm. *Here, take my seat,*" Carter mimicked. "Damn, you flirt with everything in a skirt. I'm surprised Evelyn lets you out of her sight."

"I can't help it if I'm just naturally full of charm."

"You're full of something!" laughed Carter.

"Are you looking forward to being with the same woman the rest of your life?" asked Joe. "I mean, only her?"

"Absolutely." There was nothing phony or practiced about Carter's grin.

"I don't know. I love Evelyn and all, but sometimes temptation is awfully... tempting." He could see their waitress two tables away, even shorter now in her flats, but shapely. And just his type: human.

Carter's voice dropped down confidentially. "You fool around on Evelyn? Man! I was you, I'd be afraid to."

"Afraid to what?" asked Lisa, sliding back into her spot beside Carter.

"Afraid they will forget to leave out the capers," answered Joe.

"It comes down to this, man," said Carter earnestly, taking Lisa's hand. "You love her or you don't."

Joe shook his head and drank some of his water. That seemed a bit too simple.

#

During dinner, Joe got to hear every moment of Carter and Lisa's romance, from first meeting to the proposal—when Carter had only known her a month—to moving in together. As his mind glazed over he tried to imagine what Evelyn would be doing in the warm Mexican night, but that only made him lonelier.

"Would you like coffee? Or dessert?" offered the waitress. She had been very attentive, but Joe hadn't been able to pick up any more fantasies from her, only the occasional struggle to pull the Italian names of dishes from the Chinese and English running through her head. "We have a wonderful selection of flavored coffees," she said smiling and bending back a menu to show them the list, like Vanna White with a vowel.

"No, thank you, just the bill," answered Lisa for all of them. Joe breathed a sigh of relief. He wasn't sure he could take it with good grace anymore. Despite their suits and their jobs and that big diamond, they were like two high school kids.

The worst part was that he wished Evelyn would snuggle up to him like that. He wished she would smile at him and brag about him, and call him cutesy names. Not forever—he knew this stage wouldn't last for Carter and Lisa. But just once in a while. That she loved him he had no doubt, but he wanted a little romance occasionally.

The waitress returned with their bill. "Can you pay now? I am about to finish," she said and glanced at Joe.

"I don't see why we should rush," grumbled Lisa when the waitress had taken away their credit cards.

"She's going off shift. She wants her tip," said Carter.

"You've never waitressed?" asked Joe. Of course, she hadn't. He sent Lisa an image of herself waitressing topless in a seedy bar amongst drunken, groping men. She apparently received it because she blinked rapidly a few times and was rendered speechless.

Use your powers for good, said the angel on Joe's right shoulder.

That was good, snickered the devil on the left.

When the waitress came back with their receipts, Joe found she had written her phone number on his. He smiled and tucked it in his wallet.

The bus tour was gone and it was much easier getting out of the restaurant than it had been getting in.

"So, what would you like to do now?" asked Carter, surveying the street scene.

The lit-up signs and neon letters glowing in the dusk were inviting, but not if Joe had to endure any more of the Lisa-and-Carter-romance show.

"I think I'd better get home. I have to work tomorrow," said Joe.

"Oh, well, that's too bad," said Lisa. "It was a pleasure meeting you. We'll see you again sometime."

"I'm sure you will." Had Carter even told Lisa he wanted Joe to be his best man? Would it get past her?

"I'll call you, man," said Carter with a wave as Lisa led him away.

Joe put on Claude's mirrored shades against the glow of the setting sun and headed toward the parking lot behind the restaurant. As he turned the corner he saw the little waitress standing on the sidewalk at the far end of the building. She pulled out the combs that had been holding her hair back and let it fall in a long, black river over her shoulders, then fished around for cigarettes and a lighter in her bag. Joe stood and watched her for a minute and imagined her naked.

It comes down to this, man: you love her or you don't.

Couldn't he love Evelyn and still have a fling now and then? Why did it have to be so black and white? They didn't mean anything, these little liaisons. Joe was very discreet and very careful. No more regular affairs, like with Richie. That was too risky.

He tried to conjure up an image of Evelyn to compete with this pretty little girl who was leaning against the building now smoking. Somehow he couldn't do it with the live option standing in front of him. She let smoke waft out of her mouth and pulled it in through her nose.

She looked up then, in Joe's direction, and he couldn't very well stand there staring, so he walked toward her.

"Did you enjoy your dinner?" She flashed him a smile. She had very even, white teeth.

"Yeah," said Joe, smiling back. "Are you waiting for a ride?"

"Waiting for the bus."

"I could give you a ride."

"No, Mama says never take ride with stranger." Her eyes sparkled with mischief. Her accent seemed stronger now that she didn't have to try so hard.

Joe stuck out his hand. "Hi, I'm Joe. What's your name?"

"Sue."

"There, now, we're not strangers." Joe pointed the remote at his car and clicked the locks on and off which made the headlights flash so that she could see he was driving a Beemer. He sent her a modified image of the one she had imagined earlier, of them kissing, but this time, inside the car.

She pushed off the wall and started walking toward the car with Joe. "What happen to your friends?"

"They were getting to be a bit much," said Joe.

She nodded. "Just got engaged. Think they are hotshots."

Joe laughed. "Okay, now guess how much they weigh."

She stopped and look at him quizzically.

"I mean, how did you know?"

"They so happy and giggling. And big diamond on her finger."

Joe drove to Sue's apartment, and they made out in the visitor's spot in the parking lot. He filled her mind with increasingly graphic images of the sex they would have until she practically dragged him upstairs to her tiny student flat. It was a seduction technique he had learned from Richie.

#

Joe checked his watch as he put it back on. Four a.m. Time for even night owls like him to be getting home and to bed. Sue was asleep and Joe decided to slip out quietly. Easy come, easy go.

As he leaned over to tie his shoes, she stirred behind him. "Maybe you stay?" she asked.

"Sorry," said Joe. "I just thought I'd go now...." He got one shoe on.

"I see you again?"

Joe looked down at the other shoe in his hand. "I told you I have a girlfriend." He had told her. After sex. Well, after the first time. He didn't want to spoil the mood.

"Yeah, but you here now. I call you," she announced.

"You don't have my number."

He looked back at her sad face and relented. "I have your number. I'll call you."

"You call me, or you lie?"

Joe leaned over and kissed her.

As he drove past the darkened restaurant, he heard Carter's voice again, *It comes down to this, man: you love her or you don't.*

But he did, didn't he?

#

Joe knew he should get to bed. Instead, he rummaged through the bottom drawer of his dresser until he found a stiff manila envelope.

He had taken this from the desk in the library. He knew Evelyn would have wanted him to trash it if she'd seen it, but he'd hidden it away.

It was packages of Evelyn's school photos, from kindergarten up to high school graduation. Evelyn in twisted pigtails, Evelyn with a gap in her front teeth, Evelyn's ringlets pulled back into what was more pom-pom than ponytail. Evelyn in makeup, probably for the first time. All the portrait packages were unopened, the sheets uncut, just an 8x10 of Evelyn peering through the clear plastic back of each one.

She wasn't smiling in any of them.

Maybe when you're married you won't be so tempted to stray. Maybe if you're a vampire you won't miss warm flesh in your bed.

Maybe... maybe....

Joe had opened the last package: Evelyn's high school graduation photos. This was Evelyn as she looked now and would look forever. He'd taken one picture with him to school. Was there any naiveté in her still human face in the photo? Joe had looked for it in vain. Evelyn's face didn't reveal so much emotion even then.

Marriage to Evelyn would be more complicated than going to a church and saying I do. They wouldn't grow old together, and he didn't think Evelyn could stand for him to grow old while she remained 18. She already had to remind him sometimes, "I'm not a child."

Marriage meant forever; it meant becoming a vampire.

Joe sighed, looking into Evelyn's soft brown eyes. Yes, taking her blood didn't mean he was hers. And he supposed marrying her didn't mean he had to become a vampire, although perhaps to Evelyn it would.

It was so simple for Carter: *you love her or you don't.*

I love her, said Joe to himself. He closed his eyes and smelled Sue's perfume on his fingers. *I love Evelyn.*

Then why not marry her?

Joe opened his eyes again and met Evelyn's serious, photographed gaze.

"I will."

Joe Vampire

A Modest Proposal

"**H**oney, I'm home," called out Joe as he let himself in the front door. His own car, his own house key, a job, and he still felt like an overgrown kid playing house.

"Hi, baby." Evelyn was wearing a gold and purple paisley robe, tied at the waist and nearly brushing the floor. Joe's first thought was to wonder what was underneath it. She had hunted last night, and Joe knew that was when she preferred to have sex—when she was sated and would not be tempted to bite him.

She slipped her arms around his waist, still staring up at his cropped hair. When they'd met, Evelyn had seemed so mature. He was only fifteen. Now she seemed young to him, and sometimes he was surprised to be reminded that she was older.

"I got you a present," Joe told her. He'd stopped on his way home from work to pick it up, but he hadn't planned how to give it to her. Every time he thought about it, he started to hyperventilate.

"Do I have to guess?" she asked when he made no move to give her anything.

"No. Um, let's sit down." He nodded toward the games room.

Joe slipped out of his jacket, took the two boxes from his pocket, and took a deep breath.

Just say what you mean to say! expostulated the memory of an English professor he'd had in his freshman year.

"Okay, I'm going to do this." he muttered to himself.

Evelyn was sitting on the couch, the robe slightly

askew, revealing one shapely brown leg crossed over one completely draped in purple and gold satin.

"I, uh...." he sat down beside her. She smelled like vanilla, and he knew from experience that meant she was going to taste like it too.

He set the boxes on the coffee table. "Maybe these could wait."

"You're being a tease," she scolded as he buried his face under the ringlets at her neck.

"Not me."

"Come on, what's in it?"

She had the smaller of the two boxes, a perfect cube of blue with a silver-papered lid.

Joe settled back in resignation. "Okay, open it."

Out of the box dropped a burgundy velvet jeweler's box. Evelyn flipped the lid open.

"Oh!"

Inside was an engagement and wedding ring set, the former sporting a row of small diamonds. It had a little wave to it that fit perfectly with the top of the plain gold wedding band.

"Will you marry me?" he asked quietly.

"Oh, Joe!" She flung her arms around him and kissed him.

Yes, thought Joe, *yes, let's just kiss and go upstairs and not get to the other box. Let's just do that.*

Evelyn pulled away from him a little.

"I thought you didn't believe in marriage," she said softly.

Joe gave a little shrug. "I don't believe in other people's marriages. Besides, I wasn't really thinking about a conventional, till-death-do-us-part sort of thing."

"Oh?" She raised one eyebrow.

"Open—" Joe stopped and cleared his throat, "— open the other one."

The second box looked like Snow White's crystal-lidded casket. It was the same size that would hold a fancy ball point pen, but inside it was a mother-of-pearl-handled knife with a small blade.

"What's this?"

"It's a scalpel. They had them at the jewelry store for graduation gifts, you know, for medical students. Anyway, I thought this was a better engagement gift, only you can't wear it very well."

Evelyn blinked at it and then blinked up at him. Joe smiled. He had not seen her looking so animated— human really—in a long time.

"You mean...?"

"Yeah. I figure, you know, marriage to a vampire is forever, so this would be the engagement. And when I die, that will be our wedding."

"Oh Joe," Evelyn sighed and kissed him. "I know I keep asking you, but... are you sure? There's no backing out of this, no leaving me at the altar, no divorce. Are you sure?" she asked in a whisper.

"I'm sure." Joe swallowed to quell the butterflies in his stomach. "I know what I'm getting into."

"You know you won't really be immortal."

"I know."

"You know you'll be giving up the daylight, food, normal dealings with normal people...."

"I've never had any normal dealings with normal people."

"I just—" she stopped and bit her lip.

"What? You want me to, don't you?"

"Oh, yes."

He kissed her, pushing her back against the leather upholstery. "Then let's do it," he breathed. "Gimme the scalpel."

The man at the jewelers had assured him that the blade was surgical steel, sharp, and just as functional as any ordinary scalpel.

Evelyn gave him the box, her eyes intently fixed on his.

"Are you going to drink my blood?" he asked.

"I don't have to."

"Fair's fair." It was how he had envisioned it, an exchange, followed by incredible sex.

Evelyn shied away as he brought it to the side of her neck.

"Wouldn't my wrist be easier?"

Joe's eyes traveled over her body, from her neck down to her wrist, and then over to where the scent of vanilla was wafting up from under her robe. So many places he could drink from. But Evelyn wasn't likely to let him.

"I thought this was... more official."

"My wrist, please."

"Is all of eternity going to be like this?" sighed Joe.

"Where did you want to drink from?"

Joe's eyes traveled down to her nearly uncovered breasts. "Never mind." He had no interest in causing her pain.

"If you want it to be 'official,' like a ritual, I could drain some into a cup."

"No, no, I'll do your wrist. And you'll drink from mine?"

"Alright," she agreed, then tipped her head down and batted her lashes at him. "You enjoy it, don't you?" she teased.

Joe felt a blush coming on. "Well, I mean, what could be more intimate?"

Joe put the tip of the blade against her skin, but when he tried to cut, it was as if all the strength drained out of his hand.

"What's the matter?"

"It's okay, it's okay. I just never cut anybody before."

"And you think you're ready to drink blood?" she jibed him.

"Hey, there's a first time for everything. You have to crawl before you walk, all that crap." He scraped his lower lip with his teeth and got a better grip on her arm.

This time he pushed the scalpel through her skin, into the little blue vein that ran under it. Evelyn hissed.

"Sorry!"

Blood welled up in the wake of the blade, pooled and then began to run down her arm.

"Quick, before it drips on the carpet," said Evelyn, taking the blade from his hand.

So much for romance.

Joe closed his mouth over her wrist, and at the same time felt her fangs pierce his left forearm.

Her blood didn't taste any different. Joe had tasted his own plenty of times and had tasted menstrual blood once or twice. But her blood was only room temperature, like her skin.

Joe let go first. He had to nudge Evelyn to get her attention.

"Sorry," she said in a husky voice. She licked his blood from her lips.

The cut in her wrist had stopped bleeding already. Joe watched in fascination as the marks on his forearm shrank.

"It's working already," said Evelyn, staring.

He'd done it. He'd committed to becoming a vampire, and he'd committed to Evelyn. Joe wasn't sure if he wanted to laugh or cry or throw up.

#

When Joe woke up in the middle of the rumpled, vanilla-scented king-sized bed his ears were buzzing and his head hurt. He had drunk a whole bottle of champagne and enticed Evelyn to drink from him again. It had seemed like the right thing for a celebration, and Joe figured he could make an exception for it.

Never again.

Joe drank a good deal of water in the shower, not caring that it was hot.

Like blood, he thought, and felt his eye teeth with his tongue. No, they weren't any sharper today than they had been yesterday.

It was a struggle to get dressed. He had woken late—it was nearly time for work—but he just couldn't muster up the energy to rush.

One day of being a bloodling and already I can't stand the day?

But when Joe left the bedroom the golden light from the slanted windows over the hall didn't bother him. Maybe it was just the blood Evelyn had taken, coupled with drinking, which he was not used to, and no dinner.

Joe found his timed coffee pot hot and waiting, and burned his lips on his first sip. He wished Evelyn was here. Well, she was here, but he couldn't talk to her very well. Couldn't say, *Goodbye, I'm off to work now.* He sighed, finished his cup, and headed out to the garage.

At Semple's Pharmacy, in aisle 6, an elderly woman was anxiously searching for laxatives.

"Aisle 3, at the front of the store," Joe told her helpfully. She looked up at him, startled.

Gotta be more careful, he thought. When he was tired he sometimes lost the dividing line between what people had said out loud and what they thought.

There was a kid in aisle 2 pretending to look at the magazines and trying to get the nerve up to look at the condoms on the shelf right around the corner. Finally, he did what all the other high school boys did, wrapped a hot rod magazine around the box so he could carry it up to the cashier without embarrassment.

"Why do you make it easy for them?" Joe had asked John Semple.

"Because I'd rather sell condoms to teenage boys than pregnancy tests to teenage girls," he answered easily. Joe suspected John had been a hippie in his day and developed his interest in pharmacology the same way Joe had.

"It's just you and me tonight, and Celine on cash. You interested in picking up a shift tomorrow?"

"Well, no," answered Joe truthfully, "but I guess I can if you're shorthanded."

"I wouldn't be in myself on a Saturday night if I wasn't." He looked up at Joe suddenly, the fluorescent light glinting off his shaved pate. John had recently cut off his ponytail and embraced his approaching baldness by shaving off the fringe he had left and instead growing a bushy handlebar mustache.

John frowned slightly. "You all right, Joe? You look a little pale."

"Just tired," answered Joe.

"So, aren't you going to tell me what happened last night?" asked John, perching himself on a stool between the shelves of bulk-sized jars of pills behind the counter.

"Last night?" asked Joe, thinking about feeling the sharp tips of Evelyn's fangs with his tongue when he kissed her.

"You were going to propose, weren't you? You lose your nerve?"

"No, I did it," answered Joe, grinning sheepishly. "We're engaged."

"Congratulations! So, when will the wedding be?"

"Uh, we haven't set a date yet. May be a while. Hell, we're living together. It's not like anything is going to change."

"Evelyn still in school?" asked John, turning the plastic jars so that their labels all faced out.

"No."

"What's she do?"

"Nothing."

"Nothing?" John shook his head. "Not sure I could do that."

"Well, okay, not nothing. She's taking a night course in Japanese, she manages her own money and stocks and stuff, and hey, now she's got a wedding to plan."

"Money? You didn't say she had money," said John.

"Yeah, she inherited it."

"So...are you...happy about being engaged?"

"Yeah. Why do you ask?"

"You seem kinda distracted tonight."

"I think I have a hangover. I've never had one before. Does it feel like all the elves in Santa's workshop are hammering inside your head?" said Joe as airily as he could.

"Preceded by drinking? Yup, that's a hangover."

"What should I take for it?"

"Nothing. You should suffer so you learn to drink in moderation. Well, I'm going to go do paperwork while you mind the shop," said John with a sigh that made him sound his age. "You want to put a new tape in that register? It's almost out."

"Aye aye, cap'n," said Joe with a salute.

"And swab the deck, me hearty," answered John.

"Would that be cotton swabs?" replied Joe lightly, pulling the box of cash register tapes from under the counter. "Aisle six."

John went off to his office with a chuckle.

Joe didn't feel light, though. He thumped the box up on the counter in front of him and pulled a stool over. God, there was so much noise in his head! All these people—

Clearer. They were clearer than ever. Louder and more of them, but the sensations were sharper and if he focused....

It was the blood. Evelyn's blood was working on his brain, giving his psychic powers a boost.

Ironic, when she didn't have them herself.

They were all so loud! Joe shut his psychic shutters. He could explore that later when he did not have a hangover.

Joe pulled out the spool from the old tape and started threading the new one, following the tortuous diagram on the inside of the register's hood.

You've changed. Never grow old. Never die. Party all night. Joe recognized it as the advertising line from a movie, but couldn't remember which one.

Party all night. Yeah, he was immortal now. Well, not immortal, but the next best thing to it. He couldn't get sick, he couldn't—.

Joe turned and looked at the shelves and shelves of pills behind him. Pills, pills, pills, in all their pastel colors and friendly rounded shapes. His hands began to shake.

They can't hurt you anymore.

No, said Joe to himself. *I kicked it. I'm not going back. I'm not going to let addiction control my life—*

You know better now, whispered the devil on his shoulder. *You're an expert. You know your limits and you know your drugs. You know what can deliver the feelings you want, on demand.*

No. He shut the register and it automatically chugged out a length of tape.

For instance, for this hangover—

"No," muttered Joe out loud as he tore off the extra tape. *No, no, no,* he chanted in his head like a mantra.

Joe Vampire

Party All Night

I t took Joe three tries to get the key in the lock of the front door. God, he'd snorted so much coke. It didn't help that he was wearing Claude's sunglasses even though the sun had set hours ago. The girl at his side was giggling, but he didn't know what about. Did it matter? He giggled along with her.

"Oh, man," she breathed in awe once the door was open, "you live in a fucking palace!"

"No," demurred Joe. "Just a nice little country cottage."

She giggled some more. Wisps of blonde hair floated around her face, and Joe saw a halo. An angel of light. Pale skin, pale hair, pale blue eyes....

"Joe?" inquired Evelyn suddenly. Joe was struck by the contrast between the girl before him and the vampire glaring at him from the door to the morning room. One was light and the other dark, one carefree and stoned and the other staid and sober. It seemed to him to be the most miraculous revelation he'd ever had. He wanted to put them side by side and just stare, but Evelyn walked up to him, ignoring her counterpart.

"What have you been doing?" she demanded, staring up at him. She was so little, he thought suddenly, and smiled.

"Just having a good time," he told her. Did coke work on vampires? He wondered if the girl had any more, so Evelyn could get in the groove too. She needed something. She was way too serious.

The muscles in Evelyn's jaw were flexing and Joe hoped she wouldn't scare off his new friend.

"And who's this?" Evelyn demanded.

"Joey, you didn't tell me you had a girlfriend," pouted the girl.

"Naw, Evelyn's not my girlfriend. She's my fiancée," he replied, and vaguely realized that didn't quite answer her question.

"Jo-seph," growled Evelyn.

"'Scuse me one minute," said Joe, holding up one finger to indicate the time. "I'll be right back." He let Evelyn pull him into the morning room by his belt loop.

"What are you doing?"

Evelyn really needed some coke, he decided. But the girl? What was he going to tell Evelyn? Oh yeah.

"I'm practicing," Joe whispered.

"For what?"

"You know. For when I'm—" he affected a bad Bela Lugosi accent "—a vampire."

"You're stoned out of your mind and you're practicing hunting," summarized Evelyn.

"No, I'm not stoned. Not that stoned. I just had a little... you know. Come on, baby, why are you worried? I'm immortal now, right? It can't hurt me."

Evelyn gripped his arm hard enough that pain seeped through his happy fog. "You don't even have fangs."

"Hey, well, I don't intend to bite her. But if you're hungry...." That was what he meant to tell Evelyn, to explain bringing a girl home with him. "She's, like, a present. For you."

"Get rid of her," Evelyn ordered, thrusting Joe's arm away from her.

"Okay, okay, no sweat. I mean, I proved I could do it, right? I picked her up and I got her to a safe place to bite her, right?" Evelyn just glared. "Okay, well, just let us grab some munchies."

As he turned to leave Evelyn grabbed his arm again. "Call her a cab. You're in no shape to drive."

"Okay, okay. Shit."

The girl was not in the hallway. Joe looked around and found her on the balcony above looking up through the skylights.

"Hey, you hungry?"

"Yeah. Hey, I could really go for some cheesies," she said as she tripped down the stairs, lighter than air. "You got any cheesies?"

"Your wish is my command," said Joe, bowing low. She giggled. He put his arm around her shoulders and led the way to the kitchen.

"Wow," the girl looked around. "You have a cook?"

"Just me. What did you want? Oh, right, cheesies. Cheesies, cheesies, cheesies...."

The girl hopped up on the butcher block-topped island.

"You know you're really sweet," said the girl coyly as Joe rooted through the cupboards for cheesies. He had some, didn't he? If not, why was he looking for them?

"You haven't, like, tried to get in my pants once. You're a gentleman."

"That's me," answered Joe. Pretzels. There weren't any cheesies but he saw the pretzels and had to have them. He pulled open the bag and pretzels flew everywhere. The girl started to laugh, and then they both laughed. She grabbed the shoulder of his shirt and pulled him over to her and they held each other while they laughed.

"You could, you know," she said when the fit had passed.

"Could what?" he asked, repressing a giggle.

"You could get into my pants," she answered.

"I'd never fit into your pants," responded Joe. He looked down to see that she wasn't wearing pants anyway. She had on a short skirt and... oh, and stockings. He could just see the tops of them and the little bulge under her skirt of the garter clips. And what else was under there? It was giving him a hard-on thinking about it.

"You're so funny," she said, giggling some more.

Joe felt her stocking tops and then her warm bare thighs under his hands, which seemed to be moving by themselves while he looked into her dilated blue eyes.

"I know what I want to eat," answered Joe. She smelled so good. Shampoo and soap, human musk and warmth, cigarettes, rum, and sweat. And down, down between her thighs, he knew she would smell even better. Like honey and yogurt, like warm sand. Christ, even if she smelled like fish sticks he didn't care.

Her tongue was in his mouth and Joe's hands had raised her skirt high enough to feel the satin of her panties over her hips. She must have undone the garters because as she wriggled he was able to pull the panties down and off her feet.

"Lay back," he told her, taking hold of her ankles and bracing her stockinged feet on his shoulders. Oh, the sweet, sweet smell. One hand braced him against the butcher block while he went down on her and with the other, he fumbled with the zipper of his fly.

The girl was moaning. Oh, she was really enjoying it, he thought, and then she gave a surprised "Oh!" and he thought she was coming. He was about to come himself, but she pulled away from him, hastily pulling down her skirt. Joe looked up and turned to see what had alarmed the girl.

Evelyn. Her lips were closed but Joe knew that the dilation of her pupils was not due to any of the chemicals he had been indulging in.

"Oh, uh," he ran his hand through his hair, "we were just, uh, going to, uh, get a snack."

Evelyn turned on her heel and walked away.

The girl started to giggle. "Your dick is out."

276

"What? Oh." Joe zipped himself back in. The girl was still giggling and he felt a couple giggles well up and spill out of his own mouth. It was like his stomach thought this was really funny, but his head knew better.

"You better go."

"How am I going to get home?"

"I'll—no, I shouldn't drive, and besides, uh, I'll call you a cab."

Pretzels crunched underfoot, and it took them longer than it should have to get out of the kitchen, between the giggling fits and trying to stomp on each and every pretzel.

In the front hall, the cordless phone was on the hall table, just like always, and Joe picked it up but the girl gasped.

Evelyn had brought a chair into the hall, placed it between the twin staircases, and sat on it now like a queen on a throne. An Egyptian queen, he thought. Nefertiti. She just needed the funny hat and the linen dress. She was as still and unblinking as a statue.

Before his mind could get too far off on that tangent, Joe said, "I'm just going to call her a cab."

Joe looked at the phone. He didn't know what number to call.

"Why don't you go wait outside?" Evelyn's voice carried the weight of a command.

"Um," the girl looked at the door and back at Evelyn. "In the dark?"

"There's nothing to be afraid of out there in the dark."

No, what you need to be afraid of is inside the house. Joe giggled.

Joe went over and flipped on the lights on the front of the house. "Yeah, go, I'll call you a cab, it'll be fine." He hustled her out the door, ignoring her mouthed *call me.* He never called any of them.

"How could you?" Evelyn was at the hall table now.

"I, I just got carried away, baby. I'm sorry."

Joe couldn't tell her about his desire to be near warm, living flesh. He loved her, but it was something she couldn't give him. Lovely as she was, she was always cold and dead. He could feel the difference when he touched a living person.

And instead of getting better with commitment, this craving had only gotten worse since he'd drunk Evelyn's blood.

"It's no big deal."

Evelyn's nostrils flared.

"I, uh, I can do it, though. If I was, you know, I could have drunk her blood. That way. I proved that I could do it." When she didn't respond he fell back on, "I'm sorry, Ev."

She dragged her hands back through her hair, pulling the tangled ringlets straight with her fingers. "Where did you find her?"

"Party. Uh, Carter's rehearsal dinner, you know, and then we went out to a bar, and she," he gestured towards the door that the girl was presumably on the other side of still, "was passing around a joint, and I kinda lost track of Carter, so her and I decided to take off. We scored some coke at... a bar, somewhere. And then we came here."

"Who saw you together?"

"Uh, people at the party, but at the bar, I don't think anyone would remember. I mean, the dealer, it's not like he's going to tell anyone who he sold to, right?"

"You're asking me?"

Joe shrugged.

"So your 'practice hunting'", she clawed quotes into the air, "was a total failure. You had witnesses, so if you killed her, they would finger you, and you brought her here, and, if you didn't kill her, she would know where you live and could tell the police. And you're high."

"Hey, I'm immortal now. It doesn't it matter anymore."

"It matters to me."

"Oh, baby. Look, I promise not to do it at work, and it won't interfere with us. Just sometimes I want to have a little fun. You go out and have a little fun now and then."

"I what?"

"You know, when you hunt. I know how you hunt. I don't care, it's no big deal."

The look of shock on her face was priceless. Joe wished that he had a camera. And that Evelyn would show up on film.

And then she vanished.

"That's not fair!" he shouted, but there was no answer.

#

Joe came away from the bar with a Coke in an old fashioned glass and a ridiculously narrow straw. He saw Carter sitting by himself at a table away from the dance floor and headed towards him.

"What are you doing over here in the dark? This is your party."

Carter chuckled wearily. "Lisa went to get changed into her 'going away outfit'."

"Going away outfit?" Joe imitated Carter's air quotes.

"Yeah. It isn't enough to have a wedding gown, no, you need a whole different outfit to leave the reception."

"I see."

"You'll find out, man."

Joe nodded, thinking, *no, I won't.*

"So, the sun has set. When is Evelyn going to get here? Lisa keeps asking me, *When am I going to meet Evelyn?*"

"Yeah, she asked me too."

"So?"

"I don't think she's going to come. She'd mad at me."

"What did you do?"

Joe chased the cup-shaped, machine-made ice cubes around in his drink with his miniature straw. "I, uh, you know how we went out to that bar after your rehearsal last night?"

"Yeah, I know. You disappeared. Best man and all, and poof, you're gone, like Keyser Soze."

"Well, I, uh, I met this girl...."

Carter snorted. "I knew your womanizing was going to get you in trouble eventually."

"Yeah... and I took her home with me...."

Carter frowned. "Home? You mean, like, the home you share with Evelyn?"

"Uh huh."

Carter sat back.

"It didn't go well," said Joe.

"Were you out of you ever-lovin' mind?"

"Well, yes, actually. I was stoned but good."

"You were what?"

Joe had told Carter almost nothing about his past and certainly not about his drug habit.

"Stoned. We smoked a joint and then... we did some lines."

"You mean, lines, like, you mean...?"

"Coke."

"Cocaine?"

"Yeah."

"Sweet Jesus!"

"I tried to tell Evelyn that I was practicing hunting."

Carter winced.

"She won't talk to me. Anytime I come into the room she just pops away. I don't know what to do, man. I'm half afraid that if I do talk to her she'll kick me out."

"It would serve you right! Cheney," Carter leaned forward, about to give him advice, but then stopped and leaned back again. "Why should I even help you? Tell me that. What makes you think you deserve her, the way you tomcat around?"

Joe looked at him for a minute. "You can help me?"

"But why should I?"

"'Cause you're my college roomie and that's what roomies do for each other?"

Carter snorted.

"'Cause I love her. I love her. This 'tomcatting around' is just, you know, it doesn't *mean* anything. It's over in an hour. Or so. Like I went to a ball game." Richie's remembered voice echoed in his head: *Not much point in immortal youth if you can't have fun, is there?*

"But with Evelyn, I don't just want to go to a game, I don't want to have season tickets, I want to buy the whole team. I am committed."

Carter shook his head.

"Anyway, I don't think you can help me. What would you know about it? You're so straight an arrow people use you to calibrate their compasses." He knew Carter was dying to give him advice. He just had to pretend he didn't want it.

"Believe it or not Cheney, I still manage to end up in the dog house now and then. And I have found, that no matter what happened, it is always the man's fault."

"Uh huh."

"So this is what you do."

Bingo.

"You go out tomorrow and you buy the biggest bunch of roses you can find, and you write a long letter telling her how sorry you are, and how much you love her, and how you don't want to lose her. Maybe don't use the sports team metaphor. And write it out by hand, no using the computer. And then you leave that where she's going to find it."

"And you think that will work?"

"It melts Lisa."

Joe had always thought of Lisa as having a hard, shiny outer shell. She was polished. But Evelyn.... her toughness went through and through. Solid titanium. Once she had made a decision about him, no amount of flowers were going to sway her.

"I don't know about the flowers, but the letter might work. If she won't talk to me she might still read a letter."

"Well, then try some other gift. There's always the measuring cup."

"Oh," teased Joe, "are you volunteering to fill one?"

"You want her back, you need to fill it. My days of doing that are over."

"Days of doing what?" asked Lisa as she sidled up behind him.

"My days of partying with the boys," answered Carter smoothly. He stood up and stepped back to admire her dress. "You look stunning."

Lisa had been all in glaring white in the midst of her pink-clad bridesmaids. Now they would pale beside her fuchsia silk skirt and jacket.

They kissed. Joe had the sudden mean desire to try his luck seducing Lisa, but he tossed it aside. His present predicament was his own fault, not Carter's, and Carter should not be punished for being well-adjusted and happy.

"Excuse me a minute, love." Carter left Lisa's side and leaned over close to Joe's ear. "And you stop fooling around," he said. "'Cause if she catches you again, no amount of blood or ink is going to fix it."

Joe smirked. He already had plans, post-reception, with one of the groomsmen.

#

The next night Semple's Pharmacy was quiet. It was eleven o'clock, and Celine was ringing up a customer's purchases at the front while a young couple with a new baby pondered over the diapering options in aisle three.

John was in the back office, doing paperwork, and the store was deathly quiet. Joe slipped into the storeroom. He opened one of the large plastic containers of Tylenol 4's, popped a couple into his mouth, and dry-swallowed them. He pocketed a few more, then he helped himself to one insulin syringe.

Carter had given him an idea. *No amount of blood and ink....* What about using blood as ink? He could withdraw a little blood from his own veins, like taking money out of an ATM, and use it to write his letter of apology. He had worked it up earlier in the day on his computer, but Carter was right, it had to be handwritten. He would copy it over, and that would slow him down and make his writing more legible. And he would do it in blood. That way she would know he meant it, and she would be sure to sniff out the letter no matter where he left it.

He slipped some Valium tabs in the other pocket of his dress pants, grabbed a couple new register tapes from the box to restock the shelf under the cash register, and went back to work filling the stack of scripts faxed from doctor's offices earlier in the day.

Joe was counting out chewable amoxicillin tablets by twos on the little plastic tray when John came out from the back, grabbed the other stool, and pulled it up to the end of the counter so he was perpendicular to Joe.

"Whassup?"

"I've got a problem, Joe."

"What kind of problem?"

"I just ran inventory. We're missing stuff. Tylenol 4's, Naproxen, Percocet, Diazepam—whole whack of painkillers."

Joe's stomach sunk. *Play it cool.* "Are you sure?"

John nodded, head bowed and eyes averted. He was nearly whispering. Of course, this wasn't the kind of thing you wanted customers to overhear. "The thing is, I didn't have this problem before I hired Celine."

Joe looked toward the front cash, where Celine, middle-aged single mother of three, was tidying the shelves behind the counter.

Lie.

"I can't imagine she took anything...

LIE!

"... but, well, the other night, just before we closed up, it was just me and Celine, and I went to the john and when I came back the gate was up." 'The gate' was a section of counter that flipped up. It was the only way to access to the pharmacy from the store itself.

"So she'd been back here?"

"I could have left it up myself. I'm not sure."

"Did you say anything to her at the time?"

Joe shook his head. The pills in his pants pocket felt like fist-sized rocks.

John looked around to see if there were any customers within earshot. The couple had made a diapering decision and they were chatting with Celine now as she rang up their purchases.

"I'm going to have to fire her."

Joe opened his mouth but the Devil ordered, *Say nothing. Let it happen.* He closed it and continued to count pills until John's stillness started to get to him and he had to look up.

John was watching him, his mouth a straight, hard line.

"Joe, I know it wasn't Celine."

A strangled noise was all Joe managed.

"You were going to hang her out to dry, weren't you?"

"I...." Joe's stomach was plunging down, storeys underground, like some Twilight Zone elevator to Hell.

"I thought I'd give you chance to come clean," John sighed, then shook his head. "You're fired, Joe."

The elevator hit bottom. Joe blinked.

"I won't call the police," continued John quietly. "You might not be so lucky next time. If you use me as a reference I will tell the truth, so don't."

"I—"

"Give me your keys and take off your coat," John gestured to the white lab coat with Semple's Pharmacy embroidered on the left breast. "Your jacket is at the back door."

"I—"

The look John gave him forestalled any more attempts to object. It wasn't anger; it was pity. Joe couldn't think of anything to say anyway. Not only was he a thief and an addict, he was a liar who had been willing to throw a fellow employee under the bus. Joe rushed to strip off the lab coat as his face burned and tears started to spill over his lower lids.

He caught sight of Celine at the front of the store, looking worried. He didn't deserve her concern.

Joe tore out of the parking lot, but a few blocks later he pulled onto a side street and parked where an overgrown maple shaded out the streetlight.

He had lost his job. Worse, he had lost his source. If only he had known, he would have stocked up. Instead of taking a few pills here and there, he would have helped himself to whole plastic mayonnaise-jar-sized bottles from the storeroom. He had a key. John trusted him.

John had trusted him.

Joe dug in his pocket and dry swallowed a few capsules without even looking at what they were. He wanted numbness.

The job didn't matter, he told himself. It wasn't like Evelyn cared. She had never asked him to pay rent or anything. The only expenses he had were his food. Now he was free to do whatever he wanted with his time. Working nights at Semple's Pharmacy, waiting on the recluses who wouldn't come in when the store was busy, and helping people who needed immediate relief for embarrassing conditions wasn't so great. Nor was filling the backlog of faxed scripts. Tidying the shelves. Replacing register tape.

Helping people. Being respected. Being treated like an adult. Being trusted.

Joe put his forehead against the steering wheel and cried.

Mother's Little Helper

Joe woke up in the green bedroom feeling too achy to keep sleeping and too tired to get up. He had been rationing the painkillers he had left, hoping to wean himself off of them, but now he was overdue for a dose and there were none left.

He had not seen Evelyn since he came home from Carter's rehearsal dinner with that girl. He would think Evelyn was in the house somewhere, but when he got to the room, she was gone. Or he would think he felt her watching him, but when he turned, there was no one there. It was more like being haunted than stalked. If she didn't want to talk to him yet, he was willing to give her time and space. He took the fact that she was checking up on him as a good sign. At least he hoped she was checking up on him and it was not just drug-induced paranoia. Being ignored would be worse. He remembered what had happened to Andy, how she had avoided him until he forced the issue, and then kicked him out. Joe did not want Evelyn to kick him out. He had nowhere to go, and besides, he didn't want to leave her.

Joe had moved to the green bedroom in order to give her space and to get some himself. Even if he was truly alone during the day he didn't want to be in the bedroom with Evelyn's things: the bed where he had given up his virginity, the table that she had once compared him to (favourably for him), the closet that was full of her sexy going-out-hunting dresses and her conservative business clothes.

"Fuck."

Joe got up and peed. The only thing in the medicine cabinet was a bottle of ibuprofen. He took four caplets for his aches and pains and shut the mirror again.

You look like shit.

His eyes were puffy and shadowed, and his cheeks and chin were rough with tiny spikes of strawberry blonde stubble that looked like tiny gold needles when the light caught them.

Oh to be happy again.

Cocaine will do that. Or crack. It's cheaper.

Fuck off.

He'd been happy the night he brought that girl home. He'd been flying so high he didn't even realize what an ass he was being.

Ride it out and get straight.

There was no way he could go to Evelyn and apologize unless he was sober, and there was no way he could bear to confront her while he was aching and craving. If only he had one last pill to take the edge off. Or maybe two. She wouldn't know he had anything in his system, and then he could stand to apologize, and if she accepted it and they were okay again, then he would have the strength to really kick this habit.

Again.

Existence was a pain. Being a bloodling was not helping him out with either his addiction or withdrawal. Frog had it totally wrong.

Joe flumped down into the green velveteen armchair. Evelyn's mother had been a pill popper, and all of her things would have been left behind here. Not in the room. The closet was as empty as the medicine cabinet. Or had Evelyn just junked everything?

The nursery, whispered the Devil in his ear. *All those boxes....*

Joe checked the time. Hours till sunset. He bounded up the stairs to the third floor, suddenly energized.

The trunk Simms had been sleeping in had been empty, except for Simms himself, of course. But the others? Joe moved boxes to the floor and wrangled with the rusty hasp on a blue metal steamer trunk.

Inside was a mound of white tissue over gauzy white fabric. He pulled out a bridal veil, and below that, the yellowed satin and beads of a wedding dress.

Happily ever after, for richer or poorer, till nothing do us part.

Just one or two pills. Something to take away the pain so I can talk to her like a man instead of whining. Something so I can be my old self.

Old self conjured up an image of himself in his white lab coat with Semple's Pharmacy embroidered on the breast. He pushed that thought away.

Joe dug in the trunk and encountered a dried bouquet and a flower girl's yellow dress and white patent leather Mary Janes. He stuffed everything back in without even wondering whose they had been.

He cleared more boxes off a wooden chest. Inside it smelled good. He pulled up a green velvet gown. Its lining was rotten and it tore as he lifted the dress. How old was this thing? 1920's? These were not Evelyn's mother's things. There were not going to be any drugs in here. Joe dropped the dress back in and shut the lid. He had better put it back in order. Even if Evelyn no longer slept in the closet, now missing its door, she might notice and wonder.

He lifted one of the boxes, and there, under his nose, written in neat, squarish Sharpie letters were the words *Alicia, personal effects.*

Joe dropped the box on top of the chest and tore off the packing tape. Deodorant, contact solution, a purse, and two makeup bags. With trembling hands, Joe unzipped the first makeup bag.

Jack. Pot.

It was a veritable pharmacy. The bottles all had different doctor's names; some bottles even had different patients' names on them. Some of the bottles had a mix of pills and capsules in different shapes, sizes, and colors, while others held only one type of medication, presumably the original contents. Joe twisted the lid of a bottle of Percocet and swallowed a little orange, oblong tablet.

He clutched the bag to his chest.

Who are you trying to kid? You don't want just one pill.

Joe wrenched the lid off and took a second and third tablet.

#

Joe drifted slowly into consciousness. The TV was on in front of him, an endless stream of light and movement and sound without meaning. He flipped his lower lip with his fingers and listened to the flapping noise it made. He couldn't feel either finger or lips. He was numb and safe.

This can't go on.

I want it to.

That supply of meds is not infinite. You need a plan to wean yourself off before you run out again. Then you can make up with Evelyn.

Evelyn.... He wished that she was with him inside this soft fluffy cloud of well-being. He missed her. The longing was enough to cut through the codeine and everything else.

If you want Evelyn back you have to get clean.

Crashing from the state he was in now was not going to be enjoyable, and Joe knew if he didn't plan he would just keep dosing himself in order to stay there. He needed limits. He needed to gradually reduce his intake and his dependence.

He had once taken an elective course in Greek mythology, and Joe had learned that in every tragedy there is a point where the hero could change course and turn things around but doesn't. Joe was at that point. He didn't want to miss his opportunity.

You did it once, he reminded himself.

I need a plan.

Joe floated up the stairs to the green room, which he had started to think of as his room. The makeup bag was lodged out of sight inside the base of the armchair, inserted through a slit in the lining. He lay down on the floor and fished it out.

You are never going to be anything but an addict.

Shut up!

Joe sat up and opened the bag. Inside the tops of the pill bottles had been labeled. M break. M lunch. M dinner. M bed. T break. T lunch. And so on. He gave a delighted chortle. He was smarter than he thought. He had already hatched this plan.

"Thank you, Joe," he said to his past self and laid back on the rug again, hugging the bag to his chest.

Everything is going to be okay.

#

Bright sunlight slanted across the grey and black granite kitchen counter. Joe looked down at his sandwich. How long had he been standing there, with the butter knife in his hand, staring off into space?

He was on day five of his weaning off plan. It seemed like he had been overly optimistic when he set it up. *Too aggressive.* If it was too aggressive, it would not work, he would backslide.

You will only backslide if you let yourself.

Joe scraped butter over his toast. He craved... chocolate? Music? Booze? How could he crave something he never used? That was the beauty of being multiply addicted: he could not pinpoint his craving. If he knew which little pastel-colored pill would take it away, he would be much more likely to go find one.

I could just take my afternoon dose early. Then take the bedtime allotment after lunch. I can skip the bedtime. I'll just sleep through any cravings.

You will, huh?

The downside was that he was pretty indiscriminate about what he did take to quell the craving, hence being multiply addicted.

You are full of shit.

I'll go for a walk. Fresh air, sunshine, that will help.

He cut the toast into two triangles. Then he realized that the phone was ringing. It had rung once or twice already, and he had heard it but hadn't processed the meaning of the sound.

Joe lifted the receiver of the kitchen extension. It had one of those extra-long cords that twisted and tangled and ended up leashing you even closer to the wall than if you had a regular cord.

"Hello?"

"Is Frog there?" It was Asha's voice, not demanding, but sounding frightened.

"No, Frog isn't here. You took him home, remember?"

"I took him home," she sighed, "but he's gone again."

Silence for a minute. How long had it been since they rescued Frog?

Asha was talking in his ear. "He wasn't making any sense. He had some story about vampires and women in cages and.... His mama didn't want to send him to the hospital...." Her voice trailed away.

"Asha?"

"He's gone and disappeared again, but... but it's weird." She sounded as tranquilized as Joe was, and that made her easier to talk to.

"Yeah. Frog is weird."

"I mean his disappearance. He.... His mama got up yesterday morning and he was gone, and when she looked out in the back yard there was this... this burn mark in the grass."

"What?" Joe felt like someone had just slapped him.

"It was like someone had lit a fire, but, like in a line, like six feet long. The grass was all burned away from the spot, and around the edges, it was singed. The only thing they found was a couple of these little, what did they call them? Not grommets. Little... things that they say was used to fasten a sign to a stake."

Joe could see it, clear as day. Clearer than if he was imagining it: the grass burned away from the blackened earth, and the rivets between the fingers of a police officer. Great, he had finally accomplished it: he was inside the head of someone on the other end of the phone line. Only he didn't want to be.

"There's a house for sale across the street and the sign is gone, tore up, and the stake missing, and in Frog's garage there's a knife and wood shavings." Each image was as clear to him as memory, coming from Asha's brain, not his own. Joe closed his eyes and that made them more real. "And someone said Frog use the shavings to start the fire, only if he did that, why they still there? And what did he burn? Nothing missing. And that's the only clue. He didn't take nothing, not his coat, not his wallet, nothing. But he's gone."

"He's...." Joe envisioned what happened. A sharpened stake, and crazy Frog throwing himself on it like an old Roman on his sword. That would kill a bloodling as sure as a vampire if he impaled himself on it. And then the sunrise....

Asha gave a cry and Joe's eyes popped open. He had just broadcast his thoughts to her. He quickly pulled out of her head and shut his mental shutters.

"No!" wailed Asha.

"Asha, I—"

But she was breathing in gasping sobs like someone had punched her in the gut. Joe closed his eyes.

You listen. You deserve to listen to her grief. You didn't save Frog, did you? You led that pale, annoying amphibian into a nest of vipers and it killed him.

"He's gone, Asha," Joe whispered as gently as he could. "He couldn't take it, I guess. What he saw." Joe was careful not to send his memories of the dungeon and of Frog in his top hat and bare feet on the cold concrete to Asha.

Asha's sobs got quieter, but not less intense, like she had moved away from the phone. Joe listened. Her tears lashed him like a penitent's whip.

Her sobs ebbed and flowed, and eventually abated into hiccups. She never hung up the phone. Joe eventually pressed the off button and set the receiver down gently, as if it was made of lightbulb-thin glass. Asha's crying continued to echo in his head. Their psychic connection wasn't broken.

Fuck the plan. He needed a fix.

#

Joe stood in the kitchen doorway and wondered how he had gotten there. Had he popped? No, he couldn't pop. Evelyn's blood had not given him that power.

Vampire blood—what good was it anyway? Ketamine—that could make him fly, and codeine could make him float like he was on a cloud. But this blood wasn't doing anything for him at all.

Now he was in the front entrance hall.

"Joe?"

He looked up to see Evelyn on the landing above him, like Juliet on her balcony. He wanted to see her step off the rail and float down to him.

"What are you doing?"

And then she was gone, and when Joe looked around he found her on the other side of the big round hall table. He didn't know if she had popped or walked down the stairs. She had not floated.

He tried to tell her about Frog, but all his words were log-jammed in his throat.

She gave him a quizzical look. A small frown formed on her forehead. Her pretty forehead. Her beautiful brown skin and her ringlets and her little hourglass figure and her soft thighs showing below her short skirt....

"Joe?"

"Frogilldemsef."

What the hell? That garble was not what he had meant to say. His lips were like rubber.

What had he meant to say anyway? Something about Frog....

"Joe? What is wrong with you?" She was moving closer, or Joe was floating towards her, he wasn't sure which.

"Burndisefup."

He was not this stoned. He was a pharmacist now, not a desperate kid trying out whatever was offered and even things that weren't. He knew what he was doing.

"What have you taken? God, Joe, your lips are blue!"

Evelyn was closer now. She looked worried. What *had* he taken? He dug in his pocket for his aluminum foil, but there was nothing but lint.

"I juh.... I juh...." And then Joe fell down.

Joe Vampire

When Joe woke it was dark. Pitch dark. And noisy, like there was a party going on somewhere nearby. It reminded him of Richie's bar when the ghosts came out, but he wasn't in the Lazy Susan. The bar had a particular smell to it of must and age and spilled beer. No, Joe smelled.... plastic.

Plastic?

He tried to move and found that he was hemmed in on all sides. The walls around him gave a little, but he didn't feel like he could possibly break through them.

"Don't panic," came Evelyn's slightly muffled voice. Joe flinched at a cracking nose near his head and suddenly there was light.

Evelyn was in front of him, lifting the lid from a large plastic container away.

That was what the walls smelled and felt like. A plastic bin. As he sat up he saw that this was the bin their Christmas tree had been in. There were little plastic pine needles in the bottom.

Joe sat up. He was in the Christmas tree bin in their walk-in closet. Evelyn's clothes were on his right and more of Evelyn's clothes were on his left, and his own, taking up only half the rod.

And Evelyn herself was standing in front of him, not live, but real. She wasn't hiding from him anymore.

Joe looked down at the bin. "Why...?"

"What do you remember?"

Joe opened his mouth to answer, but, oddly, he had no idea how he had gotten into the Christmas tree bin. He tried to pull up the last thing he remembered doing, but...

... Asha crying and Frog self-immolated in his weedy back yard.

Joe swallowed. "Frog is dead."

Evelyn's mouth dropped open. "What?"

"He... he killed himself. I don't understand. Why am I in here?"

"You passed out," she told him.

"I passed out," he repeated. Well, he had done that any number of times lately. He had never woken up inside giant Tupperware before.

"I thought... I was afraid you wouldn't make it through the day. I wanted to keep you safe."

Considering he had blacked out, he felt pretty good right now. Alert, awake, no aches, no headache. Except for the noise.

"Safe? I could have suffocated in this thing! You should have called 911."

Evelyn just stared at him.

"Is there a party going on downstairs?"

"What? No."

"What is all that noise?"

Evelyn cocked her head to one side. "What noise?"

"People. Talking, singing, laughing, and carrying on." Crying. *Crying?* And then there were just random images, tastes, feelings....

Psychic noise. More noise than he had ever heard before. Joe looked around, trying to locate the source. It wasn't coming from one direction; it was coming from everywhere.

Evelyn reached up and pressed her fingers to the side of his neck. They didn't feel cold to him like usual. She stepped back and gave him a sadly sympathetic smile. It was hard to focus with all the commotion in his head.

"Ev?"

"You didn't make it through the day."

Joe stared at her, trying to figure out what she meant.

"You've become—"

"No!"

Joe pushed past her and ran into the bathroom. God, he had not died, he was not a vampire. He couldn't be! He wasn't ready for that. He—

He was worried about what he might look like in the mirror, but when he leaned on the sink the mirror in front of him was empty. He put his hand against the glass and his fingers were not twinned by the silver backing.

When Evelyn touched his back, he jumped. He had not seen her behind him in the mirror, and not heard her steps over the noise in his head. *Shut up!* he told the voices, but it did no good.

Joe turned back to the mirror and stared. He was upset—terrified actually—but he wasn't breathing hard and his heart wasn't pounding.

"Oh God," he whispered.

"Come," said Evelyn gently. She took his hand and led him out of the bathroom. The Christmas tree was slumped in a corner of the room, like a post-holidays reject. They sat on the edge of the bed.

"How did I...?"

"You OD'd."

"I...?" Joe gave a humorless chuckle. "I OD'd? No. I wouldn't do that. I know better. I am a pharmacist."

The truth in Evelyn's eyes made him look away. "You couldn't talk right. You were slurring all your words. And your lips and your fingers were blue. And then you passed out and I couldn't wake you. So I brought you up here, but after what happened in the blue room.... I decided to put you in the Christmas tree bin. I knew you'd be safe."

Her voice was like velvet, but the words....

"I killed myself with pills?" Joe shook his head. *I can't really be that stupid. Can I?*

WOULD YOU ALL SHUT UP!

Close your mind. It was Richie's voice but Joe wasn't sure if it was a message the live and present-day Richie, or a memory. Either way, Joe shut his mental shutters.

Ah, that's better.

"What happened, Joe? Why did you go back to it? You kicked it once."

"I...." Joe ran a hand over his hair. In all the time he had known Evelyn she had never gotten a haircut, so he supposed his own short crop was the hairstyle he was saddled with. For eternity.

"I don't know. It just—things got out of hand."

"I know this isn't what you wanted. I know you wanted to be a bloodling, like Richie. But it beats the alternative, right?"

What did I take? He could see pills in his palm, and he could identify each one by its color and shape. But when had he taken them?

Evelyn touched his chin and gently turned his head to get Joe to look at her. "Tell me about Frog."

"Uh, Asha called to say..."

You are a vampire.

"... that he had disappeared again, only there was a burn mark..."

You have fangs.

Joe poked at his teeth with his tongue. They didn't feel any different. Maybe it required the smell of blood to make them come out. He leaned towards Evelyn but he couldn't smell anything and nothing happened.

Evelyn touched his cheek again and turned his gaze back towards her. "There was a burn mark?" she prompted.

"Like a fire in the back yard."

You are going to need blood.

"He—it looks like he took a stake from a sign, and probably sharpened it—"

You are going to need to hunt.

"—and, um, I think he impaled himself. Outside, in the back yard. And then the sun—"

You are never going to see the sun again.

"—got him."

"Asha thinks he's disappeared again?"

"I, um, I don't think so." He had been so lax in letting Asha see his ideas about what had really happened.

You could end up a burn mark on the lawn.

"Look at me," said Evelyn. She stroked his face. "It's going to be okay. Nothing can hurt you."

"Except the sun."

"Except the sun, but we have a solution for that."

Joe glanced at the Christmas tree bin and snorted. It seemed like a joke.

The voices had snuck back into his consciousness again, babbling away, and with them came a storm of sensation and emotion. Each thing pelted him individually, like hail.

"Stop!" he cried and covered his ears with his hands, but that didn't help. He closed his mind.

"What is it?"

"Psychic noise! But there's no one around for miles out here. Why can I hear them so clearly?"

"Didn't the Mater say that your powers would get stronger when you—"

"Oh, fuck, yes." Joe dropped his hands from his head. He just had to keep his mental shutters closed. All the time. They had a tendency to slip open when he was home.

"You need—"

"Don't say it."

"But you do. Blood is the cure-all. You will feel better."

"I—I just don't think I can—"

Hunt.

"Honestly, Joe, blood will make you feel better. It will help you sort things out. Here." She offered him her arm, pale side up.

"No, no, no."

"I've drunk from you often enough."

Joe stood up. "That's how Claude does it. I saw it in Frog's head, only I didn't quite get it until now. The women drink from their customers and he drinks from them."

Evelyn gave a brittle laugh. "He's a blood pimp."

"I need to go out and do this for myself." Joe was started pacing. "I feel fine. I feel finer than, well, ever, I think. I don't—there's no hangover, no withdrawal, no cravings. I just feel, kind of, you know, restless." He stopped and looked at her. "I can do this."

"You might want to take a little time and get used to this first." She walked up to him and put her hands against his chest. "Drink." She tipped her head to one side, exposing her brown neck.

"I.... Okay." Joe bent over her neck, his arms wrapped around her. *I vant to drink your blood,* said a comic Dracula in his head. He inhaled, but Evelyn had no smell. "How do I...?"

"I know!" Evelyn went to her jewelry box and retrieved the pearl-handled scalpel. With it, she made a small cut on her inner forearm and held it up to Joe.

"Taste."

Joe licked the blood welling up tentatively. He expected the same tinny taste as the first time, but this was different. This was mesquite-grilled steak and truffles and—

His eye teeth ached, and then they moved. He felt them sliding down. A touch of his tongue assured him that they were sharp. He took a few steps towards the bathroom to take a look at them in the mirror before he remembered.

They didn't stay out, though. Joe felt an unswelling and poked them with his tongue. His eye teeth were still sharp, but the same length as all the others in his mouth.

"They're gone."

Evelyn extended her arm under his nose again. Joe gave a sharp inhale as his fangs descended. Her blood smelled so good!

Evelyn took away her arm and tipped her head again. "Now, let's see if you can use them."

Joe bent over her neck, but his fangs slid back in.

"I can't." *Fuck.* "I just can't."

The cut on Evelyn's arm was already healing. She made a determined face and pressed the scalpel into the side of her neck.

"Try that."

Joe bent over her neck again. Oh, yeah, he had fangs. In spades. He licked at the blood and his nose filled with the aroma that was all his favorite foods, but none of them.

"No licking." Evelyn grabbed the back of his head and pull him closer. His fangs sank in with almost no resistance, and then....

It was not liquid that spurted to the back of his throat and down, it was a red glow, like the coals of a fire. It suffused him, going somehow straight to his network of veins and arteries, and spreading out through his body.

It was, without a doubt, the best thing he had ever had. The best food, the best drink.

The best drug.

"Enough, Joe." Evelyn tapped his shoulder but Joe ignored her. A little more. A little longer. It was so good.

"Joe?" She tried to wedge her arm between them and Joe gripped her tighter. "Joe, let go!"

Joe didn't want to ever let go. He didn't ever want this feeling to end.

"Joe, stop!"

But Joe didn't want to stop.

Suddenly Evelyn was torn out of his arms with the speed and force of a hurricane. Joe's fangs sucked air, and it made them ache like ice cream on a bad tooth.

"I said stop!" Evelyn was on the other side of the bed, her own fangs down, and her pupils dilated to black out her irises. Blood ran from twin gouges on her neck, and she pressed a hand to them to stem the flow.

More!

Joe couldn't speak. With his dilated gaze he could see so many details, down to the fine hairs on Evelyn's cheek.

Could he throw himself over the bed and tackle her before she disappeared? Or should he feign contrition and get close to her that way?

Stop it!

Evelyn took her hand away from her neck. The gouges were sealed with new, pink skin. She blinked and her fangs and eyes went back to normal.

I hurt her, and I don't care. I just want more.

Joe turned away. The voices were back and he slammed his mental shutters.

"Is it always.... It's not like cocaine, is it, where you only feel that high the first time?" Joe asked.

"Warm, human blood is better."

Joe needed a warm human. Now.

"I'm going out."

"Joe!"

"Hey, I can pop, can't I?"

"Joe, you—"

And in the next instant, Joe was in the back room of the Lazy Susan. He was pleased to discover that it didn't make him at all nauseous. The lights were off and it was empty, but there was enough light seeping under the door for him to see clearly.

The smell. He could tease each component of it apart now. Beer. Rum. Whisky. The sweet rotting smell of spit gathered and dried in Richie's sax. Years of dust, mostly shed human skin cells, in the carpet. Sex, perfume, food, mouse droppings.

And blood.

And voices! The ghosts were loud. Joe shut his mind again. *Stay closed.*

At the door, Joe stopped himself. He couldn't just walk out from the back room. Richie would know. He needed to think this through.

Joe thought about blood, inhaled the faint smell of it coming from down the hall, and willed his fangs down. They obliged. Getting them back in was a little harder, but he managed it. He did this a few times to practice.

I hope I can do that when I need to.

Joe took a deep breath, but he found that he didn't need to settle his nerves. He knew he was nervous, but he didn't feel it. No rapid heartbeat, no adrenaline. Damn. *Dead calm.* Joe smiled at his joke and popped himself into the alley behind the bar.

Some small animal went tearing away. Joe could smell its blood too. Not nearly as appetizing.

He walked around the end of the block and entered the Lazy Susan through the front door, like an ordinary mortal. Richie was at the bar, and when he looked up at Joe his face fell into lines of disapproval. He didn't say anything until Joe was up at the bar and he could growl, "What the fuck, man."

Richie's familiar musk was stronger now, more complex. It was a smell Joe associated with pleasant back room afternoons. He opened the tiniest door in his mind and projected a collage of memories and a warm bath of desire. Joe forced his fangs into hiding and said, "I just came by to check up on you. I wanted to make sure you were okay and that Claude hadn't come around."

Richie was receiving the psychic push of lust. His pupils dilated, his face softened. Joe didn't dare peek into his mind in case it revealed Joe's own.

"We all doing fine," answered Richie. "I still don't want you coming here as long as you have business with Claude."

"That's all over with."

"Yeah?"

Joe smiled at him, keeping his teeth hidden. "I've got a hankering for old times," he said. "No point in having eternal youth if you can't enjoy it."

"You don't say? So you took a drink from the fountain?"

Joe leaned forward confidentially, and when he spoke he whispered so he wouldn't open his mouth enough to expose his fangs. "I have to say it's made things harder than ever."

Richie smiled slyly. "Well now, can't leave you in a state like that. You want to come on back to the office?"

Leroy, seated on his stool, rattled his newspaper. Richie gave him a glance. "Watch the bar, Leroy."

"Richie..." whispered Leroy as Richie walked past him.

"Keep your comments to yourself, old man," Richie snapped.

Joe met Leroy's eyes and Leroy put his newspaper up between them.

In the small and untidy office, Richie turned to Joe. "I am not going to be visited by Claude, am I? Or the Mater? Or the ghost of Christmas Past?"

"No, man. I just came to see you." Joe reached out to give Richie a hug, sending a potpourri of warmth and friendship. He tried to rein in his bloodlust and think only about sex, but he could see the pulse beating in Richie's neck. He got one hand on Richie's upper back when his fangs betrayed him.

"Hey!" cried Richie.

Joe stopped for a second while Richie stared open-mouthed at his fangs, but the smell was too enticing. He tried to pull Richie to him, and Richie kneed him in the groin. Joe went down.

Apparently, his pain receptors were still functioning like normal.

"Are you a goddamned—" Richie stopped himself short of shouting the word vampire. Then he started kicking Joe. "Get out! Get the fuck out!"

Joe covered his head with his arms.

"You come in here, intending to just take from me! Fucking—fucking...." Apparently, there was no word bad enough.

Joe expected Leroy or a patron or someone to bust in the door any minute, but it didn't happen. In his fury Richie was heating up, sending out his scent more strongly. The scent of blood.

Richie, his one-time lover.

Richie, who was willing to abandon Frog to Claude.

Richie, who didn't hesitate to show Joe his one-time tryst with Evelyn.

Richie, whose wide eyes betrayed his fear.

Richie, who was pumping warm blood in a place where no one was going to check on their noise.

Joe launched himself at Richie and got him in a bear hug where Richie could not effectively hit or kick or knee him. His fangs went right through Richie's shirt and into his shoulder.

Joe Vampire

Blood.

Evelyn was right. This was better: more warming, and more complex. Evelyn's blood had a dull, red glow like the last heat of a fire, but Richie's filled him with orange light, like sunset or molten metal.

Time stood still while Joe was latched onto Richie's shoulder, but eventually, the feeling started to pale and wear out. *So, it's possible to be sated.* He realized that Richie had stopped struggling and pulled his fangs gently and carefully from Richie's shoulder. When he met Richie's gaze his eyes were dull with hate.

Joe let go of him and Richie stumbled back into his desk chair.

"You fucking bastard," whispered Richie, and turned away.

"Are you okay?"

"Get out."

"Richie, I—shit. I'm sorry, Richie. I—"

"Get out!"

"I'm sorry."

Joe popped himself back to the alley. The night was bright. At first, he thought the sun must be rising, but the sky was a uniform color and his watch said it was just after 9 pm.

Evelyn had been right. He needed blood. His restlessness was gone and he had a feeling of well-being that no drug had ever delivered to him.

Evelyn had been keeping this from him.

As if.

Joe began walking. He wasn't looking for more victims, he was just looking. Seeing, smelling, tasting the air, sampling the thoughts and feelings of people he passed, who didn't even know he was there because they were on the other side of brick walls.

He was completely safe in the night city. He was the thing to be feared.

#

"Joe?"

Joe lifted his head. He was on the floor in the walk-in closet, his feet in the Christmas tree bin, which was on its side. He remembered falling down just a few minutes before.

"Joe?" Evelyn opened the door, flooding the small room with artificial light, and gave an audible sigh of either relief. or exasperation, or both.

"I started feeling heavy and I popped back here, but I think I cut it a little close."

Evelyn took hold of the bin, and Joe pulled his feet out so she could set it upright. "You know you can just pop right into the container." She put the lid on the bin and snapped it down on either end. "It doesn't have to be open. Try that."

Joe did. Inside the container was dark and claustrophobic, but what did it matter when a whole day only felt like a few minutes? He popped back out.

"There, now, we can stuff it under here where it's a little less obvious." She shoved the bin under the clothes hanging on his side of the closet. "How did it go last night?"

Joe tried to breeze past her and out of the closet, but Evelyn disappeared before he could touch her. He looked up to find her on the other side of the room.

"I'm sorry, Ev, I'm really sorry. I got carried away last night. It was," he shook his head, "it was amazing. But it won't happen again."

I'd really rather have warm, human blood.

"You're certain?"

"Swear to, to whatever. I don't want to hurt you."

But you will, whispered the Devil in his ear, *if you need to, if you're hungry, if she's handy. And that's going to be hard if she doesn't trust you.*

She was still looking at him skeptically.

"Really." He opened his arms, inviting her for a hug. "I can hunt. I did it last night."

"And how did that go?" Evelyn stayed where she was and Joe decided to let it go for now. She would come around.

"Fine. Great. No problem."

"Really? Where did you go?"

"Uh, just, you know, wandered until I found a likely candidate."

Joe stripped off his shirt. He could smell Richie on it. His musk, his aftershave, the lingering scent of the Lazy Susan itself, and Richie's blood. There was a little smear of it on the front placket.

"Anyone who can identify you?"

"No, well, yeah, but he won't."

Joe popped himself across the room to his dresser. It was fun now that it didn't make him nauseous. Evelyn was right, it saved so much time. There was still some effort involved, though.

"I know it's tempting to vamp people you know. It's easy to get close to them. But it's really a bad idea."

Joe laughed. "It's fine. I don't need you mothering me. I got this."

"Who was it? Not Carter."

"No, not Carter. Look, it's all good. I went out my first time and scored. Blood, not, you know, scored like as in drugs. It was easy. I learned a lot from your journals."

He looked over at Evelyn to check her reaction and she had disappeared. He looked around and was dismayed to find her lifting his shirt from the laundry hamper.

"What are you doing?"

"You were at the Lazy Susan." She put the shirt to her nose. "Is that—? Richie? You bit Richie?"

Joe popped across the room and snatched it from her hand.

"Why are you in my business?"

Evelyn took a step back.

"You've drunk his blood. What does it matter?"

Joe popped back to his dresser and found a T-shirt to wear. It didn't matter that it was winter. He wasn't going to be cold no matter what he wore.

When he was dressed he turned to see Evelyn still watching him.

"Joe, after we ran into Richie at that first council meeting, he called me. He propositioned me. Me and you and him: a threesome. I turned him down. When you were taking lessons from him...?"

"He suggested it, just like you said, a threesome. I turned him down too." Joe shrugged. "He didn't seem to take offense."

"And last night?"

Joe blinked. What could he say? The truth was not an option. He picked up his comb, looked at the empty mirror, and threw it down on his dresser.

"I didn't do anything with Richie last night but drink from him. And what does it matter what I did or didn't do anyway? You fucked him. Besides, I learned how to hunt from you. From your journals. How else would I do it besides seducing people like you do?"

Evelyn was very still, then in a small voice she said, "That's what you said when you brought that girl home. What's good for the goose is good for the gander."

The girl! Oh God, that fucking girl. How could I have been so stupid?

You know perfectly well how and why you were so stupid.

He turned on Evelyn. "Well? Isn't it the same?"

"I know what you read in my journal may have given you the impression that I jump every guy I sink my teeth into, but it's not like that." Evelyn's words pelted Joe like sleet. "Not anymore."

He had assumed that. Maybe not that she screwed every guy, but that she enjoyed a tussle now and then. He had never cared one way or the other. It hadn't really had any impact on his own promiscuousness, other than that he had intended to use it as a defense if it ever came up. Like now.

Evelyn spread her hands. "Do you have nothing to say?"

"Why am I on trial?"

Evelyn gave a huff of frustration and disappeared. *Goddamn!*

"Evelyn!" Joe rushed out to the rail above the front hall, then popped himself to the morning room. Evelyn wasn't there. Not in the games room or the library. The kitchen?

Joe's shoes crunched on something on the floor of the kitchen and he flicked on the lights. The floor was strewn with bits of pretzel, most of them crunched to powder on the floor, but what he had stepped on were Claude's sunglasses.

Death and the Maiden

Richie's blood glowed within him for days. It boosted his mental powers: Joe could pick out one person from the psychic noise and spend hours following the thread of their experience. It was better than television. His connection with Asha had stuck. He watched her competent hands run sheets of upholstery fabric through an industrial sewing machine, then toss the finished car seat cover onto a pallet. He felt the undercurrent of her grief.

Evelyn didn't avoid him, like last time, but she barely spoke to him, and then only about strictly factual things. *Did you put the garbage out? Is there gas in the car?* Joe didn't worry about it. She would come around. After all, she hadn't kicked him out. And if he got over being mad at her he might write her that letter.

He had no good reason to be mad at her, and he knew it, but he had to wait until he stopped feeling it. He told himself his emotions were just too tangled and complicated right now to figure out and avoided thinking about them at all by following the lives in his head.

After several days he started to get restless again, and his mental control weakened. With the glow gone he felt less substantial. He flexed his hands and poked himself and he seemed solid enough, but it was like he was hollow inside.

In the green bedroom, Joe located his stash. Even if he was so drugged up he couldn't remember what he had taken or when he always had the presence of mind to hide it in the same place. Drugs were more important than self-preservation. And judging by how many days of decreasing doses from his weaning off plan he had used up at once, self-preservation had not been important to him at all.

Obviously.

But now? Now he really was immortal. He had gone through Death's door and come out the other side. Could the pills hurt him?

More importantly, could they help him?

Joe knocked a mix from one of pill bottles into his hand and looked at it. A Valium, half a Percocet. He tossed them to the back of his throat and swallowed them with a glass of water.

The water almost made him retch. It tasted like rotten fruit and mold and oil and bleach. He ran the tap again to see what color it came out, but the water ran clear. It smelled bad. Good thing he didn't need to drink it.

Half an hour later, feeling no effects, Joe took a couple more Valium and another Percocet. He cracked open a can of cola to wash them down with, but it smelled so bad he dry swallowed them instead. Half an hour after that he crushed seven Percocet to a powder with the back of a spoon and snorted them up a rolled-up dollar bill.

Nothing.

It made no impact on his restlessness, his clarity of mind, his vision. He could not sleep. There was no sleep anymore, only that moment of death that spanned the daylight hours.

Might as well throw it all away.

Joe tucked the bag back into the rip in the underside of the armchair in the green room. He wasn't quite ready to let it go.

#

"I'm, um, going to go out," he told Evelyn one evening. He tried to make it sound as casual as possible.

Evelyn took a long look at him. "Do you want company?"

Joe wasn't sure if that was an olive branch, or an attempt to chaperone. Joe shook his head. He didn't need help. He knew how to seduce women and he knew how to hustle men. Evelyn would only be a liability in her present mood.

Joe put on his coat which he knew he didn't really need and went out to the garage. He would drive to.... Where? Campus? Semple's? That thought was fleeting. Not the Lazy Susan; he didn't want to repeat that violence.

But how could the hunt be any other way, once the prey knew it was prey?

You are starting to sound like a real member of that club.

Joe put his car keys into his pocket and popped himself to the park next to his old house.

The house was not the first place he looked, but it was the one that held his attention the longest. All the other things in the park—the swings, the merry-go-round, the sparse grass and dry stream bed of a path that bisected it—were the same. On the other hand, what had been his house was now a jagged section of roof and part of a fire-blackened wall.

Can't go home. Not that he would want to. He had often wished that home was different, even tried to pretend that it was, to see if that made a difference, but it never had.

The park was empty. It was 3 a.m. and all the little kiddies—good and bad—were home asleep by now. *Except me.* He had often passed the nights sleeping on the merry-go-round.

And then he heard someone coming. She was humming to herself and her too-large winter boots thumped on the sidewalk. Joe sat down on a bench and waited to see if she'd come through the park.

In a few minutes, she appeared, bundled up in a puffy purple coat and only as tall as the chain-link fence that surrounded the park. She had her arms wrapped around a pillow and was chewing on one of her beaded cornrow braids. She was maybe ten years old.

"Hey," said Joe when she was about fifteen feet away. She stopped, startled, her eyes so wide Joe could see the white all around her brown-black irises.

"Aren't you kind of young to be out so late?" he asked with brotherly concern.

"I'm just going home," she said. She didn't seem to be afraid of him, and she kept walking along the path, which would take her within a few feet of his bench.

Joe could smell the pickle from her fast food hamburger, the dryer sheets that had tumbled with her pajamas, and someone's perfume that had rubbed off on her.

And her blood.

"Does your mama know where you are?" he asked.

"No," she answered, too innocent to know she ought to lie. "I'm supposed to be sleeping at my cousin's, but my Grandma snores too loud, so I'm going home."

She had stopped now, five feet from the bench. Joe's fangs were pushing and the night seemed less dark as his pupils dilated. He could see the pulse in her neck and her slight wrists. He could almost hear her heartbeat.

"Does your grandma know you left?"

"I didn't want to wake her up. It's only across the park."

So no one knew she was gone. No one was looking for her or expecting her.

"Where's your house?"

"Just over there, past the burned one." She came closer, gesturing toward the street. Joe could hear it now, *ba-bump, ba-bump, ba-bump,* quick and lively.

"Yeah? I used to live there."

"Yeah? Was you in the fire?" she asked excitedly.

"No, this was a long time ago." *A lifetime ago*, he thought.

"Oh, 'cause the guy who lived upstairs, he got out, but the lady who own the house, she died. She put something on the stove to cook and then she fell asleep watching TV and the stuff in the pan burned and started on fire and she didn't never wake up. She didn't get burned, it was smoke hay-laytion."

"Inhalation," Joe corrected her. "You're pretty brave, walking past that house after dark."

Big dark eyes turned on him. It hadn't occurred to her to be afraid.

Bump-bump-bump-bump, went her heart.

"I mean, if she died in the house maybe her ghost is still there."

The girl studied the house and then slowly looked back at Joe.

"Hey, mister, maybe you could walk with me? It's not far."

"Sure." Joe held out his hand. "C'mere."

You're so good, you can seduce anyone.

She came toward him, still watching the house in case a ghost should appear.

Ba-bump ba-bump ba-bump....

Joe took the pillow out of her arms and put it on the bench beside him. He pushed an enveloping blanket of affection over her, and images of romping puppies and kittens. A smile lit up her face.

Shush-shush, shush-shush, shush-shush, went the blood in her veins.

When he grasped her other arm the smile faltered.

"It's okay, I'm not going to hurt you," he promised in a gentle voice. He put an arm around her. She was stiff, but she didn't resist. He could feel her confusion. Joe knew the dissonance in emotions when an adult said one thing while doing the opposite, and the paralysis it led to. He was counting on it.

Joe brought one hand around from behind so he could pull her head to the side and at the same time cover her mouth.

—*bump-bump-bump-bump*—

"It'll all be alright."

Are you talking to her or yourself?

I'll be gentle and I'll hold her tight so there's no tearing and heal her up afterward. I'll just take a little. She won't even remember.

Shush-shush, shush-shush, shush-shush. He could feel the pulse in her lips under his fingers.

It was a relief to let his fangs down.

—*bump-bump-bump-bump*—

—*shushushushushush*—

Joe leaned over the girl's exposed neck and bit as gently as he could. There was no resistance in her skin; his sharp teeth slid right in.

This was better than Richie. Her blood was bright, like a blue summer sky. It had no weight and no density at all. It filled him like helium. Whatever had been bothering him—what had been bothering him?—it was annihilated in the warm gust of blood coursing down the back of his throat. He heard a moan and realized it was himself. It was a great night to be undead.

The flow began to ebb and Joe's fangs started to feel loose in their sockets, no longer thrust down by hunger. He pulled them as gently as he could from the girl's yielding skin.

"Okay?" he asked in a whisper and licked droplets of blood from her neck. She was heavy now.

"Hey?" Joe loosened his fingers from her mouth. She was still staring at his old house, looking vainly for the ghost.

318

"Hey," repeated Joe, jiggling her a little. She was as loose as a rag doll.

Joe listened.

There was no *ba-bump*.

There was no *shush-shush*.

"Come on, it's okay, it's okay, hey, come on kid, it's okay...."

She laid limp in his arms, the way Evelyn had the one time he'd slept with her during the day, back when he had been mortal.

Joe stared at her. Her mouth gaped half open like a dead fish, and her lips were livid with the imprint of his fingers. He hadn't meant to do this. All he wanted was a little blood.

"You can't be dead," he whispered. He pressed his ear to her chest just in case he was mistaken. There was silence inside the quilted coat.

It couldn't happen just like that, could it? So quick and quiet and... It was just a mistake. He'd slipped, he'd lost track of time, and he hadn't listened to her heart to make sure it was keeping up the beat. She was so limp it felt like she had no bones.

What was he going to do? He couldn't leave her here. She was so little and fragile and.... He couldn't just leave her. Joe scooped her up in his arms and popped back to the house.

#

In the light of the chandelier hung high over the marble floor of the hall, the little girl looked bad. Her skin was ashen, her lips were colorless, but her wide eyes were the worst, open and unseeing and frightened.

"Evelyn." He tried to call but it came out as a whisper.

319

He hugged his limp little burden closer. How much did she weigh? Sixty pounds? Seventy? How could he have done this? She was only a child. She was wearing pink pajamas with snowflakes on them. Small, frail, defenseless, innocent, trusting. She didn't deserve to die; she didn't deserve to be attacked; she certainly didn't deserve to meet a vampire in the park.

And what was he going to do with her now? The idea of burial seemed obscene. Heaping dirt over her little body was repulsive. He had already done enough harm. Joe sank to his knees.

"Evelyn," he whispered again.

This time she appeared in front of him.

"Joe?" She stooped over the corpse. "What did you do?"

"I couldn't—" No sound would come out of his throat.

"Take a breath, Joe," said Evelyn, locking onto his gaze with her brown eyes. "Breath in. Now tell me: what happened?"

"I didn't mean to kill her. I took too much."

"She's just a child!"

"I know, I—" *I what?*

Evelyn crouched down. "Where did you find her?"

"The park." Joe slipped from his knees to sit on the floor so he could support the child's weight on his legs.

Evelyn put her hand to the girl's neck to feel for a pulse. Her fingers came away bloody. Even though Joe was both sated and horrified, he didn't know how Evelyn could resist licking them clean.

"What am I going to do?" he whispered. "Maybe... maybe I should take her back."

"What?"

"Take her back to the park."

"No, you should not do that."

"But—"

"No!" Evelyn's voice was sharp. "Look at her neck. You don't want anyone to see that."

"But—"

"But what?"

"What am I going to do with her?"

Evelyn sighed. "Give her to me."

"Why?"

"I'll take her somewhere she won't be found."

Joe looked down at the girl. Her eyes were still open.

"Come on, Joe, let me have her. You know there's nothing else to do."

Evelyn lifted the child from Joe's lap. She didn't look so small in Evelyn's arms. Together they disappeared.

Joe just sat and stared at the floor. He could see the park in his mind's eye, and suddenly he was back there.

No, no, no!

Joe popped himself home again and found Evelyn brushing snowflakes from her hair. There were cinders and snow on her shoes. She gave him an odd look.

"Never again," he vowed. "I will never touch a child again."

"Why the hell did you touch one in the first place?" Evelyn hissed.

"I...."

"You are six feet tall, Joe. You know the streets. You could be taking down drug dealers. You could be putting the fear of God into guys like Ricardo. But instead, you choose a defenseless little girl?"

"You don't understand!"

Evelyn planted her fists on her hips. "What don't I understand?"

"It's so easy for you!"

The pitch of Evelyn's voice and her eyebrows went up. "In what way?"

"I don't know." Joe put his head in his hands "I don't know."

"You need to develop some self-control, Joe."

Joe laughed. *Self-control!* If he had any self-control he would not be a vampire now. He laughed until he wept, and when he looked up, Evelyn was watching him with that little frown line between her brows.

"It's just another addiction, isn't it?" He gave a joyless laugh. "You want it, you need it so bad you'll do anything, hurt anyone...."

Evelyn was suddenly in his face. He hadn't seen her move; she had popped. "No, Joe, you decide what kind of person you are going to be. You decide what kind of vampire you are going to be. This is not out of your control."

She got up and walked away from him, and after about 5 steps vanished altogether.

Joe laid down on the marble floor. It was cold and hard, like the floor of a crypt. That was where he should be. He should be dead. That overdose should have killed him and he should be dead and resting in his coffin.

The world would be a better place, and God knows it would be easier on me.

Why was it so easy for Evelyn? Where did her reserves of self-restraint come from?

Maybe Frog had it right. Maybe we are monsters.

How could he have drunk the life out of a little girl?

But it was so easy.

Joe followed his mental thread to Asha. She was lying in bed now, warm and comfortable and safe. And not alone, he was surprised to discover.

We should get some sleep, baby, murmured her companion. The voice and the soft body beside her were female.

Asha had chosen life. Asha had rejected vampires and the half-life of darkness. She endured the grief of her mother's passing and Frog's final disappearance, and through those experiences the knowledge of her own mortality, and still she chose a mortal life.

Asha snuggled up to her girlfriend and Joe withdrew from her head. He didn't want to see her happiness.

Carter had turned it down too when Joe had asked, theoretically of course, if he was interested. Joe didn't try to find his roommate in the psychic soup. It was bad enough to see Carter's smug, newly-married face in person; Joe didn't want to experience it from the inside.

And Richie? Joe didn't want to think about Richie. He didn't want to remember the look in Richie's eyes after he stumbled into his desk chair, betrayed and hurting and weak with blood loss.

What about Claude? He had never been in Claude's mind before, but now that he was a full-fledged vampire, could he find it? It was like sniffing out one particular flower from a field of them. He picked up a likely thread and tried it. No, not Claude. He sorted through until he found another one. Another. After a dozen or so he picked one up and started to follow it when it suddenly terminated.

You have all the subtlety of a neon sign.

That was Claude, and Claude saw him coming and shut him out. Joe didn't push. He didn't have the energy.

All the best vampires are psychopaths.

Joe rolled on his side. The floor was cool, and he could feel that, but he didn't feel uncomfortably cold. Would he lose the ability to react emotionally too? Was he doomed, as a member of *that club*, to lose his compassion and see mortals as food? *They are food.* Joe closed his eyes. That was all the little girl had been to him, an opportunity to slake his thirst.

Picturing the park took Joe back to it. He opened his eyes and saw dry grass and a cigarette butt at eye level. The ground was as hard and cold as the floor had been. Across the street, a window in one house flickered with the blue light of an insomniac's television, and in another, a nightlight glowed in a child's room. Joe wondered whether a gentle tap at the door or window of either could deliver him another meal.

Joe got up and walked to the bench where the little girl's pillow lay like a napping ghost. He was going to pick it up, but he stopped and let it be. It was her tombstone. *In memento mori.*

More from habit than anything else Joe went and stretched out on the merry-go-round. He had spent so many nights lying here, wanting to escape the hell that was his childhood and youth. Looking back now, as an adult, he realized how many options he had, but back then he had been too frightened, too ignorant, and too cowed to pursue them.

And now? What are your options?

He had missed his chance, as the hero of his own Greek tragedy, to fix things.

Joe pushed at the ground with one foot so that the merry-go-round turned and the stars wheeled above him like a time-lapse film of the night sky. With his vampire vision, he could see all the colors of the Milky Way.

The beauty of the stars mocked him.

Just stay here. It's easy, so easy. Just stay here and let yourself get heavy at dawn. The sun will make sure you never hurt anyone again.

The merry-go-round squeaked under him, and he felt the vibrations of the sound through his back. He could always change his mind at the last minute. He could always pop back to his Christmas tree bin. But frankly, he was content on the cold metal wheel.

Commitment

Joe Vampire

ABOUT THE AUTHOR

MJ Gardner is a web developer by day, who lays in bed at night and wonders, what if....? Her stories have been published in *Mad Scientist Journal, Luna Station Quarterly, Plan B* and *Saturday Night Reader*. She self-published her first novel, *Evelyn's Journal* in 2015. She also publishes a movie review blog called *Movies Off the Beaten Path*.

Gardner currently lives in Windsor, Ontario, Canada with her partner, Karen Hobden, and her cat Zoom. She is also the virtual curator of *The Suicide Museum,* an art project/work of fiction/website.

Website: http://mjgardner.com

Facebook: https://www.facebook.com/mjgardnerwriter

Twitter: https://twitter.com/WebDivaMJ

Wattpad: http://www.wattpad.com/user/webdiva

Movies Off the Beaten Path:
http://quirkymovies.blogspot.ca/

The Suicide Museum: http://thesuicidemuseum.com/

Joe Vampire